# Anointed

A David and Goliath Novel

Book One of the Davidic Chronicles

by

Greg S. Baker

# Anointed

A David and Goliath Novel
Book One of the Davidic Chronicles

by

Greg S. Baker

Printed by CreateSpace, An Amazon.com Company
Available from Amazon.com and other retail outlets.



ISBN 13: 978-1721565993
ISBN 10: 172156599X

First Edition

All Scripture quotations are from the King James Bible.



This is a work of fiction based on the Holy Scriptures as presented in the King James Bible. All characters and events resembling real people and events outside the Scriptures is wholly coincidental.

# Other Books by Greg S. Baker

**Christian and Christian Living**

*Fitly Spoken – Developing Effective Communication and Social Skills*

*Restoring a Fallen Christian – Rebuilding Lives for the Cause of Christ*

*The Great Tribulation and the Day of the Lord: Reconciling the Premillennial Approach to Revelation*

*The Gospel of Manhood According to Dad – A Young Man's Guide to Becoming a Man*

*Rediscovering the Character of Manhood – A Young Man's Guide to Building Integrity*

*Stressin' Over Stress – Six Ways to Handle Stress*

**Biblical Fiction Novels**

The Davidic Chronicles

Book One - *Anointed*

Book Two - *Valiant*

Book Three – *Fugitive*

More to come…

**Young Adult Adventure Novels**

Isle of the Phoenix Novels

*The Phoenix Quest*

*In the Dragon's Shadow*

More to come…

www.TheDivineIngredient.com

*To my wife, Liberty. Your name says it all.*
*You are my liberty. Without your love and*
*support, I would never have penned these words.*

# Acknowledgments

These novels represent the fulfillment of a burden to create more interest in the Bible and people it speaks of. No work of this magnitude is the sole product of a single individual.

My Saviour, Jesus Christ, is of course the One I believe laid such a burden upon me. I pray that this work exalts His name and helps expand His kingdom.

I am grateful to my beta-reading group. Each person was instrumental in pointing out specifics that enhanced this work. Elizabeth Speers was most diligent in her efforts to help make this novel stand out. Her contributions were immeasurable. Other readers in this group helped as well, specifically my beautiful wife, Liberty, Trent Cowling, Josh Geisler, Diane Frazier, Erica Lerisse (and her children), and my mother-in-law, Judy Bulmer.

My editor, Linda Stubblefield, has been a partner-in-crime in the editing world for some time now. An editor's contribution can never be underestimated.

# Author's Note about Biblical Fiction

### What Is Biblical Fiction?

Biblical fiction can have a variety of meanings, but essentially for my purposes, the genre is similar in nature to historical fiction. In biblical fiction, the author takes the true events and people of the Bible and expands upon them into a fuller story of "what might have happened" that connects separate events into a broader fictional, but possible, story.

In such a novel, I would expand upon the historical facts mentioned in the Bible and present a possible fuller picture of what the Bible describes. An entire novel could be based on those few chapters, filling in fictionally all the blank areas.

For example, David mentions to King Saul that he had killed a lion and a bear. The Bible does not describe those events, so in a biblical fiction novel, I might write the scenes surrounding those events as they might have happened while staying true to the biblical account. This work is not intended to be Scripture or to replace Scripture. Instead, my intent is to bring to life a possible fuller picture of the characters and events that the Bible describes.

This book is similar to what preachers do when retelling a Bible story from the pulpit. They embellish the story, add emotional responses or reactions to the characters, and extrapolate events and actions in ways that depict logically what might have happened or how biblical characters might have felt. Still fictional—but logical fiction.

Scriptural footnotes have been added to show where a biblical fact is anchored in the story.

My desire is to ensure that the biblical facts are the mainstays and core of the story while the fictional aspects are forced to revolve around those facts to bring a cohesive narrative that remains true to the biblical record. I won't bend the facts or alter them to present a more "entertaining" story.

Again, to be clear, this book is not meant to be Scripture or to replace Scripture of any sort. Except for what the Bible says, the rest of what I write is fictional—my best guess based on the information the Bible shares as to what might have happened.

These stories are meant to be fun and adventurous while remaining true to the biblical account. These novels are not children's books, though they are suitable for children. I am writing predominantly for a more mature audience, that of teenagers and adults. I don't sugarcoat the men and women in the Bible. They were often thieves, liars, murderers, adulterers, and bloodthirsty warriors. I decided not to reduce the violence and other horrible deeds that the Bible describes. I aim to present an entertaining story, true, but also one that will hopefully inspire the reader to see Bible stories in a broader sense. These were real people with real problems who made real mistakes but who lived real lives that God wanted us to study and know.

So, enjoy!

# Table of Contents

# Map of Israel

At the Time of David's First Anointing

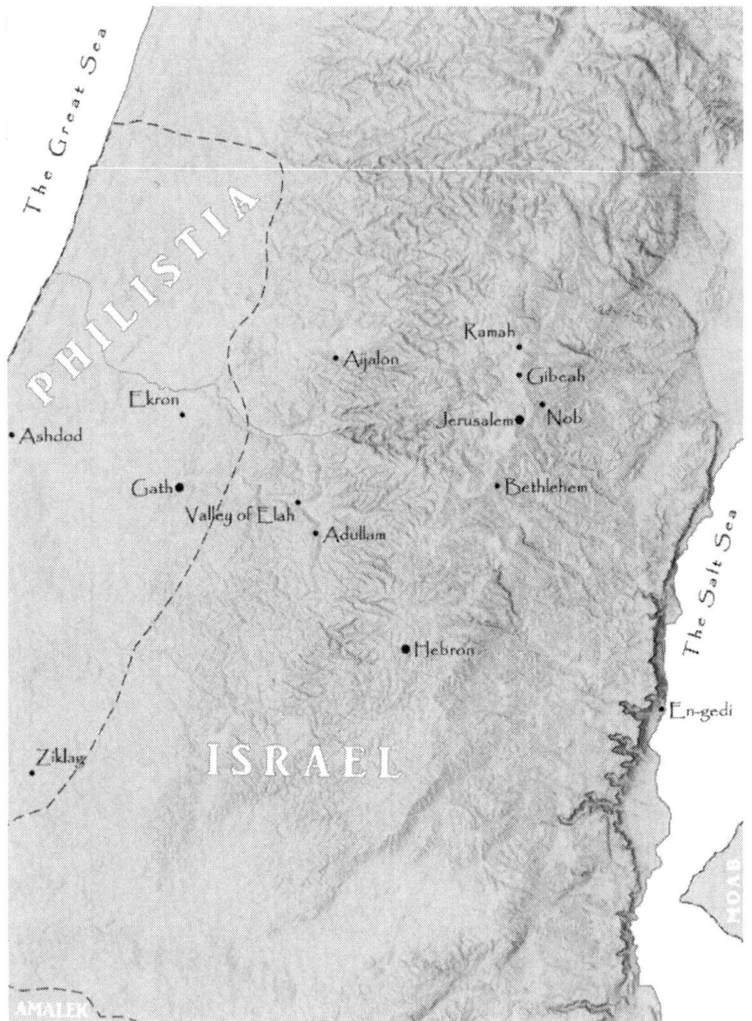

# Prologue

The smell of burnt flesh and hair lay heavy in the evening air. Jesse inhaled deeply, his long, white beard swaying ever so slightly with the gesture. His love of offering sacrifices to Jehovah was more than a sacred duty, but a way to express his gratitude and love. Peace offerings[1] were among Jesse's favorites of all the sacrifices. He just didn't like the way this one had gone. It felt…off.

But the source of his anxiety wasn't something he could immediately identify.

The temporary altar smoldered with the remains of the sacrificed heifer. Most of the meat had been removed by the elders of Bethlehem who had been called to the sacrifice and who would use the flesh as the main course of the feast held in the city.[2] The elders were beginning to disperse back to Bethlehem in anticipation of the meal.

Jesse, like the other elders, had come to the sacrifice at Samuel's request. That he'd been called to such a sacrifice was to be expected. Jesse's great age,[3] wealth, and wisdom virtually demanded that he be a part. What felt odd was the fact that the old seer[4] had also called Jesse's sons to the sacrifice. None of the other elders had been asked to bring their sons.

With a wry shrug, Jesse turned to leave with the other elders to the feast, motioning for his boys to follow, but a robed figure moved out of the lengthening shadows of the early evening and confronted

---

[1] It can be assumed that Samuel offered a peace offering (Leviticus 7:12-21) here, because later he says he would not sit down until David comes. This hints at sitting at a table and eating. The peace offering is the only offering that all the participants could eat of and the one most likely to be shared with others, thus Samuel's "calling" of the elders to the sacrifice. Another example can be found in 1 Samuel 9:12-13.

[2] 1 Samuel 16:2-5.

[3] 1 Samuel 17:12.

[4] 1 Samuel 9:9.

Jesse. The seer laid a hand upon Jesse's stooped shoulder, stopping him. For a mere moment, Jesse felt terror.[5] He swallowed it, forcing himself to look into the eyes of the man who could single-handedly call down thunder and lightning from the heavens and destroy entire armies.[6] Jesse knew firsthand that the LORD God was with Samuel and would cause Samuel's words to come to pass.[7] Many felt dread when Samuel spoke lest his words bring down ruin and destruction upon them. This was not a man to trifle with.

"Be at peace, Jesse, son of Obed," the old seer said, his voice a strange mix of obvious age and youthlike power. Jesse found the voice both compelling…and a little scary. "The LORD requires your presence yet a little longer. We will join the others afterward."

"My lord, I—" Jesse began, questions springing to his mind, but the aged eyes of Samuel glittered darkly. Jesse bowed his head. "As you will, my lord."

"Wait then," Samuel said, his voice soft, yet somehow managing to convey a command Jesse dared not disobey.

Unsure, Jesse's sons waited, standing near the pair of old men and glancing uneasily at each other. Jesse could guess what they were thinking. The seer's reputation and judgments had become legendary in Israel. Only one man had been rumored to stand up to him, to dare to disobey. That man was King Saul.

Rumors swirled like eddies of a receding tide about the degrading relationship between the Great Seer and King Saul. Whispers in the dark hinted that Samuel refused to see the king, that messengers were turned away, and that messages went unread and unheeded. The king sat in his house, stewing in his festering ire at Samuel even as smoke rose from Philistine weapon forges across the border. Trade with the Philistines had all but stopped, and rumors of shepherds and merchants gone missing near the border had reached even to Bethlehem. Everyone knew what that meant.

War was coming.

---

[5] 1 Samuel 16:4.

[6] 1 Samuel 7:10, 12:17-19.

[7] 1 Samuel 3:19.

And the two most powerful men in the nation would no longer look each other in the eye.

Jesse looked at his sons, a spike of dread piercing his heart. If war came, he knew what King Saul would do. He would take Jesse's sons and fling them into battle. Jesse was old, his youthful vigor now gone. He could not go in their place. It was a terrible thing watch one's children go to war.

Finally, the elders had all disappeared, leaving Samuel alone with Jesse and his sons. The seer's hand dropped from Jesse's shoulder, and the two old men regarded each other uncertainly. Something in the Great Seer's eyes hinted of fear. That, more than anything else, unnerved Jesse.

"My lord," Jesse said, trying to cover his unease, "I am your servant." He bowed over his staff, but only slightly. His aching back wouldn't allow for much more.

Samuel stood about a handspan taller than Jesse, his age somewhat indeterminate. Jesse didn't know which of them was older. However, the Great Seer still retained a measure of his physical power. He stood straight, his gray beard falling to his flat, lean stomach—unlike Jesse's rather obvious paunch. The gray hair of his head, likewise, fell to his waist—a testament to his lifelong Nazarite vow.[8] Samuel's hands, gripping a well-worn walking staff, though wrinkled and veined with age, remained un-gnarled and strong.

Samuel's eyes closed briefly. When they opened, Jesse saw the Samuel of old, the one he had once witnessed call down thunder and rain from a clear sky, the one who had demanded his own integrity to be judged before God and the people with cool confidence in his unshakable honor.

His voice firmed as he spoke, "Jesse, son of Obed, abide yet a moment longer." He hesitated, like a man weighing the inevitability of having to perform a disagreeable job. "I am come to anoint a new king over Israel," he announced.

[8] 1 Samuel 1:11.

Jesse stared, his mouth dropping ever so slightly. He didn't figure much could surprise an old man anymore, but that…that did it. Samuel regarded Jesse solemnly. Despite the power of the announcement, Jesse had detected a measure of pain in the seer's voice—a sorrow that bespoke of great disappointed love. Samuel didn't want to be here. He didn't want to perform this duty.

Jesse kept his eyes locked on the seer's. Instinctively, he knew there was more. "Is this true?"

The old seer offered a slow nod of resignation. "It is as I say. Yet there is more, Jesse, son of Obed, for the LORD has provided our people a king from among your sons."

"One of my sons?" Jesse asked, blinking, his long eyebrows nearly hiding his dark eyes.

"Yes. The LORD has rejected Saul from being king, and He has sought out another man, a better man,[9] to lead His chosen people. That man is among your sons." Samuel stepped away and turned to Jesse's seven sons. He swept them all in with a glance of his piercing eyes.

The men stood in a ragged line before the Great Seer. They'd heard his announcement, and they'd exchanged a whispered ripple of anticipation between them. Jesse knew his boys. He could read their eyes like a scribe reads a scroll. He saw fear in some, ambition in others, and in a few, he saw humility. Then the import of the Great Seer's words struck home. *A king? One of my sons?* He studied his boys with new eyes.

Eliab, Jesse's oldest, stood tall above his brothers, and if rumor was true, he stood nearly the height of King Saul himself. He was a powerful man, a man of war. Most men were these days. Most men trained to fight even as they performed a trade. This training had been a command of King Saul from years ago when he was first establishing his rule.[10]

Abinadab, Jesse's second oldest, had a restless spirit, but a commanding presence. He was a leader of men. He cared not for

---

[9] 1 Samuel 15:28.

[10] 1 Samuel 8:11-17.

flocks of sheep and had long since entered King Saul's service, rising through the ranks until he now captained the garrison of soldiers near Bethlehem.

One by one, Jesse looked at each of his children, and if the truth were known, he figured each of them would make a decent king—except one. Maon.[11] Jesse studied the young man, his youngest but one. Jesse had tried, the LORD knew he had tried, but Maon had no regard for the faith of his fathers. Even now, Maon stood sullenly behind his brethren, his small mouth pulled into a thin line of barely contained anger, resentment bleeding off him in waves. Jesse didn't know what to do for the lad. He was headed down a dark and lonely path.

Jesse's thoughts ended as Samuel motioned for Eliab to step forth. "Pass before me and present yourself before the LORD your God."

Eliab stepped forth, his confident manner a good match for his well-muscled physique. He passed between the Great Seer and his brothers. Samuel cocked his head as if listening. With a sigh, he shook his head. "The LORD has not chosen him."

Jesse's eyes widened. "Surely? Eliab is—"

Samuel's wave of the hand cut him off. "The LORD does not see as a man sees. We may look upon the outward appearance, but the Lord sees the heart. The LORD has refused him. Say nothing more."

Jesse clamped his mouth shut and motioned for Eliab to join him. He could sense his son's disappointment, but Eliab, at least, had sense enough to say nothing.

The Great Seer then motioned for Abinadab. "Pass forth," he commanded.

Seeing what happened to his brother, Abinadab, stepped forward a bit less sure. He drew himself up, however, and marched by Samuel as if parading. Jesse nodded to himself. If war were

[11] Maon is fictional. His story is an attempt to explain why eight sons are mentioned in 1 Samuel and only seven sons of Jesse mentioned in the genealogies, 1 Chronicles 2:13-15.

looming on the horizon, then Israel would need a soldier. Abinadab would be perfect as their next king.

The seer once again seemed to be listening. He shook his head. "Neither has the LORD chosen this one." He motioned Abinadab toward Jesse. "Stand forth with your father."

Abinadab joined his older brother and Jesse. He hid his disappointment better than Eliab had, but then Abinadab was a solider at heart. He followed orders.

Jesse couldn't figure it. His first two sons were by far the most experienced and well-balanced of all his sons. Why had they failed? He felt frustrated. He didn't even know the criteria by which they were being evaluated.

The old seer motioned to Shammah. "Pass before me and the LORD."

Shammah was the thinker in the family. He handled most of the business dealings with the family—something for which Jesse would ever be grateful. Thinking about it, Jesse could see his third son becoming king. He had the intelligence, and people instinctively trusted him. True, Shammah had a penchant for craftiness, particularly in business dealings, but then that proclivity should make a great quality in a king.

But the old seer was already shaking his head. "The LORD has not chosen him."

One by one, Jesse's sons passed before Samuel until only Maon remained. The old seer studied the young man intently as if able to pierce Maon's wall of anger and resentment. Some sort of understanding passed between the two for Samuel did not call Maon forth. Instead he turned to Jesse. "The LORD has not chosen these. Are all of your sons here?"

Jesse hesitated. By the process of elimination, only one son was left that could be chosen. But he could hardly credit the thought. It was ridiculous! Why—

"Is this all of your sons?" Samuel repeated, his eyes boring into Jesse's orbs.

"There remains yet one," Jesse said, feeling as if someone else had control of his mouth. "The youngest. He keeps the sheep."[12]

"Fetch him then," Samuel commanded, "for we will not sit down[13] at the feast until he comes."

Feeling as if everything in his life had suddenly been tossed upside down, Jesse turned to his other sons. "Go get David."

---

[12] 1 Samuel 16:11.

[13] 1 Samuel 16:11.

# Chapter One

David crouched behind the large rock, his sling held loosely in his right hand. He'd chosen the perfect place for an ambush. The enemy either had to pass right below him or make enough noise coming down the slope of the hill that David could easily pinpoint their location. He settled down, allowing his weight to distribute evenly over his leather sandals and forcing his muscles to relax. He slowed his breathing, worried that his own exhalations and pounding heart would drown out the faint sounds that would warn him when his opponents were within range.

He cocked his head, listening. Only his eyes moved as he scanned the deepening shadows around him. Low-lying shrubs gathered heavily to his left, but to his right, the hill sloped down, dotted by large boulders and short trees. Somewhere out there, the enemy crept through the dusk, trying to find him. David smiled, knowing he had the advantage.

He waited.

There. His ears picked up the slight sound of someone trying to move carefully through the brush above him, and movement from below betrayed the second enemy as he darted from tree to rock to tree again. David grinned. *Too easy.* He now knew where both of his enemies were.

They were dead. They just didn't know it yet.

Carefully, David reached into a well-oiled satchel and pulled out a dark-brown object and dropped it into his sling pouch. Hooking the middle finger of his right hand through a loop at one end of the string, he then took the knotted end and pinched it between his thumb and index finger. He let the sling dangle and took a deep breath.

As happened every time he prepared to sling, time seemed to slow to a crawl for David. His heightened senses distinguished every sound, the breeze as it wafted through the trees, the cricket chirping its welcome of the coming night not fifteen paces away, the plaintive bleating of his father's flock of sheep just over the rise, and the careful tread of his would-be attacker as he moved through the brush. He perceived, more than saw, the other assailant peering toward David's hiding place, no doubt wondering if the shadows hid more than darkness. David knew instinctively what would happen next.

David stood. By the time he came fully to his feet, the sling was in motion, building up tremendous speed. Relying completely on where his ears had perceived the stalker to be, he launched the sling's missile before even coming fully erect or his eyes could make out the crouched form moving toward him.

The stalker cried out in pain as the missile took him full in the chest, the force of the blow knocking him over. In the same motion, David dipped his free hand into his satchel, came out with another missile, and had the sling spinning before the second assailant had time to truly register David's exact position.

David let fly—his second missile streaking off in a blur and splatted dead center in the second attacker's forehead. The defeated attacker, a fifteen-year-old, cried out in pain and surprise as the fat date spattered wetly, and the hard pit inside completely knocked the boy off his feet.

David strolled over to the youth, his nephew, looking mighty pleased with himself. "Joab, do you know what you did wrong?"

"I let you hit me with a rotten date," Joab complained, wiping juice from his forehead from the overripe fruit. Joab's skin was darker than David's, and the youth's square face foretold of the flat face he would one day grow into as a man. "Why'd you have to hit me in the head?"

"The Philistines wear armor in battle," David explained, offering a strong hand up to the prone boy. "Bronze[1] dents, but not

[1] The KJV translators rendered the Hebrew word *nechôsheth* as "brass," but modern-day brass did not exist in David's day. The alloy used was copper and tin which, today, is commonly known as bronze. The term "bronze" had not yet been introduced into the English language at the time of the KJV translation, so "brass" was used for any type of copper alloy. Therefore, in today's usage of the words, Goliath's armor was bronze, not brass.

that much. The forehead is often unprotected as are the knees…hit the knees if you want to cripple a man, but if he's running, such a feat could be difficult."

"I'd just be glad to hit my target," Joab grumbled, allowing David to pull him up.

"Practice, Joab. You are getting better, much better. Just keep at it. Abinadab thinks the Philistines may invade again, and I for one am going to be ready." The fervency in David's voice broke through to Joab, who nodded wordlessly.

The light tread of the first attacker joining them caused David to glance over his shoulder. "Abishai, you made too much noise trying to sneak through the brush."

The fourteen-year-old, Joab's younger brother, rubbed ruefully at the wet spot that stained the front of his tunic. "But this time, I knew where you were hiding," he boasted.

"Knowing your enemy's location is not the same as being able to take him down—not when he's in a superior position. Since there were two of you, one of you should've stayed high and slung dates at me to keep me pinned down. The other should've flanked me and forced me to either reveal myself to the first or risk being hit by the second. That's what you did wrong. You should've worked together, particularly against a superior fortification. As good as my position was, it becomes a weakness if you really knew where I was…" David gave Abishai a penetrating look. "…which I very much doubt."

The young man's face tightened in stubbornness. David recognized the signs. He spent much more time with his two younger nephews than he did with his own brothers. His older sister, Zeruiah, had another boy besides Joab and Abishai, a sturdy lad by the name of Asahel, but the fleet-footed[2] youngest brother had remained at home to assist his father in sheering sheep—something he complained about loudly and bitterly. He knew that his older brothers played these wargames with David, and he wanted in on the action. Being the youngest of his own brothers, David could

[2] 2 Samuel 2:18.

sympathize with Asahel. Except for Maon, his older brothers were more like uncles than siblings.

Maon was closer in age, but David had never gotten along with his brother—often fighting over trivial matters. Though some of it wasn't so trivial in David's eyes, particularly when they fought over religion. David found comfort and purpose in Jehovah Elohim.[3] But Maon languished under the strict teachings and observances. Maon perhaps didn't disbelieve, but he certainly didn't care to believe if he could help it.

Shaking his head, David absently shoved Abishai, who gave a startled yelp, stumbled back, tripped, and fell heavily on his rump.

"What was that for!" the boy whined.

"For betraying your brother," David replied, trying to put sternness in his voice. "You were hoping I would be too distracted with your brother that you could sneak up on me. You dangled your brother as bait all because you wanted the glory of the *kill* for yourself."

"It's just a game," Abishai muttered, climbing back to his feet.

"The Philistine dogs won't care about your games," David snapped. "They will kill your father, kill your mother, and kill you—or raise you among their heathen gods. How would you like to bow before Dagon, Abishai? May Jehovah protect us from soldiers like you."

The boy's face turned ashen. It wasn't often that David snapped at him like that, but rumors of war had David on edge. He was nearing his seventeenth birthday soon, and that put him only three years away from being able to follow King Saul into battle. But every boy knew that if invasion did come and their cities and families were threatened, it wouldn't matter what age you were. Everyone would be needed to fight off the invaders.

David said a silent prayer to Jehovah, asking Him to watch over Israel.

---

[3] Jehovah (or *Yahweh*) is typically translated as LORD in the Old Testament. *Elohim* is typically translated as "God" throughout both books of Samuel and is the most common usage of "God" for this story.

"Enough," David said, rubbing Abishai's dark hair, so unlike his own. David's hair, as did his skin, tended toward the lighter side—perhaps a trait inherited from his mother. At nearly seventeen, he cut a striking figure—at least he hoped the girls thought so. Despite his youth, he had a man's build already; his arms and legs were well-muscled from years of herding sheep and practicing with the sling and staves. He could outrun every man in the village, and he was by far the best shot with the sling. Not as tall as his eldest brother, David nonetheless was above average height.

He honestly didn't mind being a lowly shepherd, but he, like most boys in every village and city throughout Israel, had been training all their lives to fight. Enemies surrounded Israel, and only the grace of Jehovah Elohim had kept the Hebrews from being enslaved again—but the memory of slavery ran deep in every Hebrew consciousness. *Never again.*

"Let's see to the sheep," David finished, pushing Abishai ahead. The youth darted to the top of the ridge, but Joab followed more slowly.

"What do you suppose the Great Seer wants with grandfather?" Joab asked as they trudged up the hill.

David shrugged, warding off a pang of disappointment at having been excluded. "He came to offer a sacrifice to the LORD God."

"But don't you think it strange? Why here in Bethlehem? Father says that the Great Seer hasn't left his house in Ramah since King Saul destroyed the Amalekites." Joab swung an imaginary sword. "Wish I could've been there," he muttered. He broke off in mid swing, realizing he'd sidetracked himself. "Why would the Great Seer come here?"

It was a good question—one that also nagged at David. When he had learned that Samuel had called his father and brethren to a sacrifice, he had been so excited…to see the Great Seer, to talk to him! What an honor! But then his father had left him behind to tend to one of his many herds of sheep. That decision hadn't been unexpected, but it had hurt. Servants tended the other herds, so why couldn't one be found to take this one? David really wanted to meet Samuel. Of all the men in the kingdom, above even King Saul himself, David wanted to talk to the seer of the Most High God. To enquire at his feet, to know directly the will of Jehovah—David couldn't imagine what that was like.

His fingers itched to find his harp. In the melodies he played, he could lose himself in his imaginations of what it must be like to be in the presence of Jehovah. If David had one regret, he wished he would've been born a Levite instead of being from the tribe of Judah. To serve as a priest of God and to be in the presence of God as Samuel lived must be the most incredible experience in the world.[4]

A shout broke his reverie. David looked up to see three of his brothers running toward him. David froze, wondering if his playing with Joab and Abishai had allowed any of the sheep to stray. The stupid beasts did that sometimes, but generally, they didn't like straying too far from David. He glanced at the animals. Most were lying contentedly near clumps of grass, though a few had jumped to their feet, startled by Eliab's shout. David made a quick count. They all seemed to be there. He sighed in relief.

"David!" Eliab shouted again. "Come! We must go to our father."

David ran the rest of the way to his brothers. "The sheep, Eliab, who—"

"Maon will look after them. Come quickly. You must present yourself before the Great Seer."

David's heart skipped a beat with excitement. "The Great Seer wishes to see me?"

Eliab and Abinadab exchanged glances. Maon just glowered. Obviously, he didn't like his role of taking David's place with the sheep.

"Father commands you to come," Abinadab cut in. "We must go now."

---

[4] Psalm 17:15, 43:4, 63:1-2, 84:10.

"Of course," David agreed. He flicked up his shepherd's staff from where it lay next to a rock and tossed it to Maon. "They seem ready to bed down for the night, Maon. But watch Little Itchy. She likes to wander over the hill when no one's looking."

"I know what to do, David." Maon's face darkened even further. "I don't need you telling me."

David felt a flicker of anger flash through him. *Why does he need to turn everything into a fight?* "Sorry," he muttered, feeling anything but. He turned to his other brothers. "I'm ready."

His brothers nodded, and Abinadab turned to his young nephews, his face and tone taking on that of a captain who brooked no nonsense. "You two, get. Go home. By the LORD God of Israel, you had better not follow us."

Joab and Abishai turned without a word and scampered away toward Bethlehem.

The pace his brothers set forced David to nearly run to keep up. On a far slope, the light of the sacrificial fire beckoned to David. There stood the man of God, and David was to present himself before him and, by extension, before Jehovah. He tried to think of what he'd say—*no, best to say nothing. Best to just listen.* He'd always wanted to meet Samuel, and only once had he ever seen the Great Seer during one of Samuel's circuits through Israel[5] before he had stopped his travels in recent years.

Sooner than expected, David's brothers escorted him to the top of the hill and into the dying light of the sacrificial fire. The mixed smell of burnt flesh and hide reached David's nose, invoking a deep reverence in him. The altar was temporary, smaller than the one Samuel had built in Ramah,[6] but it represented the very presence of Jehovah Elohim—His God, the God of Abraham, Isaac, and Jacob—the God of Moses.

David knew the stories. His father often recited one before the evening meal. He knew them all by heart, and he often sang songs

[5] 1 Samuel 17:15-17.

[6] 1 Samuel 7:17.

of those times—some of which he had composed himself. David's favorite was "The Song of Moses."[7] This song had been handed down for generations, sung at banquets, at festivals, and in every home. The beauty of the song had inspired him to learn to play the harp.

But more than anything else, the altar represented a means of connecting with Elohim. At such a holy place a man could find forgiveness and reconciliation with his God. David couldn't help himself; he walked up to Samuel, who stood before the altar, staff in hand, a capped horn slung over his outer robes, and wearing a stern and implacable expression, and David fell on his knees. Such a place required reverence, humility, and submission.

David kept his eyes squarely on the patch of dirt and grass before his knees. It felt right to kneel on Jehovah Elohim's creation, to feel small rocks digging into his knees, his toes, creating small grooves in the dirt. There, he waited.

And waited.

He could hear his brethren whispering to themselves. David knew his father stood apart from them, no doubt watching with anxious eyes, but daring to say nothing. This was between the man of God and David. David didn't know why. He didn't understand why Samuel wanted to see him, but David would not disrespect the Great Seer, for Samuel did nothing outside of the word of God.

Finally, Samuel spoke. His voice seemed infused with power and authority, and David felt a little thrill of excitement. "The LORD has chosen you, David, son of Jesse, to be captain over the people of Israel, His inheritance."

David felt his legs tremble. *What?* He nearly got up and scrambled away. King Saul was the LORD's anointed! *Not me!* The rumors of Samuel's fallout with Saul were true! *This*—David's thoughts were cut off when he felt thick oil poured over his head.[8] Almost David ran, but as if sensing his fear, an aged, yet powerful,

[7] Exodus 15.

[8] 1 Samuel 16:13.

hand fell on David's shoulder, keeping him in place, and so the oil ran off his head and streaked his cheeks.

"The LORD God of Israel has commanded me to anoint you, my son," the seer said. "You will be king after Saul. Your task will be to lead the LORD's people and protect them." Something in Samuel's voice nearly broke when he said that. Something profound had just happened—something David didn't understand. "Rise, David, son of Jesse, and look upon me."

A Spirit of peace and purpose came over David in that moment.[9] It was like he could sense the truth of Samuel's words, and they resonated with him on a level he had never before experienced. The Great Seer had spoken truly. David looked up into the Great Seer's eyes, his face wet with the oil, and saw sorrow there, and David perceived the source. Samuel feared for Saul and for David. Samuel, above all others, knew what this new anointing would mean.

Infused with new strength of his own, David rose smoothly to his feet and stood facing the aged seer. Samuel had not yet removed his hand from David's shoulder. Leaning forward, the Great Seer kissed David on the forehead amid the oil that still clung to his brow. "Be at peace. The LORD God of your fathers will be with you, and the day will come when you will take your place at the head of our people."

David found his voice. "Is that day now?"

"Nay. You are not yet ready. But be warned, the Spirit of the LORD has departed from Saul this same hour and has now fallen upon you, my son. Men will sense this Spirit upon you, and like Saul did, you will become a new man with a new heart.[10] Men will gather to you. You will be a beacon of light in dark times. I have seen this. But you must hide this anointing from Saul as best you can. In the day he learns of it, he will no doubt seek to kill you."

"What must I do?" David inquired, not a little worried. He had never met King Saul, but he admired him greatly for what he had done for Israel. The last thing he wanted was for the king to hunt

---

[9] 1 Samuel 16:13.

[10] 1 Samuel 10:9.

him. Something in David clicked into place. No matter what this anointing meant or what Samuel wanted him to become, David vowed never to betray his king. He'd die first.

"Abide. Be patient. Do nothing." Samuel looked over David's shoulder to Jesse and his brothers. "Do not speak of this. Hide it deep in your heart for, if Saul ever learns of what took place here, he will use you to get to your son, your brother. You will all be in danger."

David risked a glance at his family, and from the various, furtive looks they exchanged, he figured they would keep quiet, though they obviously did not seem very happy about the situation. Only his father, Jesse, seemed to look on approvingly. That itself was enough for David.

Jesse moved forward and joined Samuel and David. "We will not speak of this, my lord. God's will be done."

Samuel's wise eyes scanned the men gathered around the dying fire of the altar. The sun had not quite set, but shadows lay heavy across the land. Samuel nodded, apparently satisfied. "So be it. I will return to Ramah."

Jesse was scandalized. "No, my lord! What of the feast? It must be eaten before the new day begins."[11] He scanned the sky, looking for stars, but it was not dark enough. "A new day will be upon us soon, my lord. After the feast, I beg of you to stay at my house lest some danger befall you on the way."[12]

Samuel shook his head. "Be at peace. I fear not the night, and you may preside over the feast in my place. It is permitted as the sacrifice has been rightly finished. But I cannot abide here. Saul must not learn of this." His eyes lingered on David. "Know that I will pray for you all."

Jesse looked at his son, David, and nodded curtly. "As you wish, my lord." Turning to the rest of his sons, he said, "Go before

---

[11] Leviticus 7:15.

[12] Traditionally, Jewish days run from sunset to sunset and becomes official when three stars are visible in the night sky.

us and inform the elders that I will be there presently to join in the feast."

As a group, they moved away uncertainly, whispering to themselves. David heard disbelief and fear in their voices, and now that the moment had worn off, he too began to feel a measure of fear. He turned to the Great Seer, but the aged man had already begun to walk off, his back straight, his strides long, leaving only David and his father standing together.

"Son, are you well?" Jesse asked.

David reached up to wipe away some of the olive oil that threatened to run into his eyes. He honestly didn't know how to answer his father. What could he say? Samuel had anointed him as the next king of Israel, but he wasn't allowed to say anything? How could this be kept a secret? "I don't know what to do, Father. Tell me, please?"

Jesse placed both hands on his David's shoulders, forcing the young man to look into his eyes. Shadows played with Jesse's white beard, making it look darker than it should. His eyes, surrounded by wrinkles, held strength and conviction that David needed right then. "Son, listen to me. I won't pretend to understand what this anointing will mean for you. I can't begin to comprehend the burden you now carry. But if this is the will of Jehovah, we will see it through. For now, we will do as the seer has commanded. We will wait and do nothing. We must hide this from King Saul."

A thought struck David. "What about Maon? Does he know what happened here?"

Jesse sucked in a large breath, and David could see some of the strength leave his father. David knew how much his father agonized over his wayward son and the potential danger he represented. No one knew exactly what Maon was capable of. "He knows that the Great Seer came to anoint a new king." He hesitated. "He knows that none of your brothers was chosen, so he'll think it is you, but we can tell him otherwise."

"You wish me to lie?"

Worry lines creased his kindly father's face. "We must create doubt in him. The doubt will be enough to stay his tongue."

David felt a flash of fear. "Do you really think Maon would tell King Saul?"

For a long moment, Jesse said nothing. His eyes shifted away from David's and looked off into the dark night. David couldn't even begin to guess what his father was seeing. Then in a voice drowning in sorrow, he answered, "I really don't know. I just don't know."

# Chapter Two

Jonathan, son of Saul, marched down the hallway, his scowling face driving servants out of his way like a battering ram smashing through weakened wood. His father shouldn't have recalled him home—not with the Philistines stirring and certainly not with more border raids taking place. Jonathan was needed back with his men. Not here. Not now. Irritation had built into a towering rage over the last few days as he imagined what might be happening now that he wasn't with his men.

He hardly felt the weight of his armor or the heavy sword strapped to his side. He had long gotten used to battle dress. He carried his helmet under his left arm, his only concession to being indoors. The thick soles of his leather sandals slapped against the cobbled floor of the hallway, and each slap was accompanied by a snarl of impotent frustration.

Fortunately, even though this was the king's house, the building wasn't overly large—not compared to other kings' houses. Jonathan's father had never really had the time or the inclination to build one of those palace-like structures that other kings favored so much. The house was utilitarian in construction, lacking the grandeur and excess most people would associate with a king's residence. That didn't mean Saul hadn't indulged in some degree of fancy. Gilded wood and carvings were abundant throughout the house.

A guard stood at the end of the hallway before a single, unadorned oak door. Beyond lay the king's chamber where King Saul held court. Jonathan ignored the guard and shoved the door open without slowing one bit. The room beyond was by far the largest one in the house. But even then, it seemed crowded with the twenty or so people who lined the walls or stood before the thick wooden chair where Jonathan's father, King Saul, sat.

A banner depicting the tribe of Benjamin hung against the wall behind the chair, a concession to Saul's familial roots. Saul was a wartime king, and he knew it. The Philistines could invade at any moment, and the king had to be ready. Besides, their western enemy was not the only threat to Israel. Even while sitting in his chair, he had a javelin and sword resting nearby where he could easily lay hands on them.

Something was clearly bothering Jonathan's father, for he too was dressed in the best bronze armor that the few smiths of Israel had been able to produce. The armor glistened brilliantly in the light streaming in from windows. The builders had artfully focused the light on Saul's chair, but the darker corners required a few oil lamps to compensate for the size of the room.

Other than his armor, Saul wore a thin gold crown, more of a circlet really, with two rubies affixed to it. A golden armband, wrapped around his upper right bicep, was the only other ornament revealing his kingship.[1]

Looking at his father's armor, Jonathan almost paused. He had not expected this. Typically, his father wore his state robes when home. *What changed?*

Jonathan shoved his way through the crowd until he faced his father. "Why have you summoned me, my lord? Is it because the border is as peaceful as a suckling child?" His voice bled with sarcasm. "I am needed there, Father."

Saul sat stiffly in his chair, one elbow resting atop an armrest, and his head sunk down into his large hand. Jonathan couldn't think of a time when he'd seen his father so fatigued, so tired. At his son's words, Saul dropped his arm and looked up, meeting Jonathan's glare with one of his own.

Jonathan recoiled, sucking his breath in sharply. Saul's eyes looked haunted, the skin dark, gray, and sunken. Red lines seemed to throb in the whites of his eyes, and the brown irises had lost their luster, looking…dull, listless. His once brown hair and beard were speckled with gray and looked grimy. His face looked more lined than Jonathan remembered. The once powerful jaw and square face

[1] 2 Samuel 1:10.

seemed somehow…shrunken. But anger and bitterness were cast around his features to a degree that Jonathan couldn't match. His own fury melted away to be replaced by worry.

Saul glanced away, allowing his gaze to take in the rest of the group of men standing before him. "Now that my son is here, we can proceed. Abner, report."

In contrast to his king, Abner, Saul's captain over the armies of Israel, was a short, stocky man who had one of the sharpest minds Jonathan had ever met. The man's intellect, rigid principles, and lack of any humor whatsoever had always intimidated Jonathan, but his unflagging loyalty to his cousin,[2] the king, made him like an uncle to Jonathan. And despite the many battles the captain had fought, his hair remained black, without a gray strand anywhere to be seen. His unusual blue eyes remained focused and sharp, and his body fairly rippled with muscles under his mail shirt and armor.

Abner turned slightly so that he could address everyone. "War is coming. Our spies have reported that the kings of Gaza, Askelon, Ashdod, Ekron, and Gath met a week ago. We know not what they spoke of, but the lords of the Philistines would not gather unless they intended to march to war." He hesitated. "The situation is most serious, for they can field an army that exceeds our own twice over."

Jonathan nodded. Abner's conclusion seemed reasonable, matching what Jonathan himself had both witnessed and surmised. Despite the severity of the danger, something in Jonathan looked forward to the conflict. He hated sitting around doing nothing, patrolling the borders, and drilling men. He wanted to fight. He dreaded what invasion would mean for the villages and towns caught in the coming destruction, but personally, he looked forward to the giving and taking of blows. He idly scratched the palm of his right hand, his sword hand.

"I will muster the armies along the border, Father," Jonathan declared. "We'll meet the Philistine dogs when they march. It is

---

[2] 1 Samuel 14:50 (Jonathan and Abner are first cousins, once removed.).

because of this threat that I question being recalled. I need to be there—with my men."

Saul's dark eyes returned to his son. "No. You will remain here. Abner will see to the armies."

Jonathan's lips compressed tightly, and with a fierce act of will, he kept them closed. Now was not the time to keep challenging his father, not like this.

The king sat a bit straighter, anger flaring in his eyes, and he raised a clenched fist. "Jehovah Elohim will deliver the Philistine lords into my hand. This I swear!" But then he fell back against his chair, seemingly deflated. "Would that Samuel were here," he muttered darkly, rubbing at his temples again. "Samuel, why do you abandon me in my hour of need?" The words, hardly whispered, still carried to everyone's ears. Many of the king's advisors and servants exchanged nervous glances.

The silence that followed felt heavy, like the sudden realization of impending and unavoidable doom. Then Doeg, the Edomite, stepped forward. Jonathan frowned. He'd never been overly fond of the chief herdsman.[3] The man's reddish hair, probably a legacy of his people's sire, Esau,[4] lay in ragged curls atop his head. The man's eyes shifted too much, and he wore a sneer like a man would wear an old, but beloved, knife. "I have news of Samuel," he said, his raspy voice hard on the ears.

Saul's eyes snapped up. "You will speak of him with respect!" the king roared, nearly coming out of his chair. Doeg flinched and cringed, much to Jonathan's satisfaction. "You will address him as the Great Seer, Edomite, or I'll see you spitted on my spear."

Doeg dropped to his knees, his forehead touching the stones. "Yes, my lord! My humblest apologies, Great King."

Saul stared at the man, hands clenching reflexively. Jonathan frowned. This wasn't like his father. His temper had always been more even than that. True, Saul's falling out with Samuel had weighed heavily on the king's heart, and despite the two years of

[3] 1 Samuel 21:7.

[4] Genesis 25:25.

silence from the seer, Saul had remained his usual steady, if not jovial, self. *So what changed?* Clearly, something had.

At last, Saul settled back. "What news then?"

Doeg lifted his head and looked about like a cornered animal. He brushed aside his hair with one beefy hand. "The Great Seer made a journey to Bethlehem, my lord. His movements were reported to me by my herdsmen along the way."

"Samuel departed Ramah? Why wasn't I informed of this?" Saul looked to Abner.

The captain bowed low before answering. "My scouts have been sent to spy on the Philistines, my lord. The Great Seer has not left his home in over two years. How could I know?"

With a cry of utter rage, Saul sprang to his feet and slammed his fist into his heavy chair. The wood backing cracked, split, and then toppled over, hitting the stones and skidding a few spans toward the back wall. Saul stood over it, glaring at it as if it were a fallen enemy that refused to die. His heavy breathing and clenched teeth bespoke barely suppressed rage. Jonathan felt the first stirring of dread. Something was horribly wrong with his father. What evil spirit was this?[5] What had come over his father?

Saul spun around, glaring at his servants. "I would know what business the seer had in Bethlehem. Does he abide there yet?"

Doeg spoke quickly, "Nay, my lord. He has since returned to his house in Ramah. It was only upon his return that I learned of it."

"Cousin, summon Samuel to me. I would know the meaning of this!" Then muttering to himself, he said, "That old man is plotting something. I sense it."

Abner cleared his throat. "Is that wise, my king? Would you risk the wrath of Jehovah Elohim in the very hour that the uncircumcised Philistines threaten invasion? My lord, we still lack the smiths to produce iron weapons in any real quantity,[6] and bronze is still too rare to count upon. We are still sorely outmatched, both in weaponry and in numbers. If we are to win this war, we will need

[5] 1 Samuel 16:14.

[6] 1 Samuel 13:19.

the Great Seer—and probably the company of prophets who have gathered to him.[7] We will need Elohim's favor, my lord. I fear antagonizing the Great Seer would put us all at risk."

Saul was the tallest man in the room,[8] now that he was standing. He glared at his cousin, but the loyal man kept his eyes calm, unchallenging. Jonathan didn't know how the captain could do that. Finally, Saul sagged, his body lowering by spans. "See to the army, Abner. Prepare as best you can for invasion. I would not have the uncircumcised Philistines breaching our borders without resistance. I would know where they intend to cross."

"Aye, my lord," the general agreed.

Jonathan stepped forward. "What of me, my lord?"

Saul waved a hand at his oldest and heir. "I need you here, my son. I have need of your advice and strength in the coming days. When the time is fitting, the two of us will ride forth into battle. And by the grace of Elohim, we will prevail and drive the dogs into the sea."

With the way his father looked and his strange behavior, Jonathan thought this plan the best one he would get. As much as he wanted to return to his men and be in the forefront of the battle, he recognized his duty to his father. Right now, his father needed him more. "As you command, my lord," Jonathan said, giving his father a deferential bow of his head. That seemed to ease some of the tension from his father's eyes.

The king glanced at Doeg. "Speak to your herdsmen. Speak to the elders of Bethlehem. Discover the seer's purpose and send word." Still on his knees, Doeg began to nod effusively, but froze when Saul held up a warning finger. "Disrespect not the elders there, Edomite. Know your betters."

"Aye, my lord! Aye, my lord!" The herdsman scrambled to his feet and scuttled away to do Saul's bidding.

---

[7] 1 Samuel 19:20.

[8] 1 Samuel 10:23.

Jonathan watched him go, but he couldn't help but wonder what good could come of it. Doeg was much akin to a half-beaten dog. You never knew if he'd lick your hand or bite it.

# Chapter Three

David absently fingered his harp strings, trying to find the right frame of mind to play. He sat atop a large slab of rock, half of which was buried in the ground, but its sloped side rose gently into the air, a perfect place to sit on a warming spring day and play his harp. His father's sheep grazed around him, content to ignore him and eat.

He sighed and raised his face to the sun, trying to think. The warmth would bring a ruddy glow to his checks and face, marred only by the very beginnings of a beard. He longed to grow it out like his brothers, but he still had a few years before it would fully fill out. He smirked at the thought and strummed a few strings, the notes clear and vibrant as they filled the space around him. A few of the sheep paused and looked balefully at him.

The chords, soothing as they were, did little to dispel the turmoil that raged in his thoughts. Nearly a week had passed since the seer's visit, and his family had all but refused to say a word about the monumental event that was destined to change David's life. It was frustrating and at times infuriating. On one hand, he felt like the winner of a desperate and frantic race, in which he was the only runner, and no one could ever know of his victory. On the other, he was rightly terrified to reveal that the Great Seer had anointed him the next king of Israel. If any of Saul's servants learned of the anointing, so would King Saul. And Samuel had made it very clear that such a discovery would likely end in David's death.

David ground his teeth together. *Why me?* No answer came. Not that he really expected one. He sighed again and plucked at the strings of his harp. He let the music flow through him, rejuvenate him as he used the chords to reestablish his connection to Jehovah Elohim. He found himself playing the melody of his favorite song, *The Song of Moses*. He sang, "The LORD is my strength and song…He is become my salvation."[1] He hummed for a time, allowing his muscles and mind to relax. He sang a few more verses, finishing with a flourish, "The LORD shall reign for ever and ever!"[2]

He listened as the music and words faded into the countryside. The sheep just grazed away in contentment, used to the sounds of the harp. David shrugged, allowing a grin to spread across his face. At least the sheep knew what they were supposed to do. He then began a complex rhythm of his own composition, trying out words and thoughts to see if they fit the melody, but recent events continued to intrude in his mind, and he soon found himself distracted—but at least no longer so melancholy.

He put aside the harp and brought his knees up to his chest. He sat staring out across the Bethlehem countryside. Lost in thought, he never heard his brother's approach until Maon spoke.

"So idle, brother?"

Startled, David bolted upright and spun around to face his slightly older brother, grabbing his sling as he did so. Maon stood next to the boulder, regarding David with one eyebrow raised and sporting a half sneer that he reserved especially for David.

"It is not wise to skulk about like a cur," David warned. "I might have done you harm unintentionally."

Maon shrugged. "Doubtful." With a spring, he vaulted up onto the slope of the boulder and lay back, elbows keeping him elevated to stare at David. "You've been distracted these last days. Tell me truly, my brother. Have you given weight to the old seer's words?"

"Show some respect," David snapped back. "Samuel is a great man."

"Perhaps. But he is *old* nonetheless. Did he anoint you king as he claimed his task to be?" He had mocking singsong tone to his voice. "I sought for oil on your brow, but I saw it not."

There it was. The conversation David had been dreading. Surprisingly, Maon had waited much longer than David had expected. But David was ready. He looked away from his brother,

---

1 Exodus 15:1-2.

2 Exodus 15:18.

giving a casual shrug. "Nay. I came before him as beckoned. He said I was not chosen, but I didn't know what he meant until later."

David could feel Maon's eyes boring into his skull from the side, but he refused to look at his brother.

"Peculiar," Maon said, his voice languid. "The old man seemed certain that one of *Jesse's* sons was to be the next king."

"Even great men can be mistaken."

"It is well then, because if King Saul ever discovered it, I would think he would be most displeased."

David tried to keep his voice casual. "Doubtless. It is well that we have nothing to fear. Besides, what concern is it of yours? Your distaste for our king is well-known."

Maon snorted. "Saul is worshiped like a god. All for what? Because he delivered us out of the hands of the Philistines once or twice? Things have not improved under his hand, and without Philistine protection, we're more vulnerable than ever. The land was at peace when under their rule. The Amalekites, the Moabites, and the Ammonites feared to incur the wrath of the Philistine lords. But once they were gone, we've had more bloodshed and more death than ever! What has been accomplished? I know well of the rumors. I know that the Philistines are preparing to invade again. But if we'd left things alone, we wouldn't be facing these problems now. Nay, Saul's done us little good and a great deal of harm."

David could hardly credit his ears. "You believe that, truly? The Philistines took our women! They slew every smith in the country to deny us iron weapons! They forbade us from worshiping Jehovah Elohim!"

"You make too much of it," Maon disagreed. "These things happened in the beginning, but once things settled down, we had peace and stability. The Philistines kept us all safe. And if they forbade the worship of the God of our fathers, then that was their right. Their gods, after all, proved superior."

"How can you say that? King Saul drove them out. The Philistines fell to his hand. Their gods are nothing!"

Maon rolled his eyes. "If such were true, then why did their rule last for so long? Where was your precious Jehovah during all those years?"

"We'd turned our backs on Elohim. We had strayed from the commandments of our God."

"And that is the God you want? One Who punishes us for not doing all He demands? At least the Philistines have a pantheon of gods to choose from. And life was not all that bad under their rule."

David rolled his eyes. "How would you know, Maon? Neither of us were born. But I know the stories. We were slaves."

"And we aren't now? Saul takes anyone he wants! He takes our women and makes them servants in his house. He's taken our fields…our flocks—anything he wants! It doesn't matter to him."[3] Maon snorted in disdain. "Come, David! What is the difference? We are still slaves. If Saul is Elohim's chosen, then He is no different than the Philistines."

Both David and Maon were standing now, facing each other in barely suppressed rage.

Maon's lips pulled back in a snarl as he finished, "The only difference between the two is that now we live in more fear, more death, and more slavery."

That did it. David decided to redecorate his brother's face with his fist. He struck out, his fist flying instinctively to its target. Maon must've been expecting it, for he ducked, and David missed cleanly. Before David could recover, Maon tackled him right off the rock. They hit the ground hard, David underneath. All his breath left him, and he gasped, eyes wide in shock.

Maon had been trained, as had David, by their older brothers. Both knew how to brawl and fight with anything at hand. Since Israel had few iron weapons available to them, the Hebrews had learned to fight with anything. They'd become rather proficient with fists, slings, and any sharp instrument that came to hand.[4]

---

[3] 1 Samuel 8:11-17, 14:52.

[4] 1 Samuel 13:19-21.

Still trying to get his breath back, David brought up his knee sharply. Maon blocked with an elbow, which freed David enough to hook his brother with his other leg and twist. Maon grunted as he spun away. Still gasping, David rolled to his feet, and turned, fists coming up.

Maon had found his own feet by then, and the two squared off, glaring angrily at each other. David had fought with his brothers many times before, but since he was the youngest, he usually fared badly. Fortunately, David knew how to take a hit, and he quickly found his breath again as he circled his brother. The last time the two had sparred, Maon had beat David. This time David vowed a different ending. No more sparring. His brother needed to be taught how to respect.

David gathered his feet for a leap when an animal roar of triumph shattered the air around the two young men. David and Maon both jumped reflexively, turning back to back and looking for the danger. The sheep bleated in terror and scattered, running without regard to direction or thought.

"There!" Maon cried, pointing.

David turned to look. Not two hundred cubits[5] away, a young male lion was dragging a lamb off into the trees. The lion looked half-starved, probably why it was bold enough to attack the herd in the presence of a shepherd in broad daylight. David could see the lion's ribs under its nearly beige coat. The darker mane nearly matched the tuff of dark fur on the lion's tail, which switched rapidly back and forth in excitement. Within moments, the lion had dragged its kill into the trees and disappeared.

"A lion," David hissed. He darted over to the flat rock and picked up his sling and satchel. He settled the pouch straps around his shoulders and then hefted his shepherd's crook. He started after the lion.

---

[5] A cubit is thought to be 18 inches or a foot and a half, often measured from the elbow to end of the longest finger. Obviously, this measurement will vary from person to person.

"You mean to pursue this creature?" Maon called. "David, it's a lion!"

"It has the taste of blood now," David replied, looking back over his shoulder. "If we don't slay it, it will continue to prey on the flock."

"We should get help."

David halted and shook his head. "We need to find it quickly. The animal will finish its meal soon and either disappear or begin hunting again. I'm going. You know what will happen if the lion just started killing indiscriminately. We could lose the whole flock!"

Maon hesitated. "Wait a moment," he called. He jogged up to David, who tensed, wondering if his brother intended to finish their fight. Maon noticed and rolled his eyes. "Don't be a fool, David. Here." He drew out a short iron knife bound tightly to a wooden hilt and presented it to David. "Take this."

David stared at the knife in amazement. After King Saul's victory over the Philistine army at Michmash,[6] the army had spoiled the dead and wounded, gaining for itself many of the only iron weapons Israel now possessed. Where had Maon gotten one, even one so flimsy looking?

Maon read the question in David's eyes. "I stole it from a drunk solider." He grinned. "One of Abinadab's men, actually."

David's eyes narrowed. "Thou shalt not steal," he quoted from the Law. "You should not have taken it."

His brother snorted. "Thou shalt not bear false witness," Maon also quoted. "Pray tell, what did Samuel say when you met him?"

David snapped his mouth shut, his eyes smoldering.

"Alas, I thought not. Do you wish the dagger or not?"

David snatched the knife. "Thank you."

"Be warned, David, do not risk your life needlessly. Track the lion to its lair if you must but keep watch over it only. I'll go fetch our brothers. We'll slay it together—safer that way."

---

[6] 1 Samuel 14:31-32.

David didn't understand his brother's changed attitude. Maon walked the edge of blasphemy almost joyfully, and he seemed to despise David at times, but at other times, he was thoughtful and showed genuine concern. But he spoke sense. There was no need to chase the lion down of his own accord. That lion looked to weigh four times as much as David. No doubt the beast could crack David's skull open with a single bite of its massive jaws—and it was hungry. It would not likely run away if David encroached too closely but would defend its kill with a ferocity that David knew he couldn't match.

"I'll be careful," he promised Maon. "But hurry."

Maon nodded and took off toward Bethlehem. He ran smoothly in a loping gait that retained speed and endurance at the same time. At least he wasn't dawdling.

David turned back to the trees where the lion had vanished. He figured the lion wouldn't go too far, wanting to eat. Taking a deep breath and a firmer hold on his shepherd's crook, he jogged to the grove of trees. He saw the blood trail left by the lamb. At least tracking the beast wouldn't be too hard.

He edged into the trees, walking slowly. He almost took out his sling, but the dense trees and undergrowth wouldn't allow for a good throw or line of sight. The same problem also existed for the crook. The staff was nearly four and a half cubits high, at almost two spans taller than David himself. So unless the lion had taken its kill to a large enough clearing, the crook would do him no good.

"It's not as if I'm going to fight the beast," he muttered to himself as he set the crook against a tree and set down his sling and satchel. He took a firm hold on his only other weapon, Maon's iron dagger. He breathed a silent prayer to Elohim for safety and to hasten Maon on his way, and then he moved stealthily through the trees. He noted the direction of the breeze and shifted course to make sure he'd come upon the lion downwind.

He'd spent his entire life outdoors it seemed. He knew how to stalk animals and men. He moved lightly, making sure to avoid twigs and leaves that would give him away. His leather sandals had been oiled the day before, so they moved fluidly with his feet, making not a sound. Soon he heard the messy chewing of the lion as it tore feverishly at the dead lamb, sucking down great gobs of flesh in hasty bites.

David froze, carefully scanning the brush in front of him. He couldn't see the lion yet, but he was close, very close. He gripped the dagger tighter, wondering what he should do next. If he came too close, the lion could simply charge, and in these close confines, the lion would have all the advantages. Still, David couldn't let the lion escape either. He needed to do something.

Uncertain, David moved a few more cubits to the right, trying to get a better angle on the lion, and he inadvertently stepped on a twig. The sound, like pottery cracking on stone, split the silence. The lion suddenly went perfectly quiet as if the beast had never existed. David froze, his heart thumping in his chest so loudly that he figured the lion could hear it. *What now?* David scanned the surrounding brush, looking for the lion, seeking escape routes, and hoping for his brothers—*what is taking them so long?*

The lion roared in rage, and a tan blur leaped out of the brush right at David. He screamed, throwing himself to the side in a desperate gamble to avoid the lion's charge. Pain suddenly stabbed through his body as the lion's razor-sharp claws narrowly missed his abdomen and raked across the flesh of his left arm instead. his flesh. David rolled over into the brush and slammed up against a tree trunk. He needed to move fast. The enraged lion would be on him in a second.

But the pain did something else to David. His fear evaporated like water on heated rocks, leaving him focused. Angry. Ready. Determined. The lion needed to be stopped. David knew instinctively that the lion had gone mad with rage. The beast would kill everything and anyone that got in its way. The flock of sheep was in danger, but so were the shepherds. This lion was a killer, and when it finished with David, it would be a killer of men.

As if possessed by a different spirit, David moved even as time slowed. He saw the lion pivot with frightening grace, saw its muscles bunch as it prepared to spring at the man who dared to interfere with its meal, saw it commit to the spring, and David leaped upward.

He twisted in the air as the lion smashed into the tree trunk below, its head lifted in rage and teeth snapping mere finger widths from David's face and its claws raking the bark of the tree. Somehow, David managed to come down on top of the lion. He instinctively grabbed the mane around the lion's neck, and he managed to sneak one arm under one of the forelegs and hook it over the lion's neck. So positioned, David squeezed tightly.

The lion went berserk.

David could honestly say that he had never experienced anything quite like the frenzied next few moments. The lion, desperate to get at its tormentor, rolled over, claws raking the air, teeth snapping, and spittle flying everywhere. The weight of the roll nearly crushed David, but he held on, determined to keep his perch because to let go would be to die.

Only then did he realize he had lost his dagger somewhere along the way. David searched the ground frantically for it and finally spotted it a few spans away. With strength born only of Elohim, David maintained his hold on the lion's neck and stretched his left hand out to the dagger and managed to snatch it up. Without hesitation, he plunged the iron blade deep into the lion's neck.

If the lion had been berserk before, the enraged beast now went utterly mad. Despite his best efforts, David was wrenched off, and he flew away to land in an unsightly and painful heap in a low-lying bush.

With a roar of his own, David shook off the pain, surged to his feet and charged back into the fight. The lion was turning in circles, snapping insanely at the dagger still buried in its neck, and so failed to notice the wild young man as he flung himself at the lion once again. David didn't try to get on top of the lion this time. He simply waded in head on and grabbed the embedded dagger by the hilt with one hand and the lion's mane with the other, much like grabbing a man's beard[7] under the chin. David's momentum forced the lion back on its haunches, where it scrabbled frantically to keep its balance, even as its head came up more level with David. Withdrawing the blade, he plunged it into the lion's neck three more times in rapid succession while holding the lion's snapping jaws away from his face.

For the briefest of moments, their eyes locked—the lion's tempestuous fury matched against David's implacable sense of necessity. Necessity won. The lion managed to hook its paw over David's left arm, burying its claws into the flesh, but before the beast could add new cuts, its strength gave out. The light died in the lion's eyes as the animal slumped to the ground, dead. David let it go and stepped back, watching as a large pool of blood gathering beneath the beast's head.

David stood over the fallen beast, his eyes a bit wild, and his breath coming in great gasping breaths. He felt a sense of exultation as well. He had done it. He'd killed a lion![8] And just as suddenly, the sense of purpose and strength vanished from David.

He stumbled backward, collapsing into a sitting position as he began to tremble all over. He felt a strange chill and then pain. Blinking, he stared at his arm. Long bloody, gouges ran from forearm to elbow. Blood dripped from the wounds, splattering the dried leaves upon which he sat. His ribs hurt too. Well, in truth, *everything* hurt. Man simply wasn't meant to fight the power of such an animal.

It came to him then that his victory hadn't been his own. Jehovah Elohim, the God of his fathers, had been with him. He shouldn't have been able to defeat the lion. Not with the wounds he'd sustained. Something had come over him and had given him strength and power. The Spirit of the LORD.

Awe washed over him as he realized the truth. Maybe Samuel's anointing had meant something real after all. Maybe Elohim really was with him.

---

[7] 1 Samuel 17:35.

[8] 1 Samuel 17:34-36.

Ten minutes later, David was still sitting and shivering beside the dead lion when men broke through the underbrush and came upon him. They slammed to a stop, astonished at the sight of David sitting next to the slain lion.

"By my father's gray beard," one man muttered, "the lad's slain the lion by himself."

The others murmured, staring at David as if he were the guardian angel set to protect Eden. David didn't recognize any of them. *Where are my brothers?*

Then Maon pushed forward. He looked at the lion. Looked at David. And looked back at the lion. "You were not content to keep watch over it," he said just loud enough for David to catch.

David gave his brother a wan apologetic smile. Surrounded by strangers, he would've gotten up, but his legs were still trembling, and he feared he'd just tumble over again.

"Are you hurt anywhere else?" Maon asked, gesturing to David's arm.

"Nay." A lie. He hurt everywhere.

A curly redheaded man strode around the lion and knelt next to David. "This is truly remarkable, lad. You are a mighty man of valor indeed to have slain a lion with naught but a single dagger and to only come away with such minor wounds."

The man's voice was nasally, as if he had a head cold. David instinctively didn't like him. David also noted that the man conveniently ignored what the dagger was made of. With so few iron weapons available, that should have at least prompted a comment. But the man, obviously not a Hebrew, ignored it. David tried to place the man's nationality. He spoke Hebrew well, but with a thick accent. *Edomite perhaps?*

"Come," the man said, "let us get you back on your feet and away from this place. It is fortunate that your brother found us, though it looks like our help is not needed except to patch up those wounds." He pulled David to his feet, and David had to grasp the man's arm to keep from falling over. He felt faint. The curly redheaded man grinned. "It is called battle shock, lad. Happens after a particularly nasty fight. Fear not. You're in good hands."

David looked at the man and decided that there was no harm in being polite. "Thank you. I'm David, son of Jesse."

"Well met, lad. I am Doeg, King Saul's chief herdsman."

A spike of dread, like a chill that raised goosebumps on the arms, shivered its way up David's spine. A whisper of warning told him to be very, very careful. These men were Saul's servants. And Maon had brought them. David didn't know what it meant. Had his brother sought out these men on purpose or had their meeting been coincidence? Either way, David was in more danger now than he had ever been from the lion.

# Chapter Four

"Very well, lad," Doeg announced, plopping himself down on a fallen tree trunk. "Your sheep have been rounded up. Your arm bandaged. Your possessions reclaimed. Tell us the tale, lad. Tell us how you slew the lion!"

David winced, hoping the men around him would interpret his expression as one of pain and not of anxiety. He sat among strangers, except for Maon who stood outside the circle of men, his arms crossed, and wearing an amused look. Some ten men of Doeg's herdsmen sat in a circle around David. For the most part, they were Hebrews, but at least two were Moabites and one looked to be an Amalekite. That last was strange, for most of the Amalekites had been destroyed by Saul at Elohim's command.[1] But apparently not all. David had heard of many renegade Amalekites who still troubled Israel, raiding many of the border towns and villages. *What is one doing among Saul's servants?*

"Aye, loosen your tongue, lad!" shouted one of the Hebrew herdsmen, taking a wineskin and drinking deeply. He wiped his mouth and passed the skin to David. "Drink! Tell us the tale!"

David took the wineskin, eyeing the men around him. He had wanted to go home, but the men had refused to let him, saying that they wanted to hear the tale of his kill first. The men had helped him round up his scattered sheep, cleaned and bandaged his arm, and even skinned the lion for him. The hide was stretched between two short trees. They'd also dressed the lion and had the meat slowly roasting over a fire not far away. They had turned the incident into a festive occasion.

Tipping back the wineskin, David took a swallow. The liquid was mostly water, cut with wine to ensure that the water was drinkable. Common herdsmen like these couldn't afford more than watered wine. They'd used some of it to clean his arm and the

[1] 1 Samuel 15:20-21; 2 Samuel 28:18.

various other cuts and scrapes. The bruises and his sore ribs would just have to heal on their own. Oh well. He'd heal. David handed the wineskin back to the man who immediately took another long pull before handing it to the next man.

They all looked so eager as they waited for him to begin his tale. He saw admiration and excitement. None doubted he had actually killed the lion, but all wanted the tale which would be told again and again to their families and friends. The story would be embellished, of course, and no doubt they would soon be telling of how they had personally witnessed the fight firsthand.

So he told them, starting slowly, trying to recall as much detail as possible. But he stumbled over the words, unsure how to present it right. So many of the details were fuzzy even to his own brain. Everything had happened so fast. It wasn't working. He couldn't tell the story right. It lacked something. He fell silent, staring at the waiting men around them.

They urged him on with their eyes, saying nothing, waiting for him to continue. David bit his lower lip. How? His eyes fell upon his harp. He reached over and picked up the instrument, strumming the strings and sending vibrating chords into the air. Yes. This was how he could tell the story—in song.

Closing his eyes, he began to play. The notes felt right, flying off his fingers as he set both hands roaming over the strings with increasing speed. He then sang the story of the hungry lion and how he had laid it low. The words came of their own accord, the melody attuned to the lyrics. He sang of the might and power of the lion, its hunger, and its savage hunt. He swept the men up in the story, caught their imagination, and took them to a place where beast, enraged at being interrupted in its kill, tested its mighty strength against puny man. David sang of the Spirit of the LORD, how Elohim stood with David in that moment of death and delivered the lion into David's hands. He caught the essence of the LORD's Spirit in the melody and sang with a passion he'd never before felt. The glory belonged to Elohim. And then the song ended.

David opened his eyes slowly as the last of the notes faded off into the landscape around him. The men sat spellbound, some with mouths hanging open. They had never heard its like before. Indeed, David felt drained. He had given himself into that song. Part of him would forever be bound to it.

The men began clapping, pounding their thighs or hands in appreciation. Doeg, the Edomite, clapped with the men, but he wore a different expression, something born of cunning. David didn't know what to make of it. The only person who did not clap was Maon. He still stood beyond the circle of men, arms folded across his chest. He regarded David strangely, and not in a friendly way. It looked as if David's brother had come to a decision of some sort, but what it could be, David had no idea. Still, knowing his brother, David doubted he would like it when he found out.

Doeg rose and slapped David across the back. "Well done, lad. That was a song fit for a king." His raspy voice made it sound mockingly, but then that could just be David's imagination. "We will honor this tale and your song, young one."

The men began talking to each other, hands gesturing as they retold the story in their own words. Listening, David grew despondent. Their words lacked the spirit of his song, and they did not give glory to Elohim as David intended. They were giving David the glory.

Doeg sat down beside him. "Perhaps you can aid me, lad. I hear tell that the Great Seer came to Bethlehem not a week gone by. Have you heard of this perhaps?"

David grew very still. Here it was. Samuel had predicted this. He needed to tread carefully. "Aye, I heard of this."

"Good. Good. I myself am a follower of your Elohim," Doeg said, his eyes alight—not with the fervor of conviction, but with the fervor of something else…greed? Perhaps. "I hold the seer in great esteem and would know of his comings and goings. Know you the purpose of the seer's visit? Perhaps you know of what he sought?"

"Sought? I know not. The Great Seer sought nothing other to offer a sacrifice to the LORD."

"Ah," Doeg said in a placating tone. David frowned in suspicion. "It was a grand sacrifice then?" the redheaded man continued. "All of Bethlehem was witness?"

"Nay," David said, shaking his head. "He called only the elders. If you wish to know more, you must speak to them."

"All the elders were present?"

"Aye."

"Perhaps your father was among them?"

David hesitated. Jesse was indeed among the elders of the city. Jesse owned the largest flocks of sheep in this region and brought a level of economic stability to the area that would otherwise be lacking. His advice and counsel carried great weight in Bethlehem. This fact was well-known, so there was no reason that this Doeg would not know of it.

"Aye. My father was there—along with all the elders."

"And did your father speak of it to you?"

David shrugged, trying to be as casual as possible. "Some. He gave no particulars except to say that the Great Seer had come to worship the LORD."

"Of course, as it should be." Doeg's eyes had narrowed to slits. His curly red hair hung down nearly in front of them, giving his eyes a shaded, evil look. David cared not for the man at all. "But I heard tell that Jesse's sons were there too—"

"I was not called," David cut in sharply, his heart suddenly racing. "My brothers were there indeed, but I remained with the sheep. Someone had to watch the flocks."

"Ah. Of course. But is it not strange that of all the elders, your father alone brought his sons to the sacrifice?"

Fear crept into David's heart. The man was leading him on. Clearly, he had already discovered that David's father and brothers had been at the sacrifice. Was he trying to catch David in a lie? He cleared his throat. "It is not for me to question the Great Seer, Edomite. I cannot reveal the mind of the seer. Would it not be wiser to speak to the seer himself?"

The man's smile revealed several missing teeth. "Be at peace," he said in his gravelly voice. "I merely seek to satisfy my curiosity. The seer has been loath to leave his house these past two years, and when he does, he travels here for a sacrifice. Why here? What was his purpose?"

"To offer a sacrifice to the LORD," David said. "What else could it be?"

"Aye. What else."

Thankfully, the man fell silent. David looked nervously around for Maon, but sometime during the conversation, his brother had disappeared. David didn't know what to make of that. At least the Edomite couldn't question his brother and discover David's lies.

David stood slowly to his feet, wincing as his body protested the mighty effort required to even perform that small feat. "I must be gone," he told the men. "I am most grateful for the help and for the company. Though I'll miss partaking of the lion's flesh." He shrugged good-naturedly. "It was but a scrawny beast at best, so I leave it to you, my friends. Enjoy!"

The men cheered him. Only Doeg remained silent, frowning. He gave David a nod that could have been one of approval or dismissal. It didn't matter so long he could get away from the Edomite. The man was entirely too curious about what had happened when Samuel had come to Bethlehem.

Gathering his possessions, David moved away from the men and out among the sheep. His sheep were mingled with the sheep of Saul's. The herdsmen had other flocks and herds of cattle, but the hills around Bethlehem were not that conducive for cattle grazing, which required more flat ground. Sheep could graze practically anywhere, and the hilly, rocky terrain interspersed with grass suited them just fine.

Putting his hand to his mouth, he let loose with a call into the air. His father's sheep immediately lifted their heads from where they mixed with Saul's sheep. The rest totally ignored him. David called a second time, and the sheep came bounding to him, bleating incessantly as they gathered around. David used his crook to get them started toward Bethlehem and made a quick count. Only the lamb killed by the lion was missing. *Well, that's good news anyway.* Still, it bothered him to lose even one.

As he walked, the sheep followed along placidly. They knew the routine. He would only need to keep the occasional lamb from straying too far. Walking did, however, give him time to think. Something would need to be done about that Edomite. But what? If the man became too suspicious, he would dig even harder or report his doubts back to Saul. The last thing David wanted was for the king himself to come down here and confront the elders of Bethlehem. And Saul would do it too, if he thought it necessary.

Hopefully, Doeg had been given enough to pacify his curiosity. The herdsman was obviously intelligent, or he'd never have been given authority over all of Saul's herds. The man had already latched on to the one hole in the conspiracy to hide the true purpose of Samuel's visit. Why had only Jesse's sons been invited to the sacrifice? He fervently hoped the herdsman had been satisfied. David's very life could depend upon it.

David still didn't know why Samuel had chosen him, of all the men of Israel, to anoint as the next king of Israel. Despite Samuel and Saul's falling out, Saul was a beloved king[2]—for the most part. Maon certainly didn't feel any loyalty. But most Israelites did. Saul had wrought a great victory over the Philistines and freed Israel from their oppression. True, Saul had taken land, fields, harvests, and men and women for his own purposes. But that seemed a small price to pay for what he had accomplished.

David doubted that most men would appreciate David's anointing. He seriously doubted that once word got out, it would take Saul long to learn of it. The truth needed to remain hidden. David had no doubt that Elohim could deliver him from Saul's hand if needed, but why even get to that point? Elohim had not demanded that the anointing be made public. If anything, by Samuel's own

[2] 1 Samuel 11:12-15.

admission, the best course of action was to simply keep quiet about it.

Sighing, David rubbed one of his bruises. He needed to inquire of Elohim. Resolved, David picked up his pace, much to the chagrin of his sheep. He set his steps toward the house of Seraiah, Bethlehem's resident priest. David would ask him to inquire of the LORD. Perhaps then David would know what to do.

David left the sheep with his father's men outside the city and marched into Bethlehem proper. The town wasn't overly large, and many of the houses were scattered about. The town had a protective wall, assuming the low rock barrier qualified as such. Over the years, the town had expanded outward to include more houses, but some had started building outside the walls in recent years. No one really considered the wall to be very protective. But there was a gate. And the courtyard beyond the gate was where most of the business of the city took place.

Bethlehem wasn't like many of the more prominent cities, but it was the home of David's ancestors since they had settled in the land. Jesse owned many of the fields in the surrounding countryside, and as had once been farmed by Jesse's grandfather, Boaz, the primary crop was barley,[3] wheat,[4] and corn.[5] Between Jesse's fields, flocks, and vineyards, he was perhaps the richest man in the region, maintaining the family wealth since the days of David's great-grandfather.[6] Sadly, David had never gotten to meet Boaz, but he did have a vague recollection of his great-grandmother Ruth[7] until she had passed away when he was just a small boy.

---

[3] Ruth 1:22.

[4] Ruth 2:23.

[5] Ruth 2:1-3, 4:17.

[6] Ruth 2:1.

[7] Ruth 4:13 (Ruth was much younger than Boaz [Ruth 3:10], so it possible that she was alive when David was born.).

Despite the town's humble appearance, Bethlehem boasted of a rich history. Rachel, Jacob's[8] wife, was buried here[9] as was Ibzan,[10] one of the mighty judges of Israel. Truthfully, Ibzan was remembered more for his prolific nature in siring sixty children[11] than for the seven years he judged Israel.

David passed by the well near the gate,[12] stopping long enough to draw some water and fill his wineskin. His arm ached and burned, adding to his exhaustion, but the water refreshed him. He then proceeded through the open gate and through the courtyard beyond. Many of Bethlehem's residents were about, trading, working, or simply talking. The elders would meet here when important decisions needed to be made; otherwise, the courtyard was a place of commerce and business. In fact, it was here, David's father had often told his boys, that Boaz officially purchased all that pertained to Elimelech and Naomi, thus securing Ruth as his wife.[13] David's home had a rich history indeed, spanning all the way back to Salmon, son of Caleb, who first settled in the region.[14] The city had grown since those days, and the flattop houses spread out around the main road through the town.

With his fears gnawing at him like a dog worried a bone, David picked up his pace. The priest's house lay just beyond. He walked up to the wooden door of the stone, two-story house and knocked. A shuffling from inside announced the presence of someone within, but David still started when the door burst open and a balding, young man thrust his head out while shading his eyes from the sunlight. The Levite blinked rapidly to adjust his eyes until they focused on David standing politely before him.

---

[8] Or Israel. Jacob's name was changed to Israel in Genesis 32:28.

[9] Genesis 35:19.

[10] Judges 12:8-10.

[11] Judges 12:9.

[12] 2 Samuel 23:15; 1 Chronicles 11:17.

[13] Ruth 4.

[14] 1 Chronicles 2:50-51.

"Ah! Young David, so good of you to visit! Come, come, why are you standing within the sun's evil grasp? You'll get burned. The young truly have no sense."

David moved up as the priest ducked back inside. Everyone knew that Seraiah didn't much fancy the sunlight. His fair skin burned too easily, and the light hurt his eyes. Despite his crusty manner, the priest was probably in his early thirties. He wore a linen ephod, an apron like garment that hung over his outer vestments and distinguished him as a Levite priest. He waited for David to pass before slamming the door shut. David nearly jumped out of his skin.

"Sorry. Sorry," the priest apologized as he bustled past. "My wife and daughters are out doing womanly things and my son is no doubt tormenting the merchants, so I am left alone here. What it is that you seek of me, my young friend?" He noted the bandaged arm. "You're injured. Pray tell, what has transpired that you have earned such wounds?"

David wagged his arm to prove it functioned. "It's nothing." He hesitated. Now that he was here, he felt out of his depth. Who was he to inquire of the LORD? Would Elohim really answer? He swallowed his fear. He had to know. "I must needs inquire of Elohim. It's important, my lord." It was customary, when inquiring of the LORD, to bring a present to the priest.[15] David had thought hard about this matter, but he really only had one item to give. He withdrew the iron dagger from his belt and presented it to Seraiah. Hopefully, Maon wouldn't want it back. "I can offer this."

Seraiah's eyes lit up. "Iron?"

David nodded.

"This is too much, son. It is not necessary."

"It is a matter of life and death, my lord. I would not want it to cost me nothing."

The priest considered. "Very well. My wife will be overjoyed to have something more reliable to use around the house." He winked at David. "Let us pray she never decides to use it on me."

---

[15] 1 Samuel 9:6-9.

David grinned. He liked Seraiah. Some of the more austere residents thought the priest was too casual, too informal at times, but the man was devout, and no one could deny that. He had not been asked to the sacrifice when Samuel had come, and as far as David knew, the man had not even so much as uttered a single word of complaint.

The priest abruptly sobered. "You are set upon this course, young man?"

"Aye."

"Then give me leave to prepare."

David stepped back on the hard-packed dirt floor to allow the priest the room he requested. The man knelt and bowed his head. David suddenly felt nervous. He had never actually done this before. His father had, on occasion, and once David had gone along, but this was the first time he had done anything like this on his own.

Because Seraiah was descended from one of the two high priest lineages, he could wear the ephod and inquire directly of the LORD. Seraiah, if David remembered correctly, was descended from Eleazar, Aaron's son. Most of the priests attending the Tabernacle of the LORD at Nob were descended from Aaron's other son, Ithamar.[16] The Ark of the LORD, however, remained in the house of Abinadab in Kirjath-jearim,[17] near King Saul's city of Gibeah.

The only other man that David knew who could inquire of the LORD was Samuel, the Great Seer. Samuel was not of the line of the high priests, but a descendant of Gershom, Levi's son.[18] But the LORD had chosen Samuel as a boy to judge Israel.[19] The last judge. Now Israel had a king like all the other nations—a king who would likely kill David if he ever learned what Samuel had done in anointing him as the next king. David shivered.

---

[16] 1 Chronicles 6:3, 24:1-6.

[17] 1 Samuel 7:1-2.

[18] 1 Chronicles 6:20-28.

[19] 1 Samuel 1:28, 7:15.

Seraiah didn't look up, but he spoke suddenly into the stillness, nearly causing David to start again. "Speak, son of Jesse. Ask the LORD what you will."

Now that the time had arrived, David didn't know what to say. He swallowed, worried that his silence would somehow be irreverent under these circumstances. Yet Seraiah merely waited. When his father had inquired, he had kept the question simple. He had just asked the question, nothing more. Taking a deep breath, David started, "Shall I hide the thing done to me from King Saul? Will he seek to slay me as thy servant Samuel believes?"

A moment passed, and then in a deeper voice than David was accustomed to, Seraiah spoke, "Saul shall surely seek to slay thee upon the day he learns that I have given the kingdom to thee, but fear not. I shall be with thee. Heed my servant Samuel's words and remain in thy father's house."

For an eternity, seemingly, David just stood there looking at the priest. Then he let out his breath explosively. He found himself trembling violently. *Saul will seek to slay me!* He knew then that he had done right in hiding this matter from Doeg, the Edomite. But what now? He cursed himself for not asking a better question. He should have asked what to do about the Edomite. He grounded his teeth together. *What course should I now take?*

A hand fell on his shoulder. David looked into the eyes of the priest. Compassion and understanding shone there. "The LORD is with you, David. What evil then is there to fear? Even if you are led through the valley of death, as long as Jehovah Elohim is with you, then there is nothing to fear."

David calmed immediately. The priest was right. He realized suddenly that the priest now knew that Jehovah meant for David to be the next king. He stepped closer to the priest. "Did you understand the words you spoke?"

"Aye." The man's eyes twinkled. "But you have nothing to fear from me. I serve Jehovah first."

"Thank you."

Seraiah shrugged. "Thanks is not—"

A child burst through the door, letting in an explosion of light that caused the priest to flinch violently. The boy, perhaps six or seven, darted between David and the priest and sprinted to the wooden ladder that led up to the second floor of the house and scurried up it like a monkey, never so much as uttering a word.

"Curse that boy! He must've caused a ruckus with the merchants." Seraiah turned to shout up to the second floor. "Get down here, boy! Or I'll be sending you to the High Priest! This much energy needs taming. Perhaps it is time for you to begin your training!"

Grinning, David edged toward the open door. He knew when to leave. Seraiah didn't notice. The priest stalked over to the ladder, glowering darkly. "Ethan! Get down here!"

David scouted outside and gently closed the door. He looked up into the sunlight, letting it play over his face. Indeed, it did seem bright. But that was good. The days ahead might be fraught with peril, but if the LORD was indeed with him, he'd handle it.

# Chapter Five

"Why is your countenance fallen, brother?" Michal asked, her voice, though smooth, cut into Jonathan's reverie like a sword through flesh.

He dropped the hard bread he'd been gnawing on and shoved it across the polished table. He glanced over at his sisters, both of whom regarded him with the same expression—a mixture of disapproval and amusement. They'd gotten it from mother…and then perfected it. He sighed, knowing they wouldn't leave him alone unless he gave them something. "I don't want to be here." He nodded in a westerly direction. "I *need* to be out there."

Merab, his oldest sister at eighteen, leaned forward, her dark hair spilling around her face. Her veil, which she wore at all times around men, gave her face a ghost-like appearance. "Father *needs* you here. Besides, Ishui and Melchishua are out *there* with Abner. They'll take care of things."

Mention of Jonathan's two younger brothers only clouded his face. He was the oldest.[1] He was the most experienced. It should be him out there preparing for the Philistine invasion. Only his youngest brother, Ishbosheth[2] remained at home. Honestly, Jonathan really didn't understand his youngest brother's role. Jonathan and his other two brothers were warriors, but Ishbosheth was not. He was more of a counselor…or something. Father had never explained it to him, but if such a role existed, he'd never seen either his brother or father utilize the position. It was as if Saul feared what might happen if all his sons died in battle. But these were not the days to be careful. These were the days for men to step up or be enslaved. His father's refusal to put Ishbosheth in harm's way made no sense to him.

Jonathan folded his arms. "Father doesn't need me here. He's got you two. And Mother."

[1] 1 Samuel 14:49.

[2] 2 Samuel 2:8-10.

Michal's face hardened in disapproval. Jonathan saw it clearly since she had moved her veil back over her hair. She did that when only eating with family. "That's not true, Jonathan," she said, "and you know it. Father's…fits are getting worse—"

"Michal!" Merab snapped. "Be respectful!"

Michal's jaw firmed stubbornly. Jonathan recognized the look. His little sister at sixteen years of age was probably the most obstinate person he'd ever met. Fiercely loyal and fueled with a sense of propriety of how people should behave and act, she could be highly critical of anyone who failed to measure up to her standards. But when she stood behind someone, she went all the way. Hers seemed a heavy burden to carry for one so young.

Jonathan decided to intervene before the two started squabbling again. "I know I'm needed here," he cut in. "I just don't want to be. I've begun to think that something is afflicting Father. He's not the same…"

Merab refused to meet his eyes, her hands unconsciously smoothing her halug—a tunic-like garment—that had been gathered at the neck with a gold broach. A silver tiara kept her hair back out of her eyes. Jonathan's sister loved her jewelry. Perhaps recognizing her own uneasiness, she popped an olive into her mouth. She also loved olives.

His youngest sister huffed. "It's an evil spirit from the LORD, and you know it. Father should have never disobeyed the Great Seer."[3]

Jonathan ground his teeth together. The seer's words still burned in his ears, galling and infuriating: "*The LORD has rejected you from being king.*" Jonathan hadn't been there when Samuel had spoken those fateful words, but Saul had certainly repeated them often enough—usually in a fit of rage. Samuel had as much as slapped Saul in the face with the fact that the LORD had already chosen someone else to replace him as king. If true, that effectively meant that

[3] 1 Samuel 15:22-23.

Jonathan wouldn't inherit the kingdom in his own right. He still wasn't sure how he thought about the matter.

Ultimately, it was all about Saul's legacy. The king suspected that Samuel would betray him and anoint someone else, so the moment they discovered that Samuel had left his home in Ramah, Saul's fears about what it meant had burst forth. Jonathan fervently wished the two powerful men could come to an understanding. He figured that the seer could intervene with Elohim and make things as they were. But Samuel would not so much as even see Saul.

He snatched the loaf of bread and took a large bite, chewing furiously while eyeing his two sisters as they ate much more demurely. Finally, he said, "I know it's an evil spirit. But what can be done? If the spirit is indeed from Elohim as you suspect, then we're all in a bit of trouble. It means God is against Father. Against us." He rubbed his hair, pushing the dark brown strands back into place. "Even the servants speak of it. They know. And if they know, the entire nation will soon know—if they don't already." He frowned deeply. "It is a bit irritating," he finished with his customary understatement.

Merab had stopped eating during his words, growing pale as the reality of the situation sunk in. Traditionally, in other nations, when there was a power shift, the new king often killed the entire family of the old king, ensuring that any future succession would fall to his own children and eliminating any potential claims to the throne. Jonathan understood. He immediately thought of his wife. What would become of her? They didn't have any children yet, but Jonathan hoped that would change. When it did, what would become of them?

Merab's voice squeaked as she asked, "What then can we do?"

Naturally, Michal had a different reaction. "What do you think, sister? We must either regain Elohim's favor or slay whomever Samuel anoints to replace Father."

The words, coming from Jonathan's sister, really didn't surprise him. Michal had a much more realistic outlook on life than Merab did, but Jonathan didn't like her frank appraisal. "Are you so bloodthirsty then?" he demanded.

Michal rolled her eyes. "Be it far from me, brother. I but spoke the words everyone is thinking—including Father. If he cannot prevail upon Samuel's support, he'll no doubt seek to slay the man Samuel anoints."

"Father is not a murderer."

His sister's eyes saddened. "Have you not seen these rages that have befallen him? Do not be so naive, brother. You've witnessed his anger." She half rose out of her own chair, glaring at her brother. "By the souls of our ancestors, Jonathan, Father once thought to slay you!"[4]

Jonathan shivered, remembering. If it hadn't been for the people, his father would've indeed killed him. He realized then, perhaps for the first time, how much of a blow it had been to his father that the LORD God had fallen silent and had refused to answer Saul's entreaties.[5] His father had been so torn by Elohim's silence that he had been willing to kill Jonathan to regain God's favor.[6]

"Your words ring true, Michal," Jonathan conceded. "But what can be done? If Elohim has chosen another man to be king over His people, then what right do we have to challenge it?"

It was a good question, one that Jonathan had been wrestling with for some time. Part of the problem was that he really didn't know how he felt about succeeding his father. *Do I really want to be king?* He'd seen how the weight of the kingdom had changed his father, how it had ground down a once humble man[7] and turned him into a man of fear and worry. Maybe it would be best if the burden passed to some other man.

But where would that leave Saul's family? That was the real question. Would they all be consigned to death? Jonathan looked around at the house. Though not as palatial as other kings' houses,

---

[4] 1 Samuel 14:45.

[5] 1 Samuel 14:37-38.

[6] 1 Samuel 14:44.

[7] 1 Samuel 9:21, 10:22, 15:17.

it was nonetheless still one of the richest and most luxurious houses in Israel. Would they lose everything if someone else became king? His father believed it so, and that was one reason why he worried so much.

Michal shook her head, causing her earrings to twinkle. "There may yet be another way."

Jonathan and Merab perked up at that. "What other way?" Merab asked.

"If we knew who this other man was, we'd need some way to bind him to our family. Make him part of our family. This would at least keep us safe."

"You speak of marriage," Jonathan said flatly. "To one of you two."

"Aye," Michal said simply. "It would be the easiest way to protect our family."

It was a common solution. Many kings would send daughters to marry into the royal families of neighboring nations. These marriages would not only cement the peace between them but would bind the two families together and give each a vested interest in maintaining the status quo and help quell potential coups.

Merab looked troubled. "I know not," she hedged.

Michal smirked. "Is that not because your heart is smitten for another?"

Merab blushed, and Jonathan raised an eyebrow. "Oh?" he asked. "Who?"

"Your armorbearer…I don't recall his name," Michal said, grinning.

"Adriel the Meholathite?" Jonathan stated, surprised. The man was a good friend, a fierce warrior, and a loyal companion.

Her face still red, Merab nodded. "You seem to favor him and so will Father." She turned on her sister. "But what of you? Would you wed this…this stranger, this usurper?"

Michal shrugged. "If I must. It would be the right thing to do, particularly if it secures our family's safety."

Jonathan studied his youngest sister. Still so young, but now very much a woman. At sixteen, she was certainly of marriageable age. Indeed, Jonathan knew of at least two men who had offered dowry for Michal's hand in marriage but had been turned down by his father. He didn't know if that had been because Saul didn't think they were worthy of his daughter or if Michal had had no interest in them and had persuaded her father to turn the men down. That she could persuade their father in such a matter was not in question. She could be annoyingly persistent.

A door burst open, and one of Saul's guards stuck his head in. He looked worried. "My lord, it's the king, he…" The man trailed off.

Michal, bound her veil across her face hurriedly even as Jonathan rose to his feet. "What is it, man? Speak!"

"It's starting again."

Jonathan swore by the blood of his fathers and barreled out of the room, nearly bowling over the hapless guard in the process. He charged down the wide hallway and burst into the large room where his father held court. He slammed to a stop in the middle of the room, taking in the entire scene. Servants hugged the walls, speechless and uncertain. And Doeg the Edomite groveled alone in the center of the floor. Jonathan hadn't seen the man in nearly a month, but for the moment he didn't care. His eyes instead focused on the large chair sitting at the back of the room.

Where King Saul raved.

The king, huddled in his chair, looked with wild eyes at everything and nothing. Stark terror[8] contorted his face, and blood ran down his chin from where he'd bitten through his lip. His body quivered like a reed shaken in the wind, and his hands gripped a javelin in both hands, his knuckles white. Well, that explained why everyone was cowering away and why Doeg was groveling on the floor.

[8] 1 Samuel 16:14 (The word "troubled" is translated as terrify and afraid in most cases. Saul was in terror.).

Jonathan swallowed his own dismay and strode forward, careful not to startle his father lest the king impale him with the javelin. He knelt before his father and grabbed the javelin with both hands. Saul's eyes looked through Jonathan. It was as if he existed in a different world—a world seen only by him.

"Father," he whispered, "come back to me. Hear my words."

Saul shuddered as he continued to clutch the javelin. Jonathan grunted as the weapon was nearly ripped from his grasp. Jonathan cursed softly under his breath. His father was strong! He pulled against his father's struggles, trying to get his attention.

"Father, it is I. Your son. Heed me, I beg!"

Saul's lips curled into a snarl, and his shaking stopped. He bellowed then, a feral shout that caused the hairs on Jonathan's neck to stand on end. With almost inhuman strength, he jerked to his feet, the force of which flung Jonathan away. *Curse that evil spirit,* he thought as he hit the floor and slid for half a dozen cubits. Pain flared as he struck, but he shook it off and rolled to a half crouch, preparing to tackle his father and keep him from killing someone with that javelin if needed.

It wasn't needed.

Saul's eyes cleared, and as before, he sagged as his strength left him. He flopped back into his chair, the javelin clattering unnoticed on the floor beside him. Carefully, Jonathan rose the rest of the way to his feet and stepped slowly up to the chair.

"Father?"

Saul looked up, his eyes showing pain, but not the terror of the moment before. He shakily wiped the blood from his chin. "My son? Jonathan? What happened?"

"You were taken by the evil spirit again, my lord."

"I was afraid," he whispered, tears standing in his eyes. "So afraid."

Jonathan swallowed. "Of what, my lord?"

"The Edomite brought word."

*Ah.* Jonathan turned toward Doeg, still lying on his face in the middle of the floor. "Rise, herdsman," he commanded, his voice barely on the edge of civility. "What word have you brought that has so unmade my father?"

The redheaded man pulled himself up to his knees, but stayed there, his eyes furtive. When he spoke, Jonathan winced. The man's voice grated against his ears. "I but did as my master commanded, my prince. I sought but to discover what the Great Seer's purpose was in Bethlehem."

"Say on." Jonathan's tone could frost the windows.

Doeg swallowed a few times but nodded his willingness. "I spoke with a few of the elders of the city and learned that Samuel the seer did indeed hold a sacrifice outside of town. I found the altar and the remains of the heifer.[9] All seemed as they had spoken to me. The only curious matter was the calling of one elder's sons to the sacrifice. They lingered after others had departed, and no one could tell me for what purpose."

"Did you speak to the elder himself?" Jonathan asked.

"Aye, my lord, to him and one of his sons, the youngest, I believe, who was not called to the sacrifice. I was told that the sons were there to assist the elders and Samuel in the sacrifice. They gathered the stones for the altar and prepared it for sacrifice."

"And you believe him?"

"Should I not, my lord? I found nothing amiss."

A growl from Saul turned Jonathan around. "The Edomite has failed me," he hissed. "He has not discovered Samuel's true purpose. There must be more. Samuel has betrayed me. He gathers prophets to stand against me." Saul reflexively reached for his javelin, and the Edomite gasped, his face turning pale, no doubt seeing his own death.

Jonathan kicked the javelin away. His father seemed not to notice as he fell back into his chair, rubbing his temples and wincing. This gave Jonathan time to consider. There could be more to the seer's business in Bethlehem, but what if there wasn't? Jonathan didn't doubt that Samuel would make good on his promise to anoint

---

[9] 1 Samuel 16:2.

another king over Israel, but it had been long since the debacle with the Amalekites. Yes, that Samuel had left his home and offered a sacrifice after such a long time was suspicious, but not unheard of. He had done this often in times past.

In addition, the Great Seer's school had grown into a compound of sorts. That could be seen as suspicious too, but Jonathan doubted the prophets gathering in Ramah was directed against his father. Still, something could be going on. He looked again at the Edomite. "Did the elders of Bethlehem request Samuel to come and offer a sacrifice?"

Doeg frowned. "Nay, my lord. Samuel's arrival terrified them.[10] They feared they had somehow caused offense. They know not why Samuel chose their city to offer his sacrifice."

"Curious," Jonathan said, troubled. Something still seemed amiss about the whole affair, but he couldn't put his finger on it. Enough. There was nothing to do about it now. Unless Saul decided to sack the entire town of Bethlehem, this line of inquiry would serve no further purpose. He looked at his father. "It may be as you suggest, my lord. However, I counsel patience. If the Great Seer had some other purpose than the sacrifice, it will become known to you in time. As far as the company of prophets, my lord, let it not rest heavy on your mind. We will keep an eye on it. More concerning to me is this evil spirit from the LORD that is troubling you. Something must be done."

One of the older servants stepped forward. Jeiel, Saul's armorbearer and longtime friend, bowed to Saul and Jonathan. "I have seen something of this before, my lords, and I believe something can indeed be done. Let my lord command his servants here to seek out a man who is a cunning player upon a harp. And when the evil spirit from God comes upon you, he will play with his hand, and you will be well."[11]

Saul grunted, still rubbing his temples with both hands.

[10] 1 Samuel 16:4.

[11] 1 Samuel 16:16.

Jonathan leaned over. "This is well said, my lord. Music could be the key to overcoming this troubling spirit."

Saul glanced up, his eyes blinking. "I care not."

Jonathan strove to keep his temper in check. "Father, I beg of you, let us search out such a man. It will do you well."

The king seemed to slump even more, and Jonathan spotted a faint tremor in the mighty king's hands. "So be it." He looked at Jeiel, his old friend. "Provide me a man who can play well and bring him to me."[12]

Jeiel, who had stood tensely erect, relaxed, a smile of relief touching his lips. He turned toward the rest of the servants in the room. "Know you of a man who can so play?"

Doeg, jumped to his feet, his face betraying a wild type of hope that bordered on desperation. "I know of such a man! I have seen a son of Jesse, the Bethlehemite. He is cunning in playing, and a mighty valiant man, a man of war." The man was practically gushing, trying to get out the words quickly. *The dog probably still fears Saul might slay him. He might be right at that.* The man continued while wringing his hands, "I dare say he is prudent in matters, a comely person, and Jehovah is with him."[13]

Before Jonathan could demand how the Edomite could know all this, his father waved his hand in a careless manner, seemingly distracted. "Fetch him then. I care not."

Concerned, Jonathan decided against pressing Doeg for any more information. He would let the servants fetch this so-called mighty valiant man and let him play his harp. Jonathan would judge the man in his own way. Helping his father now was all that mattered.

His father waved his hand again. "Leave me. All of you."

Jonathan nodded. "As you will, my lord."

As the servants filed out of the room, Jonathan tracked down the Edomite before he could scamper off to whatever hole he claimed as home. He took the man by the arm and hauled him after.

---

[12] 1 Samuel 16:17.

[13] 1 Samuel 16:18.

Doeg's face turned pale, and Jonathan glared at him condescendingly. "Stop that. I'm not going to hurt you."

"Aye, my lord."

Jonathan hauled the herdsman out into the hallway and waited for the door to close, sealing his father alone inside. He stopped Jeiel as the elderly servant, the last out, moved up. "Edomite, take Jeiel and fetch this harper of yours. I fear for my father, and if this harper can help dismiss the evil spirit, then we need him. Do not tarry overlong. I would have you gone by sunrise."

"Aye, my lord," the man agreed, bobbing his head.

Jeiel eyed Doeg, probably not relishing spending time with the herdsman. Well, Jonathan couldn't blame him. He had little liking for the man either. The redheaded man was an opportunist—willing to lick any shoe that would ingratiate himself with men of power.

Jeiel spoke, "We will leave at first light, my lord, after praying the Shema. I will attend to the details now."

Jonathan placed a grateful hand on the old servant's shoulder. "Thank you, my friend. Your service, as ever, is appreciated."

Jeiel returned the smile. "I've served your father for a long time, my lord. I will not fail him."

"Thank you. I would go myself, but we've had no word from Abner in four days. I don't like it. I may need to go see for myself what is happening at the border." Jonathan tugged at his beard, thinking. "It's all changing isn't it? It's not like it was before. Back then, we were more united, I think."

"It may not be as different as you believe, my lord. It took time for your father to gain the people's trust."

"You were there in the beginning, weren't you?"

"Aye. Your father and I sought the lost asses of your grandfather, Kish, and so Saul spoke to Samuel along the way. That is when they first met."[14]

Jeiel's smile warmed Jonathan. He'd heard the story, of course. Often, Jeiel's part in it was lost, forgotten by more monumental

[14] 1 Samuel 9.

personalities. But Jeiel didn't ever seem to be discontent with his part or lot. Too old to truly be Saul's armorbearer, he was still a good man—a man who could be trusted. "Again, I give you thanks," Jonathan finished.

"It is my duty."

"No, old friend. It is more than that, is it not?"

Jeiel smiled. "You were ever a discerner of men's hearts, my lord." He turned to Doeg. "Come, herdsman, let us prepare."

Jonathan watched them walk off, becoming lost in his own thoughts. A storm was coming. He could sense it. He would need to be strong in the coming days, and with Elohim's help, he determined to be victorious in whatever battles he must face. He prayed then, prayed for his father, his family, and his nation. Dark days were coming, and they would all need Elohim's favor to get through it.

Straightening his shoulders, he decided to find his sisters and assure them that all was well. Then he needed to return to his own house and wife. Whatever was coming could wait until tomorrow.

# Chapter Six

Laughter resounded around the table where Jesse's family ate. The sheep had, at last, been sheered, the plowing of the eastern fields had been started, and so the day's work was ended. Oil lamps burned in the corners of the room, casting flickering shadows over everyone's faces. The table, probably the best and largest in Bethlehem, stretched across the floor in front of the second-story sleeping quarters. The rambling stone building that housed Jesse's quite large family was probably the most noteworthy landmark within the city walls.

David sat at his place near the end of the table, teasing one of his young nephews. Asahel, at eleven years of age, constantly wore a serious expression. His sole ambition in life, it seemed, was to outdo his older brothers and cousins. His constant companion, Amasa, his cousin[1] and another of David's nephews, sat next to him engaged in scarfing down his bread and cheese as if he'd never eat another meal again.

Everyone was here tonight—a rare family event with so many sons, daughters, wives, husbands, and children. Some forty members of David's family had crowded into the room to eat. David idly prayed that the floor would hold up under the strain.

David eyed Asahel out of the corner of his eye, and when the lad turned to say something to Amasa, he snatched the boy's cheese right out of his hands and took a large bite.

"David!" Asahel shouted, spinning and grabbing at his stolen food. "Unhand my cheese!"

While Asahel's back was turned, Amasa calmly stole his cousin's loaf of bread. David fended off his nephew's grasping hands, smirking all the while. "You must be quicker than that," he teased.

---

[1] 2 Samuel 17:25; 1 Chronicles 2:16-17.

Growling, Asahel prepared to lunge at his uncle, but David pushed him back into his stool with a hand to the face. The boy tried to shove away David's arm to no avail. "Release me! Give back my cheese!"

David let go, looking serious. "Fine. I'll trade you for your bread then."

Asahel looked at his place atop the table and discovered his bread was also gone. He looked wildly around and then saw Amasa finishing off the last bite. "Thief!"

That started a minor wrestling match that the adults mostly ignored. This was too festive an occasion to dampen the boys' play. The sheep had yielded much wool this year, so the family anticipated quite a lucrative selling season. It was a time to rejoice in the bounty of Elohim's goodness. The whole family had pitched in to get Jesse's large flocks sheered, and the women had labored long into the day to prepare this feast.

Grinning, David returned the cheese to his nephew, who was too busy wrestling to notice, took another small loaf of bread, and dipped it in a pot of honey, carefully avoiding the disgusting goat meat that sat in a heap near the bread. *Nothing like bread and honey.* He savored the taste, letting the sweetness trickle down his throat and tease his taste buds.

Maon looked on silently. Since the incident with the lion, David's brother had not spoken to him. More precisely, Maon had grown more and more remote since David had played his harp for Saul's servants. Not that David minded all that much. He didn't have much to say to his brother.

But other than Maon's self-enforced silence, everyone else was laughing, boasting, or discussing the coming planting season. Something Ithra, Amasa's father, said while speaking to Jesse caught David's attention. "The trade routes toward Egypt are becoming dangerous. The Philistines are growing bolder in their raids, so I advise selling to King Saul. He will have great need of the wool. And there is little merit in losing men or goods to the Philistines."

Jesse considered his son-in-law's comment, his lips pursed. "Your words are wise. When we send the king the tithe[2] of the sheering, we can make a formal offer for the bulk of the wool. I do not wish to sell it all to him. I'd like to reach out to the surrounding towns as well—plus we need to distribute an additional tithe to the Levites."

Ithra leaned back, his dark skin absorbing the light of the lamps. He was an Ishmaelite who had converted to the Hebrew religion.[3] "Well spoken," he agreed in his thick accent. "What about Moab? They'd probably be willing to pay more."

Jesse shook his head. "War looms upon our future. Let us first see to our own people."

Ithra nodded. "Very well. Do you wish that I make the offer to King Saul?"

David saw his father's eyes roam over the table, looking at each of his sons and sons-in-laws. He briefly rested on David, his eyes crinkling in worry, and then he passed on. "That would be for the best. You've the most experience in trade."

David sighed in relief. For a moment, he feared his father would have him go with Ithra to meet Saul. Jesse liked to train his sons on every aspect of the business, but in this matter, David would've dreaded the meeting with the king. The family had managed to evade Saul's inquiring herdsman, but David in no way believed that he'd heard the last of the matter.

Abinadab entered the conversation. "I believe the king would be agreeable, Father. My soldiers will have great need of the wool in the coming days. The winter's chill may have passed, but it hasn't been forgotten."

Eliab leaned forward. "Will the king order you and your men to the border, Abinadab? Rumors abound that Jonathan has been recalled and Abner sent in his stead."

---

[2] 1 Samuel 8:17.

[3] Comparing 1 Chronicles 2:17 to 2 Samuel 17:25, one claims he was an Ishmaelite and the other an Israelite. I speculate that he converted to the Hebrew faith.

Shrugging, Abinadab speared a slab of cheese with his knife. "I expect the command will come soon. Abner will want to consolidate the army once he determines where the Philistines will invade."

Looking at his father, Eliab said, "Father, when this happens, I will follow King Saul into battle."

The mood around the table sobered. Everyone fell silent to listen. Jesse looked disturbed, but he nodded. "It is your place, if you so will. Elohim protect you, my son."

Eliab pulled back a bit from the table, satisfied. He turned to Jesse's third son, their brother. "And what of you, Shammah? Would you follow Saul into battle alongside your brothers?"

Shammah frowned. Like his brothers, he was not new to war or combat. All three had fought in several of Saul's campaigns against raiders and overambitious neighboring nations. But of the three, Shammah least enjoyed battle. He leaned more toward scholarship and had studied any and every scroll that his father could lay his hands on. His wife was expecting their first child, and David's studious brother had already chosen a name if the child was a boy: Jonathan, named perhaps for the king's eldest son.[4] Being a father would temper him even more, so David was somewhat surprised when he said, "Aye, I will go with you into battle."

Eliab slapped his brother on the back. "Good man! Us three then! No uncircumcised Philistine would dare stand against us!"

That did it. David stood up, fired by the vision his brother had created. "As will I, Father! I would go into battle too."

Everyone stilled again, this time looking at David. He suddenly felt self-conscious. Eliab glanced away to peek at their father and then turned back to David. "You are yet too young, little brother. You lack three summers yet before you may enter battle with us."

David's brow furrowed. "The Philistine dogs care not for a man's age, brother. They will slaughter us all the same. It is my right."

"Nay," Abinadab disagreed. "It is not. You are yet untested, brother. The time will come, but it is not now."

[4] 1 Chronicles 20:7.

*Untested?* David raised his left forearm, still in bandages from the lion's raking claws. "The LORD has tested me, brother. Every man must be allowed to fight the LORD's battles. I cannot idly abide their blasphemous tongue nor their unholy gods in our lands."

Maon snorted. "Your victory over the lion was but good fortune, David. That does not make you a warrior."

David's face clouded over, but before he could retort, Abinadab stood and rounded the table. He took David's shoulders, forcing the younger man to stand before him. "Elohim is with you, David. He gave you strength to prevail over the lion, but, little brother, Maon is correct. It does not yet make you a warrior. Do not be so hasty to see battle."

David saw pain in his brother's eyes—of horrors witnessed and scars that would never fade.

He continued, "There is another reason to abide here in our father's house, and you know it."

He spoke of Samuel's anointing and warning. But didn't that mean he should, more than any of them, go to the battle? What was the LORD's anointed but to protect Israel and deliver Elohim's chosen from their enemies? It wasn't fair! David itched to fight. He'd trained his whole life with his brothers. Why wouldn't they see? The more he thought of the Philistines and their unholy feet treading the land that Elohim had given to Israel, the more his skin crawled. He would not abide it.

Yet what choice did he have? Still…

Jesse stood, bringing all conversation to an abrupt end. Everyone fell quiet and settled back in their seats or stools. Jesse looked over his family, and David saw joy there, overshadowed by a touch of fear. The old man placed a hand on his wife's shoulder, and she clasped it in both of hers. David felt ashamed. Such talk worried his mother.

Lifting his free hand, Jesse spoke the grace after the meal,[5] "We bless Thee, O Jehovah Elohim, for the good of the land which we

[5] Also known as the Birkat Ha-Mazon and based on Deuteronomy 8:10.

have enjoyed this night. We are full because of Thy blessings upon our land, and thank Thee for such."

Everyone at the table murmured the words after, thanking God for His riches and prosperity upon their people.

Jesse then looked up and began praying the Shema, "Hear, O Israel: The LORD our God is one LORD: And thou shalt love the LORD thy God with all thine heart, and with all thy soul, and with all thy might. And these words, which I command thee this day, shall be in thine heart: And thou shalt teach them diligently unto thy children, and shalt talk of them when thou sittest in thine house, and when thou walkest by the way, and when thou liest down, and when thou risest up. And thou shalt bind them for a sign upon thine hand, and they shall be as frontlets between thine eyes. And thou shalt write them upon the posts of thy house, and on thy gates."[6]

Jesse continued, quoting from the Torah, the Law, as commanded by Moses.[7] He ended the prayer with the famous line, "I am the LORD your God, which brought you out of the land of Egypt, to be your God: I am the LORD your God."[8]

When his voice fell silent, everyone remained in their seats, also silent, taking a moment of time to reflect upon the words. For David, the words sent a thrill into his heart. He had long ago memorized them, but more importantly, he had made them a part of him. Israel's past wasn't all that glorious. People tended to forget Elohim's commandments and His mighty acts. One line of the Shema in particular always stirred David, "That ye may remember."[9] For some reason, those words burned in David. He didn't want to forget. He didn't want his people ever to forget again.

Jesse clapped his hands, indicating the devotion was at an end, and the family began talking again, beginning the cleanup. David's proclamation to go to war was forgotten by everyone except David.

---

[6] Deuteronomy 6:4-9.

[7] Parts 2 and 3 of the Shema are quoted from Deuteronomy 11:13-21 and Numbers 15:37-41.

[8] Numbers 15:41.

[9] Numbers 15:40.

The next morning found David standing in the central courtyard of the family's house. He held his staff in two hands, the worn wood comfortable as he faced his older brother Abinadab, armed with a shorter stave that represented a sword. The ground here was packed hard from centuries of traversing feet. Off to one side, a stable stood where Jesse kept some of the more important breeding stock. A door led into the kitchen and the downstairs area, and a staircase from the side led up to the second floor. Jesse was rich enough to cover the courtyard with a wooden frame roofed over with branches and a type of stucco that resisted water.

Rooms had been built against the main compound to accommodate the growing family. David himself slept on the second floor during the winter and on the roof during the summer—cooler than in the house.

David eyed his brother, twirling the staff in his hands and pacing around the courtyard, looking for an opportunity to get a strike in. Abinadab held his practice sword up near his head, point straight up, and turned in slow circles as David paced around him. David didn't have much skill with the sword yet, but the staff was something else. A shepherd always had a staff, and David had spent a lot of time wielding the longer wood.

He felt confident that he could take his brother. This time.

He attacked, letting the staff slide down his hands so that it elongated, and swung it at his brother's legs. Abinadab parried and moved in, trying to get within the reach of the longer weapon, but David stepped back and realigned his grip so that he held it equally in the middle. All the same, he barely avoided being clobbered alongside the head, just barely getting his staff between himself and Abinadab's strike.

He then rotated the staff in a blinding spin to keep his brother from raking down the staff with his sword—which, in a real fight, would likely have cut off all of David's fingers—and tried to bash his brother's head with the other end. Abinadab ducked smoothly out of the way and retreated.

"Your skill has improved, brother," he said, smiling. "But in a real battle, a shepherd's stick wouldn't hold up to a sword. They'd chop your stick in half, brother."

David snorted. "Mock if you will, but I've the mastery of you this time, Abinadab."

"Bring it then, little brother."

David did. For the next ten minutes, they struck, twirled, and lunged at each other. David took two glancing blows, one against his right shoulder and the other against, of course, his left forearm, leaving his previously injured arm throbbing abominably. He'd only managed to penetrate his brother's guard once, poking him in the stomach with the end of the staff, but if Abinadab felt any pain, he didn't show it. His insufferable grin got under David's skin, so he pressed harder.

He jabbed with the end of the staff, but his brother casually knocked it aside. David allowed the parry to add momentum to the staff as he brought the other end over in a blur of wood. Abinadab grunted, flinging himself back just in time. He rolled along the hardpacked dirt and leaped to his feet.

"Playing dirty, eh?" Abinadab said, marching right back in with narrowed eyes.

David grinned. "Worried about being bested by your littlest brother?"

What came next took David's breath away. His brother was a whirlwind of movement, his wooden sword striking like a viper, seemingly everywhere at once. David found himself pressed back on his heels, his staff desperately trying to parry the lightning fast strikes. Then he got hit, once, twice, and then a third time.

David blinked, wondering why the buildings had tilted onto their side or why his brother seemed to be standing sideways on the courtyard wall, defying gravity. A high-pitched ringing sound filled his ears. Cognitive functions returned slowly. *Oh. I'm lying on the ground.* No wonder everything looked wrong. His head throbbed for some reason. There were other pains, but they seemed like a distant memory. "What happened?" he asked his brother.

Abinadab shook his head. "We'll need to train you to the sword, little brother. You still have a way to go." He reached down and hauled David to his feet.

The world spun inconsiderately, and he stumbled to the side.

"Here now," Abinadab said, grabbing his arm and steadying him. "I hit you a little too hard, I'm afraid." He smiled. "Sorry about that."

"What?" David shouted, trying to shake that infernal ringing out of his ears.

"Sorry!"

"Oh." David shook his head and finally regained control of his body, though unsteadily. "I think I need to learn the sword," he informed his brother.

Abinadab just grinned. By the beard of Pharaoh, David hated that smug look.

A sharp banging sounded at the compound's main gate. A voice from over the wall shouted above the din of other noises, "Open in the name of King Saul!"

*Saul!*

David stood rigidly, adrenalin shoving aside his pain. He exchanged a fearful look with Abinadab. "Mayhap I am the one they seek," the older brother said.

Some of David's fear melted away. That made sense. Abinadab was captain of the local garrison and was Saul's man. Aye. That had to be it.

Abinadab strode over to the gate and pulled it open. The heavy gate opened ponderously, like a storm building on the horizon. Outside, a group of men stood arrayed before the gate. The two in front wore colors belonging to King Saul's servants. A few soldiers stood behind the servants, but no one that looked particularly important.

David could see his brother's frown. "What is the meaning of this?" he demanded of the men. "You have disturbed the peace of this house."

The lead servant bowed. "Your pardon, my lord. I am Jeiel, servant of King Saul. I bear a message to Jesse the Bethlehemite. Please inform him of our presence."

Abinadab regarded the man silently for a moment. He turned to David and gestured. "Inform our father," he ordered.

Relieved to be gone, David darted away and up the stone staircase to the second level. He found his father sitting with his mother, Natzbet, while she worked a loom, making yet another garment for someone in her growing family. "Father, messengers from King Saul have arrived. They seek you."

Jesse rose to his feet and brushed a hand through his silver beard. "Rest easy, son. We know not their purpose."

"What other purpose could they have?" David demanded, looking back over his shoulder.

"Several come readily to mind, son. Come, but stay beyond their sight."

David followed his father down the stairs. The old man took his time and arrived calmly to where Abinadab had admitted Saul's men into the courtyard. David ducked into the kitchen from which he could both see and hear.

"I am Jesse, lord of this house," his father announced upon arriving. "What message from the king?"

The one named Jeiel stepped up. His beard showed signs of gray, but he had trimmed it some—unusual for most Jewish men who tended to allow their beards to grow as they may. Saul's servant bowed again to Jesse. The man took out a small piece of parchment upon which was scrawled a few words in the Hebrew language. "Thus says the king, 'Send me David your son, who is with the sheep.'"[10]

---

[10] 1 Samuel 16:18.

David's heart seemed to want to crawl down into his stomach and hide there. *I am a dead man.* Somehow, someway, Saul had found out.

If it weren't for his father's calm bearing, David would've been halfway to the Moab border by now. But Jesse folded his hands in front of him and calmly asked, "What know you of my son, servant of Saul?"

Jeiel neither looked bothered or fazed by the question. "The king requires your son, my lord, the one named David. He is a shepherd and a harper." He turned to the men behind him and pointed to one in particular. "The herdsman there has met your son. This is how we know of him."

The redheaded Edomite stepped forward, the same one David had met after slaying the lion. The one with all the questions. The one who had questioned the family about Samuel's purpose around the sacrifice. The one who'd been suspicious of David.

David felt his heart thumping against his chest, but a spike of hatred for the Edomite flared within, nearly overwhelming the fear. For the briefest of moments, David wanted to run out and attack the Edomite pig. He forced himself to breath slowly, to take control of his anger as his brother had taught him.

The Edomite, now in the presence of his betters, bobbed his head anxiously, running his hand through his beard over and over. "I met your son after he had slain the lion, my lord…if you remember. I took word of his deeds to the king and told of his most excellent skill with the harp."

"And this slain lion is why the king wishes to see my son?" Jesse asked, sounding perplexed.

Jeiel shook his head, casting a dark look at the Edomite. "I had not heard of the lion, my lord. In truth, we seek his skill with the harp. I am told he is exceedingly skilled, and the king has need of those skills."

Jesse turned slightly toward where David hid. "David, come here, my son."

David took a deep breath. If the servant spoke truthfully, then Saul had not discovered the real purpose of Samuel's visit to Bethlehem. Not yet anyway. He tried to shake the feeling of dread that still lingered in his heart and stepped out into the courtyard. He approached the men, trying to act as confident as he could. "Here I am, Father."

Jesse eyed him, and something silent passed between father and son. David understood. Jesse could not forbid this request. It would be too suspicious and only create enemies where none now existed. Jesse's family could not afford such problems. "Gather your harp, son. You must present yourself before our king."

Jeiel bowed to Jesse again. "Thank you, my lord." He glanced at David. "Hasten then, lad, our mission is urgent, and we must leave immediately."

David hesitated. *Immediately? Why so fast?* Suspicion clouded his mind, but his father waved him off. "Go, David. I will see to the other preparations."

The youth turned and ran for the stairs, worried. He gathered his harp, sling, and satchel. He had only one other change of clothing, so he stuffed the extra tunic into the satchel. On his way down, he stopped to say goodbye to his mother. She already knew.

"Elohim be with you, son," Natzbet blessed him, kissing him on both cheeks.

He embraced her, his throat thick. He studied her lined, gentle face, wondering if this would be the last time he ever saw her.

"Go," she said, her eyes swimming with tears, "go to your father."

Nodding, he hastened back down to the courtyard where he found his father tying an ass and a young goat to a lead rope. The ass was already laden down with bread and a bottle of father's finest wine.[11] He handed the rope to David. "Deliver these to the king, son."

---

[11] 1 Samuel 16:20.

Giving gifts were common when one would appeal or petition the king. David didn't understand. He wasn't going to petition the king. The king was ordering him to come. So why the gifts?

Jesse must've read the unspoken question. They embraced, his father kissing him on both cheeks like his mother had. Then in a soft voice that only David could hear, he said, "For your safe return." The old man looked pointedly at the gifts.

Oh. They were, in a way, a bribe. Jesse didn't want the king to think that David was being taken. He wanted it to be clear that Jesse was *allowing* David to go to Saul. *Clever.* It would send the right message without insulting the king. It would mean that Saul was, in a small way, in Jesse's debt.

Jeiel bowed one last time. "Come, David. The king awaits."

*As if that is a good thing,* David mentally grumbled. He exchanged nods with Abinadab and then pulled on the lead rope, moving the ass and young goat out the gate. David felt as if all three of them were being led to the slaughter.

# Chapter Seven

Gibeah had been built on a hill overlooking a series of meadows that were dotted with pomegranate trees.[1] The city lay not far north of Jerusalem and about a day's hard walk from Bethlehem. And so it was, that as evening descended upon the land, David found himself warily trudging up the road to Gibeah and his fateful meeting with King Saul.

He'd made most of the trip in silence. Jeiel had tried to converse with him on occasion, but worry had made David short-tempered and untalkative. An ominous sense of impending doom had overtaken his heart that he couldn't shake. He knew, logically, assuming that the servants weren't lying, that Saul only wanted a harper—for what purpose, however, was beyond his understanding. Jeiel had not offered any explanation.

Thankfully, the Edomite had kept his distance, though David wasn't sure if it was him or Jeiel that the herdsman was avoiding. David blamed the entire situation on the spineless cur and would've quite happily throttled the man to death given half the chance.

The hill around the city had been fortified against attack, and troop barracks had been built just inside the wall. A significant part of the Hebrew army was still stationed here, but even as they passed through the gates, David detected the tension associated with troops preparing for war. Blades were being sharpened, armor was being polished and repaired, and food stores were being gathered. All told of an impending campaign against the Philistines.

Normally, David would've loved to stay and mingle with the soldiers—to rub shoulders with the men who were fighting Elohim's battles, but not today. Today, David went to face the king. Once within the walls, the soldiers who had accompanied Jeiel stayed behind, and the Edomite, thankfully, also disappeared, leaving just David and Jeiel to continue on.

---

[1] 1 Samuel 14:2.

Saul's house had been built at the very summit of the hill. It was grander than anything David had ever seen before, much larger than his own family estate in Bethlehem. Jeiel noticed his preoccupation. "The house is Saul's ancestral home," he explained as they walked. "His family has been living there since Joshua first divided the land.[2] The king has added to it over the years, but don't let its magnificence blind you, young one. It's not as grand as the palaces in Gath or Mizpeh."

Perhaps not, but David felt amazed all the same. He could see gilded wood, even cobbled walkways that led up to the main entrance of the house. Servants bustled in and out, some working the kitchen, others the stables, and others carrying water and even bedding. It was all so large—so much.

Before the large door, David hesitated. Normally, he'd not think twice about leading animals into a house. Most people kept a few of their more prized livestock within anyway, but somehow, David felt that it would be inappropriate to drag an ass and a kid through the rooms of Saul's house. Unfortunately, Jeiel didn't give David a chance to ask, but motioned him to continue within.

Worried, David dragged the animals in after him. The first thing he noticed was that he stood in a wide hallway, not a room. That feature, in itself, was unusual as most houses opened into a common area where the main feature was the kitchen. Hesitant, David slowed, but Jeiel again motioned impatiently. "Come, David, we must see the king."

Shrugging, David walked after the servant. A variety of wooden doors branched off this main thoroughfare, another oddity that made David feel as if he were in some exotic estate. The floor was cobblestoned, instead of hard packed earth, and the walls were made of wood for the most part. David passed gilded carvings depicting, he guessed, some of Saul's victories over the enemies of the LORD. The hallway ended at yet another oak door.

[2] Joshua 15; Ruth 1:2.

Here stood a tall man, garbed in battle array. The man's bronze mail shirt sparkled in the lamplight. Bronze leg greaves and arm bracers made the man shine like a beacon in the light. He wore no helmet, but the iron sword at his side nearly made David's eyes pop out. Abinadab owned one, but David had rarely seen it as his brother kept the valuable blade locked in the garrison outside Bethlehem. This man wore his as if accustomed to doing so every day. David studied the weathered face. The man projected strength and capableness. His beard was trimmed for battle, so as not to get in the way, and his dark hair was slicked back tightly, cut short just above the ears.

Jeiel came to a stop and bowed low. "My lord Jonathan, I have returned with the harper, David."

David sucked in his breath. *Jonathan!* The hero of Michmash![3] He nearly forgot to bow, and when he did, he forgot that he held the lead ropes of the ass and kid, so in his efforts, he inadvertently jerked the animals forward. The goat gleefully butted David, nearly causing him to topple over.

"Here now," Jonathan said, reaching out a hand to steady David. "What's all this?"

Red-faced, David glanced back at the rebellious animals. "A gift, my lord, for your father, the king."

Jonathan looked the animals over, noting the bread and the bottle of wine. He nodded. "A princely gift. You are David?"

"Aye, my lord."

"Good lad. I hear that you can play the harp passingly well."

"Others seem to think so, my lord. I often play alone though, with only the sheep to listen."

Jonathan's eyes glittered, smiling, friendly. "Some would think such an audience to be fit for any king."

David started. *What?* He stared at the older man, but Jonathan was turning to the servant. "Thank you, Jeiel. If I offer no insult,

[3] 1 Samuel 14:1-23.

please permit me to introduce our young musician to the king. I must make a report anyway. Word has come from Abner."

"I understand, my lord." Jeiel bowed and turned and walked off.

Jonathan clapped David on the shoulder in a familiar way. "Come. Let us meet the king. Worry not, for he is short of stature and his presence of little note." He grinned as he turned and shoved the heavy door open. David followed the young man inside, still dragging the animals—curse that goat! He had to jerk the goat forward since the evil beast had decided to lie down right there in the doorway. The beast even had the audacity to give David a reproving look.

Finally inside, David looked to the man sitting in the heavy chair in the front of the room. His king. Saul was dressed in a red-dyed tunic—or purple, since it was hard to tell in the lamplight. He sat ramrod straight, a silver circlet of metal held his hair back from scarred face, a face that had seen many battles. His biceps were encircled with gold bands to announce his kingly status. But here was a true man of war.

He looked to be everything that David had ever imagined, except for the eyes. The king's eyes seemed lackluster, dull and uncaring. It took a long moment for them to register the newcomers. When he did, he stood, his haggard face losing some of its care, like an ox being relieved of its yoke. *Short of stature?* Saul was easily the tallest man David had ever seen.

"Jonathan! Well met, my son." Jonathan tried to bow, but the king caught him in an embrace. "You left but yesterday, my son. What has brought you back so soon. What word?"

"I didn't make it to Adullam, Father. A messenger from Abner found me. I thought it best to bring you word in person."

The king stepped back, looking troubled. He saw David then and frowned. "Who is this?"

Jonathan spared David a quick glance. "The harper, Father. The one you sent for."

Saul beckoned to David. "Come here, lad. Fear not."

David moved closer and bowed low, careful not to jerk the lead rope this time. "I am your servant, my lord."

"What is your name?"

"David."

"David. Means beloved. A good name." The king looked beyond David to the animals. "And these?"

"Gifts, my lord, from my father." David moved over to the animals and unfastened the bottle of wine. He offered it to Saul.

The king took it and pulled out the stopper. He took a long drink. Finished, he smiled at David. "Rarely, have I tasted better. This is a gracious gift." He signaled, and one of the unobtrusive servants standing at the side of the room stepped forward. "Take these."

The servant gathered the lead rope from David and led out the animals. David sighed. Saul had accepted the gifts. That was a good sign.

"David," Saul said, "I would have you here with me. Your task is simple; when the need arises, you will but play on your harp."

"How will I know when to play, my lord?"

Saul looked suddenly sad. "You'll know. Have you your harp?"

"Aye, my lord." David hastily unslung his harp and drew it out of the leather protective pouch. It made a chiming sound as it came out, clear and vibrant.

"Good then. I would that you begin now. When I retire, my daughter will take you to the common quarters where we will find a place for you." The king gestured to the heavy chair that served as Saul's throne. "Stand or sit beyond there."

David bowed and moved to his place. From there, he had a panoramic view of Saul's court. It was an ideal position to be in if one wanted to see everything. There wasn't a chair for him, so he sat on the floor and positioned his harp to play if needed. He didn't know what the king had meant by his cryptic response as to when David should play, but he determined to watch and listen.

Now that few eyes were upon him, he made a covert scan of the court. The room was sparsely furnished except for a banner that represented Benjamin and an oak chair that served as Saul's throne, but David didn't care about them. Instead he looked for the scroll that contained the Law. He knew that the king was commanded to keep a copy of the Law near at hand so that he might study it.[4] David had only seen the copy that the High Priest read from. To be near such a holy document sent a shiver of excitement through David. But he didn't see it anywhere. Perhaps the king kept it private. *That makes sense.*

He liked the king and his son. Something about them appealed to David's sense of rightness. Saul was the LORD's anointed, Israel's deliverer and king. Different than the High Priest or the Great Seer, the king still represented Elohim to the people. This was a man God had personally chosen to lead His people. Despite his fear at what Saul might do if he ever found out what Samuel had done, David began to relax.

Jonathan was talking. "Abner reports that the Philistines have begun massing troops near Gath."

"Not Ekron?" Saul asked.

"Nay, Father. The king of Ekron has sent a sizable force to join with the king of Gath. It appears that they have a new champion. He is of the giants, Father, one of the lost sons of Anak.[5] Our spies report that he exceeds six cubits in height."

Saul's face turned hard. "Why did we not know of this sooner?"

"The giant has only just risen to preeminence among the Philistines, my lord. He has cut his way through the ranks like a lion through a flock of sheep. He's slaughtered every challenger without mercy. Father, he's already defying our God. He is an abomination."

David wholeheartedly agreed. He'd heard all his life about the giants. They were scattered when Joshua invaded the land, and a small remnant had fled into the land of the Philistines where they now made their home. He thought they'd all died out though, despite the rumors.

---

[4] Deuteronomy 17:18-20.

[5] Numbers 13:33; Deuteronomy 3:11; Joshua 11:21-22.

Saul looked troubled. "Does this uncircumcised Philistine have a name?"

"Aye. They call him Goliath. Father, he is enormous. It requires two men to carry his armor, and he can thrust his spear entirely through a man wearing a coat of mail." Jonathan hesitated. "Father, when he comes, he will challenge you. You know this."

The king nodded. "It is to be expected." He shivered. "I had hoped to avoid the sons of Anak. But if this heathen dog comes, let him come. I will remove his head from his worthless carcass and drive these uncircumcised swine back into the rocks from whence they've crawled."

David felt a little shiver of excitement. This was a true king! His king!

Even Jonathan looked galvanized by his father's words. He gripped his sword hilt tightly as if he was ready to charge the enemy at that moment.

Saul abruptly whirled about and strode over to his chair. "Enough of such talk," he declared. "Come David! Give us some music. Remind us of our God and our homeland! Remind us of victory!"

Inspired, David closed his eyes. He rarely played with them open anymore. He needed to cut out the distractions and focus on the chords. Usually, he started out slow, softly, and let the music build both on his harp and in his heart, but being in the presence of the LORD's anointed, his king, he began strongly, filling the room with the vibrating notes.

The shimmering sounds of the harp gave rise to the imagination under David's fingers. He did as Saul requested. He sang *The Song of Moses,* of passing through the sea and the destruction of Pharaoh's armies. With hardly any hesitation, David moved right into the *Well of Heroes,*[6] bringing to life God's provision as the people of Israel wandered toward the Promised Land. And then the notes turned darker, a warning, as David sang *The Song of Witness,* Elohim's

[6] Numbers 21:16-20.

song taught to Moses and then who taught it to the people.[7] Then moving up-tempo again, David ended with an impromptu rendition of Saul's victory over Nahash the Ammonite,[8] the battle that truly made Saul king in the eyes of Israel.

He finished, letting the strings hum for a moment before falling silent. He opened his eyes and found Saul and Jonathan staring at him, tears unabashedly streaming down into their beards. The other servants looked on in awe. No one spoke. No one so much as moved. David understood how they felt. He often experienced the same when he played, and that last moment when the harp fell silent and the notes could still be heard as if in the distance always sent a shiver up his spine.

Saul proffered a hand and pulled David to his feet. He embraced the young man. "Praise be to Elohim who has sent you to me this day!" He pushed David back to arm's length, strong hands gripping David's shoulders. His smile reached his eyes, filling them with pleasure and warmth. "Truly, you are a marvel, my young friend. Elohim must still favor me to send you to me."

Jonathan came over and gripped his father's shoulder. "It is well," he said, smiling at both his father and David. "The Edomite did not speak false. Is this not the surprise of all surprises?"

Saul laughed straight from the belly. He clapped his son on the shoulder. "Even dogs know how to find a good bone," he said, eyes twinkling. "Thank the herdsman for me." He then looked around. "Michal! It is good you are here. Take this marvel of a musician and see that he has a place to sleep the night. I will need him refreshed and ready in the morning."

David looked over to where Saul was speaking and beheld a wonder. A girl stood near the door—probably having slipped in during David's playing—her hands clasped before her. His breath caught. Even in the dim lamplight and from behind the veil she wore, David could see her immaculate features, the softness of her

[7] Deuteronomy 31:19-22; The song itself is found in Deuteronomy 32:1-43.
[8] 1 Samuel 11:1-12.

skin, the perfection of her hair. He swallowed hard as the girl stepped closer, her presence making his skin prickle.

Her style of dress indicated that she wasn't married or betrothed—and for some reason David was highly relived by that. Many girls were betrothed at a very young age, and most women married younger than men. This girl looked to be only a year younger than he, so the fact that she wasn't married or betrothed was unusual. Not that he was complaining, not standing so near to her.

Saul turned to take his daughter's hand. "My daughter, Michal," he said. The girl lowered her eyes demurely, a blush creeping into her smooth cheeks that not even the veil could hide. "This is David," the king added, nodding to the young man. "He will join the court. You heard his play, did you not?"

"Aye, my lord," she said, and David had never heard such a sweet musical voice. He was smitten. "He is quite skilled," she added, eying him speculatively.

Now it was David who had to struggle to hide a blush. He didn't have much experience with girls. Jesse had never found a suitable match for him, the priority having been with his older sons in that regard. And since most of David's older brothers were married and most even had children, the family line was protected, the inheritance secure. David had just never been high on the priority list when it came to marriage.

"Come," she beckoned. "I will show you where you can sleep."

David didn't trust himself to say anything, so he just nodded, and followed her out of Saul's court. In silence, they walked down the hall until they came to one of those strange doors that branched off the hallway. David just wasn't used to seeing doors inside a house. It seemed unnatural, claustrophobic even.

"This is the common quarters where the servants sleep," she explained. She pushed the door open and walked in. The large room beyond was more like what David was used to. It was still cobbled instead of dirt, but open cubicles with sleeping mats and blankets were a much more familiar sight to David.

Michal waited a moment, and one of the servants inside hastened up. "Your will, mistress?" he asked.

"We have a new addition to the king's court. Please find him a place to sleep."

The servant, a long-jawed Hebrew with a patchy beard, looked David over. He then motioned toward a corner cubicle. "There, mistress. He can sleep there. No one is using that one."

"Thank you." She looked at David. "I trust you can make yourself comfortable?"

"Aye."

She smiled, and David took note of a dimple that made his knees weak. He'd never felt like this before around a girl. *What's wrong with me?* He tried to return the smile, but he feared it came off rather sloppy. Not sure what to do or say, he made his way over to the mat. When he looked back, Michal was gone.

Still, if he didn't have a good enough reason to stay before, he certainly did now.

# Chapter Eight

The next three weeks were a blur to David. He often sat behind Saul in court, and during lulls in business, he would play his harp. He had been warned that, at any moment, an evil spirit might overtake the king, but so far, he'd seen no sign of this malevolent spirit and began to wonder if it was nothing more than a subterfuge to keep him close at hand. His anxiety returned with the fear that King Saul knew about his anointing and was biding his time before he acted. For the most part, however, Saul seemed to be genuinely fond of David. This dichotomy created a clash of emotions in his heart that saw him relaxed and at ease one moment and jumpy and jittery the next.

At one point, Saul had sent messengers to Bethlehem to entreat Jesse to allow David to continue to stand before him. The king gave the command to one of his scribes in an offhand manner, and it was obvious that he did not know who David's father was—or had forgotten.[1] The king often seemed to be distracted these days, so it was an oversight that David was more than willing to forgive. One of the servants had to get the information from David before the message could be sent. Still, the gesture had warmed his heart when Saul mentioned that David had found favor in his sight.[2] Truly, during the last three weeks, David had much cause to love his king and the king's son, Jonathan, and seemingly much less to fear.

Jonathan had taken a particular interest in David's wellbeing, and they often spent time together when David was not on duty in Saul's court. They even sparred at times, Jonathan teaching him some of the more basic skills with a sword.

The threat of war continued to hang over everyone's head like smoke over a burning village, lingering and smothering. David's position in court gave him ample opportunity to understand the military and political climate that Saul faced. Militarily, Israel was

[1] 1 Samuel 17:55.
[2] 1 Samuel 16:22.

stronger than it had been since the time of Joshua. Politically, Israel faced implacable enemies on all sides. Of these enemies, only the Philistines threatened imminent invasion, but raiding parties from the other nations were a constant threat. The Hebrews were alone, and if they were perceived as weak or injured, the other nations would flock like jackals to a fresh kill.

Their one advantage was the living God of Israel. With Elohim's help, David felt certain they would prevail. But the situation continued to be dire, and David's faith wasn't always shared by those around him. Outside of a general spirit of impending doom that hung over everyone's head and the fear that Saul had discovered his secret, David thoroughly enjoyed his time in the king's court.

And then there was Michal…and Merab, Saul's daughters. He had been instantly smitten by Michal, but after meeting Merab, he found both of Saul's daughters to be equally interesting and intriguing. In a way, it was too bad they were Saul's daughters. In his mind, they were off-limits, untouchable. Who would be worthy? Not just of being husband to one, but of being the king's son-in-law. Such a thing was beyond a simple shepherd and eighth son. He not only had little to offer a king's daughter, but his position was so far beneath her that even to consider the notion made him feel like a thief. Still, it didn't stop him from fantasizing about the possibility.

He enjoyed spending time with both girls, and on a day that Saul had departed for Nob to inquire of the High Priest, Elimelech, on some matter, Jonathan had assigned David to escort Michal to the market ostensibly to protect her, but more likely simply to give David something constructive to do. Or, there might be a third reason, and for some reason, that other possibility worried and excited him all at the same time.

"Put a hold on your fierce scowls," Michal reproved him as they made their way to the market before the gate of Gibeah. "Your countenance is as if you had tasted a fiery Egyptian dish."

David swallowed his scowl and tried to replace it with a smile.

Michal rolled her pretty eyes above her veil, an opaquer one now that she was out in public. "You now resemble a wayward mongrel that's been oft-beaten."

That was the one thing he didn't like about Michal, her sharp tongue. She was more adept at flailing someone's hide with words than anyone he'd ever met. He'd never met a woman so free with retorts. Most Hebrew girls were taught to be silent, not to interfere with the men. Not Michal. But for all that, there was something refreshing about her, a challenge that appealed to David.

"Alas," David said, "you are truly unlike your sister."

"Oh?" Michal raised an eyebrow, and one hand went to rest on her hip. Not a good sign, but then David was unwise in the ways of women, so he completely missed it. "Pray tell?" she said, a hint of warning lacing her voice that he failed to recognize.

"Well, you—uh, that is…" He stammered to a stop, realizing he'd just blundered into another trap. He bit back an ugly curse. *I'd better be careful.* Insulting the king's daughter seemed a good way to end up executed—or worse. He tried again. "My words lack dexterity, my lady. I but meant to convey that your sister does not speak her mind as you do."

Michal eyed him as they walked. She carried a basket upon her head, while David led an ass that they would use to carry anything that she might purchase. Why she insisted on carrying the basket instead of strapping it to the ass was beyond David. There was probably some womanly reason for it that defied male logic. Michal was even attended by a slip of a girl, her maid apparently, who trailed along behind the ass saying nothing. Why couldn't the maid carry the basket?

"Merab is the firstborn daughter," Michal explained. "She's more important to the family and so must guard her tongue well. As for me? Second daughters have more freedom in this matter." She giggled. "It sets father's teeth on edge sometimes."

David looked scandalized. "You would disrespect your father?"

"Don't be a fool," she snapped.

"Sorry."

She shrugged it off. "But what of you, David? Your skill with the harp is extraordinary. Where did you learn such skills?"

"Long hours watching over sheep, I guess. My mother could play, and she taught me the basics. The rest I learned on my own. There is much time to account for when watching over sheep."

She nodded at his mostly healed arm. She'd seen the wounds, and David felt fairly sure there'd be scars. He liked that. "Not always boring from the looks of it," she said. "What caused those wounds?"

"A lion. It stole one of the sheep, and I went after it."

"You were most fortunate then to survive. I've heard tales of lion attacks. Powerful beasts."

"Elohim be praised," David agreed. "My life surely hung in the balance of the beast's jaws, but for the Jehovah's deliverance."

He would've launched into the full story—he was quite proud of it, truly—but at that moment they entered the market, and her attention drifted to the booths. "Behold!" she squealed happily.

David did, but all he could see were colored silks hanging from a booth. But since she darted in that direction, David figured it was the silk that had so taken her. *Senseless female,* he thought to himself. The cloth looked like it cost a fortune.

He pulled the ass after and came to stand eight cubits or so back from her and watched. He smiled as she immediately began haggling with the poor merchant after fingering some red silk. The merchant instantly announced that she was trying to rob him and starve his brood of twelve children. She, in turn, sneered at him, and demanded that he bring them forth, and if they were truly starving, she would see them fed from the king's very own coffers. He countered by claiming his family lived in a distant city, and the silks represented his last chance to provide for them. Would she ruin an honest merchant and send his family into slavery, unable to pay their debts? He dared not sell at less than…and offered a price at a third of what he'd started at.

And so they haggled. David found it endearing, actually, as her sharp tongue often caused the poor merchant's face to flush red and his eyes to narrow in feigned shock. He would, in turn, be galvanized to create even more outrageous claims. The whole time, she stood there holding the empty basket on her head.

Out of the corner of his eye, David saw a familiar face standing in the shadows of one of the booths. He started, eyes narrowing. That looked like Maon. *Why would Maon be here?* Just as he started to go over, another man with a swarthy appearance and a clean-shaven face stepped into the shadows with his brother. With their heads close together, the pair slipped behind the booths.

Frowning, he gnawed at his lower lip. Something about that second man bothered David. He stepped up next to Michal. "Your pardon, my lady, but there is something I must attend to." He really didn't worry about leaving her alone. She had the maid, and any soldier in the area would come to the king's daughter's aid if she but lifted up her voice for help.

She started to rebuke him, no doubt, but something in his eye caused her to swallow whatever it was she intended to say. Bless her! She nodded, taking the lead rope from him and handing it to her maid. "It is well. Do what you must."

He smiled at her, grateful. She might have a sharp tongue, but she was also a very intuitive girl. That aspect was something David could very much appreciate. As he started away toward where he'd seen his brother disappear, he heard her say to the merchant, "See? Even my porter has deserted me. A great man such as yourself should be more thoughtful of a maid abandoned and all alone. What would you do if I were your very own daughter, my good merchant? Would you sell this cloth at so outrageous a cost to her? Where are your fatherly instincts?"

David shook his head in wonder even as the merchant sputtered something intelligible.

The spot where Maon had disappeared lay deep in shadows between two booths. The city wall lay beyond, and though many of the merchants would set up shop right next to the wall itself, others would leave a space behind where they would keep pack animals and other merchandise.

He slipped into the spot where'd he last seen the two men and edged back toward the wall, moving slowly. His instincts warned him that he needed to remain hidden if he were to discover his brother's true purpose for being in Gibeah. He peered around a black tent and searched the shadows next to the wall. Nothing. Edging further in, he moved carefully behind the tents and booths, seeking out his brother.

He found him about a score of cubits further on in a clearing next to the wall. The spot was completely hidden from the market out front, and unless you knew it was there, it would be nearly impossible to find. So why did his brother know of it? The other man stood with him, speaking Hebrew, but with a Philistine accent.

David's eyes narrowed, and he swallowed his hail. He edged closer, careful to keep to the shadows and not trip over any of the ropes staked into the ground. Eventually, he moved close enough to hear what the two men were saying.

"...house and know the king's mind," the stranger was saying. "This is most important, Maon. My masters will not suffer failure lightly."

Maon's scowl could be seen even in the shadows. Unfortunately, the stranger had his back to David, so he couldn't see the man's features.

"I know what I must do, Nasib," Maon said.

"It's a wonder, then," Nasib spat. "I'm amazed that you Hebrew pigs have survived so long. I know your history. Your God delights as much in punishing you as He does in blessing you."

"Elohim is not my God," Maon retorted. "I serve Ashtaroth now."

David blinked, startled. *What? Ashtaroth, the filthy queen of heaven? Oh, Maon...*

"It's your one true quality," the one called Nasib said. "I want to know the truth of these fits King Saul is rumored to have. If the man is taking leave of his wits, it will give us a vulnerability to exploit when we invade. Discover this. And if you can discover Saul's plans to defend the border, all the better. I would know where his sons are, particularly the one named Jonathan, and where the captain of their armies is—the one named Abner."

"I'll seek this out diligently," Maon said, jaw clenched tightly. "One of my brothers now stands in Saul's court. I'll get him to tell me these things."

There was a pause as Nasib digested that information. "Is this so? Interesting. I was wondering how you could promise this information when you first sought us out. Will he tell you then? Could he be tempted to join our cause?"

Maon laughed darkly. "David?" He spat on the ground. "The little fool is a devoted worshiper of Elohim. More than that, he seems to revere our once mighty king. No, he won't join us. But he will tell me what I want to know. It's a matter of the proper approach. The fool will know not that he's giving information to the Philistines."

"It is well then."

"Abide a moment," Maon said, stepping closer as the other began moving away. "What if I am caught?"

Nasib regarded the younger man in disdain. "Do not. I hear Saul is not lenient on traitors. But if you succeed, Maon, we'll enrich you greatly, and you will find a place of honor among us. We may even give you a proper Philistine name to replace the miserable one you now bear."

"That would be well."

"Aye. Wait for word from us. Do not seek us out, but if you do get the information, then come to the market every day at midday. Someone will find you."

David ducked into a tent as Nasib spun around and headed in David's direction. Holding his breath, he waited until the clean-shaven man had marched past, disappearing between two tents and then into the market. Curse these shadows. He still hadn't gotten a good look at the man's face.

Then another form moved up along David's hiding place. Maon. Rage welled up inside David like a black storm breaking over a lonely ship at sea. His brother was a traitor, not only to the nation, but to their God. He flung aside the dark flap and stepped right up next to his brother. Maon only had time to register that someone was there before David drove his shoulder into him and rammed him into the city wall. Maon hit with a satisfying crunch, and a groan of pain escaped his lips.

David didn't give his brother a chance to recover and punched him in the stomach hard enough to double him over. David then quite calmly kneed him in the face. Maon snapped upright and slammed hard into the wall, hitting the back of his head on a stone in the process. It sounded like an egg cracking. He stared at David, eyes wide and shocked before slumping down beside the rock wall. Blood ran from a broken nose and crushed lips. David felt no remorse. This man had betrayed everything he held dear. He deserved worse. Far worse. But David wanted him to know who had brought this judgment upon him.

He reached down, drew his brother up by his bloody tunic, and slammed him bodily against the wall again to make certain he had his attention. "Maon, do you know me? Look upon me and name me."

Bloodied and battered, Maon blinked, eyes trying to focus. Slowly recognition dawned. "David?"

"Aye, you treacherous dog. It is I. I heard it all, *brother*—" he spat the word out like having tasted something rancid "—I know the evil in your heart."

Despite the pain, Maon began to laugh weakly. "And what do you intend to do, *brother*? Give me into the hand of Saul and let him take my head from my body?"

David trembled from rage. "Aye. It is what you deserve!"

"And would you then join me? If you give me into Saul's hand, I will give you into his, oh, so merciful hand too."

"You speak lies!"

"Nay, I'll tell him the truth, David. I'll tell him that Samuel has anointed *you* as the next king of Israel to replace him."

David grew cold, and he stepped back. Maon moaned and slumped back down beside the wall, collapsing into a painful sitting position. "You cannot!" David protested, eyes wide in shock.

"Oh, but I can," Maon said, a wicked smile framing his crushed lips. He spat out blood and a single tooth. "And I will."

"It would mean more than my life," David said. "He will slay our whole family for this. He will perceive it as a betrayal by all who are of our blood."

Maon shrugged. "What is that to me? The ties of our family blood have forsaken me long ago. I've already been outcast because I would not bow willingly before Elohim. Have you considered, brother, the truth of Nasib's words? If you heard it, then you know the truth. Elohim is a fickle God who punishes more than He blesses. Study our history, brother! How oft have we been given over to slavery, death, and poverty all because we would not heed His ridiculous commands?"

"They are righteous commands," David hissed. "The law sets us apart. Makes us a holy people."

Maon chuckled again, and then gasped in pain. "Curse you, David. Why'd you strike me so hard? Do you hear yourself? Makes us a holy people? It makes us slaves, David! That is all we are to Elohim. Slaves. I will no longer live such. Ashtaroth is a giving goddess." He clenched his fist. "She gives her worshiper's power, David. I have seen it. I have seen the priests and wizards of Ashtaroth, and I will have my share of that power."

"You are mad, Maon," David said, stepping back and running his hand through his hair. He didn't know what to do. "Ashtaroth is a cheap harlot—nothing more than an idol made with hands. Elohim is the living God, the Creator of all!"

Maon grimaced in pain. "To you perhaps. But I've beheld her power, and I will not be enslaved again." He looked up into David's eyes. Blood smeared much of his face. "You'll have to slay me, David. I know it is in your mind to do so. I can see it in your eyes. If you slay me, then all your problems dissolve into nothingness." He spat out more blood. "Can you do it? Can you slay me now…right here? I swear not to resist. Do you still have that dagger I gave you? No?" He fumbled at his belt and drew out another dagger and offered it hilt first. It was better made than the one he'd given David before. "Take it, David. Slay me."

David trembled all over. Part of him really wanted to do it…to take the dagger and plunge it into his brother's evil heart. Part of him knew that he'd be in the right to do it. Maon was a blasphemer, an idolater, and a traitor. He deserved to die. Yet part of him could not. This man was still his flesh and blood, a true brother, sharing the same mother and father.

But he couldn't leave it like this. He had to do something. If he let Maon go, then he would continue his spying for the Philistines. If he took him to Saul, then David's own life and the life of his entire family would be at risk.

"David?" called a somewhat hesitant and very feminine voice from back among the tents. Michal. "David? Where are you?"

*Curse that inquisitive girl!* Why couldn't she wait in the market? He looked around for her and saw a shadow dart away, bearded, not feminine at all. The heat of his anger turned cold as a spike of fear slammed into his heart. Someone had been hiding in the shadows watching! He almost started out in pursuit. He didn't know what the man had overheard, but he doubted the man meant him any goodwill seeing as how he had hidden in the shadow to eavesdrop.

Michal's voice carried to him again, bringing him up short. "David?"

Before he could stop himself, David swore angrily to himself. *What am I to do now?* He dared not allow Michal to stumble across Maon. There would be too many questions.

David gave Maon a troubled, worried look and then strode off. He could hear his brother laughing weakly even as he spat out more blood. David ignored him. His brother would be a problem for another day, as would be the man who had spied on them. He also dared not forget about the clean-shaven stranger to whom Maon had been talking from the first. He just hoped he wouldn't regret the decisions of this day. Facing the lion had seemed easier by far.

He moved down to where he had heard Michal's call and found her moving cautiously toward the wall between two tents. He doubted she'd ever been back behind the merchant booths before.

"David!" she called, seeing him step out of the shadows. "There you are."

She still carried the basket on her head, but she'd left the maid with the ass out front of a currier's tent. He put on his best smile, trying to regain control over his still trembling body. His rage and fear had hardly dissipated, but he mastered them and forced them down.

"Did you think I went off and left you?" he asked lightly, trying to give her a suffering look while stepping by her and taking the lead rope from a very nervous looking maid.

Michal's eyes narrowed as she looked him over. She spotted the blood on his knee. "I wouldn't be surprised. What were you doing back there?"

"Nothing," he lied. "I thought I'd seen a friend, but I was mistaken."

She pursed her lips as he tried to unobtrusively wipe the blood off his knee. Finally, she shrugged. "Do you think then that you might be able to continue your duties as an escort?"

He grinned. Her sarcasm was strangely comforting after his confrontation with Maon and the spy in the shadows. "With all my heart, my lady. I'll see to your every whim and need on this most perilous journey to this sinister and dangerous market."

She raised an eyebrow. "I doubt that."

"Why?"

"Because you've yet to offer to take this basket and tie it to the ass."

David gaped at her dumbfounded. "But—"

"Perchance you believe I enjoy carrying a basket on my head while there is a perfectly good ass at hand? You must be an escort of little manners. Or do you think a woman should walk around with an empty basket on her head?"

"No, but—"

"Then, if your words be true, take this cursed thing!"

David felt as if the earth had shifted under him, and north was now south. He opened his mouth at least three times to object, to point out the obvious that she could've mentioned this long before tramping all the way down to the market, that she had a maid who seemed more than capable of carrying it, or that carrying the infernal thing was her idea—not his. But for each time, he snapped his mouth shut. Looking at her sly smile and twinkling eyes, he realized that this was a battle he would not win.

Sighing tragically, he took the basket from atop her head—now filled with red silk. *Women!*

The Region Around Aijalon

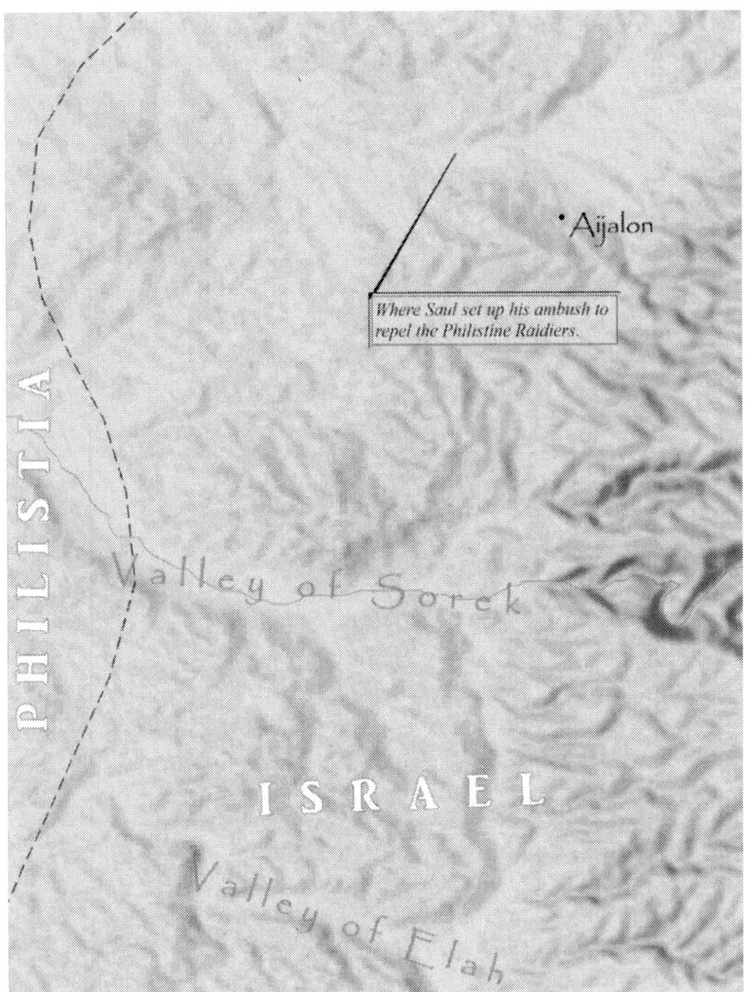

# Chapter Nine

"We've found them, my lord," the winded scout reported, breathing hard from his exertion. Jonathan carefully watched his father for any sign that one of his fits might return. Since David had come to the king's court, his father hadn't been afflicted significantly, but the harper had been left in Gibeah while he and his father had set out to intercept a Philistine raiding party. Saul hadn't wanted the young man exposed to battle. Frankly, Jonathan found this deference to be a good sign. His father had really taken to the young harper.

Saul steadied his mount and scanned the terrain ahead. Jonathan sat on a mule to one side and Abner to the other. Behind them, spread out on the slope of a hill were nearly three hundred soldiers whom Saul and Abner had collected to repel the Philistine raiders.

A messenger from Abner warning of the raid had caught up to King Saul while he'd been at Nob. The time at the city of priests had been largely wasted anyway. Once again, Jehovah had remained ominously quiet, refusing to answer any of Saul's entreaties. In response to the messenger's news, the king had returned to Gibeah to gather Jonathan and part of the garrison. They'd marched hard for two days to meet Abner who had been keeping an eye on the raiding party with a score of experienced scouts.

The wily captain knew that if he pulled all his men off the border to repel a single raiding party, he would leave other cities and towns open to attack, particularly if these raiders were nothing more than a feint by the Philistines. The Gibeah garrison had been intentionally left in reserve for just such an eventuality. They all knew that a huge army of Philistines were gathering across the border somewhere, and Abner didn't want his armies to be in the wrong place when the enemy invaded. So he'd sent for Saul and the Gibeah garrison as planned.

"What's their disposition?" Abner asked of the scout.

"Reckless, my lord," the scout answered without hesitation. He looked faintly confused. "They care not that we watch their course. I was foolish enough to have been discovered, and they but cursed me without pursuit." He shifted his gaze to the king. "My king, the raiding force numbers about two hundred."

Saul nodded and looked at Abner. "I fear you are correct, cousin. This is but a feint either to lure us away from where they will actually invade or to determine our strength and resolve."

"We have enough men here to send them home to lick their wounds," Abner declared. "I don't think we need more."

Jonathan silently agreed. The Gibeah garrison boasted of Saul's elite soldiers, many of whom were the original men who had come to Saul at the beginning of his reign. "Are they still marching toward Aijalon?"

The scout nodded. "Aye, my lord, that they are. They do so slowly, however."

Jonathan remembered Aijalon acutely. He had almost died near there at the hand of his own father.[1] The victory that day over the Philistines had been great, but it could've been even greater. Jonathan secretly blamed his father for his ill-advised vow imposed on the people not to eat anything until the victory had been fully won.[2] If the people hadn't been so tired and hungry, they'd have driven the Philistines into the sea.

His father looked uncomfortable, no doubt remembering that day as well. He cleared his throat. "I would not want the uncircumcised dogs to spoil even the least of the cities in Israel, cousin. We must destroy these raiders and send a message to the Philistine lords. What route do they take to Aijalon?"

"The easiest, my lord," the scout promptly replied. "They plan to enter the valley from the eastern pass. They'll follow the foothills directly to the city."

"How soon before they enter the pass?" Saul asked.

---

[1] 1 Samuel 14:31, 41-46.

[2] 1 Samuel 14:24, 31-34.

"We could beat them there, my lord. They aren't moving very fast."

"It could be a trap, Father," Jonathan pointed out. "They appear to be inviting an attack. They'd have to be expecting one."

Abner agreed. "True, but it may be that they expect us to repel them with our border garrisons and so leave other invasion corridors unguarded. We have enough men here to do what needs to be done. Let's turn their trap back upon them."

"Do you think they'll flee then?" Saul asked.

Abner considered. "Perhaps if they see an overwhelming force, but if we only show these, they may fight."

"If they flee, Father," Jonathan added, "it may be because they want you to pursue. Perhaps they have a larger force laying in ambush beyond them."

"If such a force exists, my lord," the scout interjected, "then we know not of it."

The king's horse—the only horse among them—snorted and stepped sideways. Saul reined in the animal tightly. "Very well then. Cousin, we will put the battle in array against them. Claim the high ground. If we can put archers on both sides of the pass, we may cut them down without too much trouble. But if they flee, we will not pursue. Let them run with their tails tucked between their legs."

Both Abner and Jonathan nodded. It was a good plan.

The company moved out quickly. Saul wanted to claim the high ground above the pass before the enemy was within sight. They cut over the large hills until the small city came in sight below them. To the east lay the pass that led to the fertile valley that sprawled to the north of the city. Moving over mountain trails, the company succeeded in securing an ambush site above the pass without incident.

The pass was wide enough that Saul didn't feel comfortable splitting up his small force, so everyone found hiding places along the southern slope of the pass. The horse and mules were hobbled safely out of sight. Scouts were dispatched to locate and monitor the approaching Philistine raiders.

Now the waiting began. The afternoon sun had reached its zenith. Lazy clouds dotted the sky here and there, and an ever-so-slight breeze came in from off the sea to the east. Jonathan inhaled deeply and tried to calm his breathing. Once the battle began, he'd be okay; the fires of battle rage would wipe away all other thoughts and fears, but the moments leading up to the fight were the worst for him. He hated waiting.

Finally, after what seemed like days, a scout appeared in the pass and ran up the slope and reported to Saul. The Philistines would enter the pass soon. The battle was almost upon them. Hastily, Saul called Abner and Jonathan to him.

"I will lead the charge," he ordered. Jonathan knew that tone. He would entertain no disagreements. "Abner, command the archers and keep the enemy from flanking me. Jonathan, attend to my right flank. When we engage, the enemy should turn to face me. When they do, sweep around me with your command and hit them on their right flank." He looked at his two commanders. "Fight well, and may Jehovah Elohim be with us."

Jonathan added a silent prayer of his own. They had not brought a priest with them, but Saul had asked that a sacrifice be offered back in Gibeah for them.

"Attend to your men then and be ready," Saul ordered. "Mark me and my charge. That will be your signal."

"Fight well, Father," Jonathan said, placing an affectionate hand on his father's armored arm.

With that, Jonathan turned and jogged away. Only a few men in the company possessed armor. Bronze, because it required both copper and tin, was much rarer than iron in these last few years, and no one had yet figured out how to adequately shape iron into the armor needed to give a man the full range of motion required for battle. His own armor clanked as he ran to take up position with his men. His armorbearer, Adriel, met him as he clanged up.

"My lord," the man greeted, "your shield."

*Good man!* Adriel had been with him since the battle of Michmash. They had stood together and faced an entire garrison of

Philistines.[3] That had been a glorious fight! He allowed Adriel to strap on the bronze shield to his left arm. He then drew his sword and held it aloft. The sword, unlike his armor, was made of iron. These days, unlike armor, there were a lot more iron weapons than bronze.

His men looked at him, their eyes glittering. He saw fear in some and battle lust in others. Both needed a speech. "Remember what we fight for this day," he said. His men shuffled and edged closer to listen. "The uncircumcised Philistines would dare to invade our land, pillage our cities, steal our women, and raise our sons as their own. But here on this ground, we will stop them. Whatever blood we shed this day will water this land and yield a harvest of valor for our children's children that shall not be forgotten."

His men raised weapons—an odd combination of swords, axes, and spears. Although more plenteous than years before, iron weapons were still not so prevalent that they could afford to outfit each company with similar weapons. The Philistines' companies of swordsmen and spearmen made them a dangerous foe, but one they intended to defeat. They should not have invaded Israel's land. They just shouldn't have.

They quickly took up positions on the slope, hiding behind large white rocks that dotted the hills thereabouts. Some burrowed down amid the cactus and shrubs, concealed from view from anyone below. Like a puff of wind, the men of Israel simply disappeared into the landscape.

Soon a troop of Philistines could be seen approaching the pass from the east. Brightly colored headdresses bobbed in the distance. Jonathan knew that the color of the tall headgear represented tribal affiliations, something he'd never been able to keep straight. Their armor consisted of ribbed leather straps that wrapped around their torso and were often studded with iron or bronze to help turn a blade or spear point. They carried round shields, many of which were covered in decorative leather. They all wore the traditional battle

[3] 1 Samuel 14:1-14.

skirt, many of which had colored tassels that hung down to their knees.

Unlike their armor suggested, however, they marched in a careless, haphazard formation. Jonathan frowned. These weren't the disciplined warriors he was accustomed to fighting. The Philistines, for whatever else might be said about them, were disciplined and fierce warriors. The ones below trudged along in unorganized groups, and even from this distance, Jonathan could tell they were laughing and joking with each other. They didn't even have reconnaissance patrols out looking for ambushes.

So much the better for the Israelites. Looking at the armor and weapons that they carried, Jonathan practically drooled over the spoil they'd find among these rich, pompous, and overconfident Philistines.

The moment neared. Jonathan's heart slowed—a strange phenomenon for one who entered battle, but his father had talked of this happening to him as well. His breathing evened out, and his focus narrowed to the task at hand. The insignificant aches of saddle soreness were washed out as he prepared for the battle to come.

The moment the Philistines reached the center of the pass, Saul and his men leaped to their feet and charged with a battle cry to Elohim and their forefathers. Jonathan's group followed only a split second behind, charging down the slope and yelling a similar battle cry. Abner's archers rose from behind rocks and brush and loosed a withering hail of arrows over the head of Saul and Jonathan.

But if the Philistines were supposed to be surprised, they weren't. The instant Saul began his charge, the disorganized lines of the enemy miraculously shifted into straight lines with shields interlocked and raised overhead to deflect the arrows. A few of the Philistines cried out in pain as an arrow sneaked through the protective barrier, but the ranks quickly reformed to keep the shield wall intact. Little damage was inflicted upon the enemy. Abner released another flight of arrows that did less damage than the first volley. There wasn't time enough for a third as Saul and Jonathan were almost upon the Philistine lines, and the archers wouldn't risk shooting their own countrymen.

With a precision born of many hours of practice, the Philistines shifted shields to the front and prepared to clash with the charging Hebrews. Jonathan gritted his teeth as he realized that the ambushers had become the ambushed. The uncircumcised dogs had known of the attack and were ready. This ruse had been planned all along.

Jonathan put the deceit out of his mind, asked the God of heaven for strength to fight the enemies of the LORD, and slammed into the shield wall with his own shield. He didn't want to use his sword quite yet. Banging away at a shield was a sure way to dull the edge of a blade or even bend it. Instead, Jonathan used his shield and momentum as a weapon.

The black-eyed Philistine in front of him wasn't prepared for the pure viciousness of Jonathan's attack. The solider literally flew backward, tossed off his feet as Jonathan heaved. Taking advantage of the sudden hole in the enemy lines, Jonathan leaped into the gap and laid about him with his sword. The enemy warrior to his right tried to turn, but Jonathan stabbed the man in the thigh. The wounded man cried out in pain and slipped to one knee. Jonathan slashed the man's throat, sending a fountain of blood into the air.

Giving the man no more thought, he slammed his shield to the left, knocking that enemy warrior off balance and into his fellow. This cleared a space around Jonathan, and he set to it, stabbing at anything in his reach. Soon he was covered in blood, though only a little of it was his own. Philistine bodies lay all around him, some with severed limbs, some moaning feebly, and others staring vacantly into space, their souls and spirits departed.

A Philistine with a crooked nose and a long scar across his forehead charged, wielding the long sharply tapered sword so favored by the Philistines. Jonathan set his feet and took the first blow on his shield. The bronze dented horribly from the impact, and only the fact that the shield had been strapped to his arm kept him from dropping it. Gritting his teeth against the sudden tingling,

Jonathan shoved forward, trying to knock his opponent off balance. The swordsman jumped back, keeping his feet. They circled.

Dimly, Jonathan realized that the battle had turned into a general melee. The Hebrews had managed to destroy the Philistine lines, but now both sides fought in chaotic groups, all mixed together. Saul fought some distance away, a group of his men rallying around him as he cut his way through the splintering enemy ranks. Around himself, Adriel and other of Jonathan's warriors fought individual battles, but by all appearances, the Hebrews were winning!

The sword-wielder stepped into another swing of his sword. Jonathan deflected the blow to one side with his shield and then stabbed forward, but his wily opponent danced away. The Philistine's tapered sword could both slash and stab, but if Jonathan could get inside the other's reach, he should be able to win this fight.

Deciding upon a desperate gamble—one he would never contemplate in his rational mind, he flung his sword at his opponent. Surprised, the man dodged to one side, barely keeping from being hit by the flying weapon. But that left him open and off balance. Jonathan launched himself forward and used his shield like a disc and swept it sideways, taking the Philistine in the head with the shield edge. The man cried out in pain, a line of blood flying out along the edge of Jonathan's shield. The man stumbled sideways, tripped, and fell. Jonathan had already drawn a heavy dagger from his belt and jumped on the dazed man, stabbing him several times until the man no longer moved.

Still in the throes of the battle thrill, he leaped to his feet and retrieved his sword, looking around wildly for another opponent. For the moment, none presented themselves. The Philistines were in retreat. Abner's archers had abandoned their bows and had joined their fellows in the battle. Outnumbered, and not ready to face Saul's most elite troops, the Philistines were clearly outmatched.

Despite that, their retreat looked organized, not the panicked rout most defeated soldiers exhibited. These soldiers were disciplined, Jonathan would give them that. He rushed over to where his father stood, directing the final push to keep the Philistines retreating. Adriel joined him. Jonathan looked at his armorbearer's blood-splattered armor and blood-stained sword and nodded. The man had made himself useful.

"Good fight," he greeted his father as he came up to the other.

"And well fought," Saul acknowledged. "What think you? Should we drive these dogs back to their homeland?"

"Are we still fearful of a larger force waiting in ambush beyond?"

The king considered. "Aye. There is that. Let's pursue them some distance to make sure they won't come back. The good people of Aijalon will sleep the better for it."

That proposal sounded good to Jonathan. He started to move ahead to join Saul's harrying force, when he stumbled to a stop in complete and utter astonishment. A man the size of a mountain, or so it seemed, came lumbering toward the Hebrew troop from behind the enemy lines. Jonathan blinked, and when that didn't work, he rubbed his eyes, but the man didn't shrink down to normal size. On the contrary, he seemed to grow even taller. No man could be that large! No man had the *right* to be that big! Truly, he was the largest man Jonathan had ever laid eyes on. This man had to be one of the sons of Anak, the giant.

The giant carried a spear in one hand and a sword in the other. The sword itself was gigantic! The spear looked to be as thick as a weaver's beam.[4] Jonathan doubted he could even get his hand to grip the haft. The man's coat of mail, no doubt, would fit four men at once.

The man's existence was an impossibility. An absurdity. He stood the height of two ordinary men, and his girth was proportioned well for his height.[5] The giant's head was thickly tattooed with religious symbols and offerings to his false gods adding a grotesque appearance to his already formidable presence.

The giant bellowed a war cry that seemed to shake the very heavens. His bristly, thick beard shook with the force of his own

4 1 Samuel 17:7.

5 1 Samuel 17:4.

shout. The Hebrew company stopped in astonishment as the Philistines parted to allow the giant through their lines. The giant wasn't very fast, but his momentum was as inexorable as an avalanche. There was no stopping it.

He crashed into the Hebrew line, swinging his sword one way and stabbing his spear another. A decapitated Hebrew head flew in a graceful arc high in the air, a look of surprise forever frozen on its face. Another Hebrew soldier found himself spitted completely through by the spear, despite his armor.

The giant roared in triumph, brandishing aloft the spitted Hebrew on his spear with just one hand. A foolhardy Hebrew soldier stabbed at the giant's leg. The giant roared in outrage and swiped his sword clean through the Hebrew. Jonathan had never seen a man cut in half before. He'd heard tales of the feat around cookfires, but no one had ever really believed it. This…this shouldn't be happening.

Another Hebrew soldier turned to face the giant's wrath. Jonathan cheered. He knew this man. This was Azel, one of Saul's elite soldiers. The man was good. Very good. In sparring matches, Jonathan won only every other bout against Azel, and he'd once seen the man take on four enemy soldiers at once and slay them all with barely a scratch in return. If anyone could take the giant, it would be Azel.

But this fight wasn't one of finesse. The giant bellowed some profane curse and swung his sword in a violent and heavy overhand swing. Azel should've dodged, should've gotten out of the way of that swing, but instead he raised his shield to intercept the blow. The huge sword crashed into the bronze shield with terrifying impact, and Azel screamed as his shield buckled nearly in half, shattering his arm in the process. He fell heavily to the ground, his left arm and his shield a mangled mess. Jonathan could see white bone sticking grotesquely from Azel's arm.

The giant kicked Azel then, snapping ribs and lifting him into the air, armor and all, to land some fifteen cubits away in a heap that only vaguely resembled a man. Jonathan paled. He'd never seen anything like it before. No man could be that strong! The giant marched over to the moaning Hebrew soldier and with one stomp of a heavy foot crushed Azel's head. Jonathan heard a sickening pop, and Azel went still, his life fleeing his broken body.

The utter carnage that the giant Philistine wrought on the Hebrew soldiers in such a short time, completely unmanned Saul's men. They panicked, turned, and rushed heedlessly away. Jonathan wanted to join them. It was as if the Philistine gods had conjured up a devil and set him loose upon the Hebrews. This was an utter disaster.

He almost fled then…almost let the fear conquer him, but his father grabbed him by the arm, stopping him. "We must rally the men," he whispered in a trembling voice.

Jonathan looked at his father. The king was terrified, but even in such a state, he knew the danger of panic. The Philistines would kill each and every one of them unless they could rally the men.

"Where?" he asked his father.

"On the slopes where we began the attack. The archers can cover the retreat, and we'll be able to take a stand on higher ground if we must."

That made sense. Jonathan rushed away to intercept the men. "To the hill! To the hill! Archers reclaim your bows and cover the retreat!"

In any other circumstances, the panicked men wouldn't have listened. They'd have just kept on running, but these were Saul's elites, men who had trained since childhood for combat and who'd fought in dozens of conflicts. These were seasoned veterans, and a commander's voice of reason brought them back to themselves.

They charged up the slope, dodging white boulders and cactus as they made their way up. Jonathan and Saul brought up the rearguard, helping the wounded as much as possible while Abner rushed ahead to organize the bowmen. Fortunately, the giant was not that fleet of foot and couldn't catch the faster, smaller Hebrews. He lumbered to a stop at the base of the slope as the other Philistines swarmed around him like ants, cursing the Hebrews and shouting profane insults after them.

A stalemate followed. The Hebrew soldiers held the superior high ground, so when the Philistines made a rush against the slope, Abner and his bowmen peppered them with arrows, leaving no small number lying at the base of the slope dead and dying. The boulders and brush made it impossible for the Philistines to interlock their shields as they'd done in the pass, making them more vulnerable to the archers. The giant ranged about in the pass, bellowing curses and raising his spear above his head, brandishing the impaled Hebrew soldier still skewered on it. Jonathan wanted to vomit.

"That's Goliath," Abner said in a sick voice at one point, pointing at the giant. "He's the Philistine's new champion."[6]

Saul stared at the mountain of a man. "Where did he come from? I know you said he was big, but by the blood of our fathers, Abner, the man is enormous! Your words did a disservice!"

Abner gave him a reproving glance. "My spies say he has brothers or cousins nearly as big as he," Abner added.

Saul shuddered, and Jonathan tried to imagine what a squad of such giants could do if they all charged together. He felt sick.

"How can we fight a man so large?" the king whispered. "Did you behold what he did to Tilon? He cut him in half. In half!"

They paused as the Philistines drew up, gathering their wounded and pillaging the dead, both Philistine and Hebrew. Goliath walked to the forefront and stared up the slope at the hidden Hebrews.

"Harken, King Saul," he bellowed in Hebrew.

Jonathan started in surprise. "He speaks our language!"

"I know you're about," Goliath continued, his voice echoing across the hills, "hiding like a rat before your betters. Crawl forth and fight me! Leave your rabbit hole and fight me like a man! Right here, right now! Let us see whose god is the greater, which people is the greater! Come king of the Hebrews. Let us fight!"

---

6 1 Samuel 17:4.

Jonathan looked at his father, but Saul didn't so much as move a muscle. This surprised him a bit. Not too many years before, Saul would have already been down there attacking the giant, but his father's pale face reflected his fear—and anger. Jonathan placed a hand on his father's arm. "It would not be cowardice that stays your feet, my father. It would be prudence."

Jonathan could feel his father trembling or was that his own trembling? Jonathan had never before felt such fear of a man. But what could be done? No one could fight that giant.

The giant waited for several long minutes, and when no answer came forthwith to his challenge, he slammed a heavy fist against his bronze breastplate. "King of the Hebrews!" he bellowed again. "I name you coward before your sons and your men! Know that when we next meet in battle, I will take your head and mount it upon a spike atop the walls of Gath. All will know then that your pathetic God must bow before Dagon and Ashtaroth." He turned and spat onto the ground.

Jonathan bristled, but his fear kept him in place. He'd seen all too clearly what the giant could do with both sword and spear. Now was not the time to die for naught.

Goliath milled around at the bottom of the slope before gesturing sharply to the Philistine warriors. They gathered into ranks and marched east, toward Philistia, which was the only move they could make. They were tired and wounded—most of them—and if they tried to reach Aijalon, the Hebrew bowmen would pick them off one by one until they were all dead. Even Goliath, apparently, wanted nothing to do with the bowmen.

Jonathan realized then that the whole raid had been nothing more than an attempt to lure King Saul into a fateful fight with Goliath. Only chance had prevented Saul from being on the frontlines when Goliath had appeared. If not for that, Jonathan knew that his father would most assuredly have been slain by the giant.

Saul and Jonathan watched the Philistines until they were out of sight. Abner sent scouts to tail them in case they doubled back, but once it became clear that the battle was over, the Hebrews slowly made their way down to the foot of the slope to retrieve their dead. The Philistine dead, abandoned by their own people, were left to the scavengers.

Wary and disheartened, the Hebrew soldiers, led by Saul and Jonathan, began their trip back to Gibeah. Plans would need to be made, and something would have to be done about the Philistine champion—if indeed anything could be done.

Jonathan glanced one final time over his shoulder and shuddered. The image of the impaled solider raised to the sky like some sort of macabre banner haunted him as he walked away to retrieve his mule.

# Chapter Ten

King Saul had returned from Nob only long enough to gather his son, Jonathan, and half the garrison of soldiers before marching to meet Abner near the border to deal with a large Philistine raiding party. They'd been gone a week, so David found himself with an abundance of free time. He spent much of it looking for his brother, Maon. He spent every day at midday at the market, trying to spot his brother and catch him meeting with his contact. Not that David had a clear plan as to what he'd do if he did catch them, but he couldn't stand the thought of his brother lurking around somewhere plotting against the king. He had to be stopped.

But David hadn't seen either man so far. He scoured the city as best he could, trying to root out his brother, but to no avail. At night, he slept fitfully, worried about a plot against the king and about the unknown spy who had witnessed his confrontation with Maon. With the king gone from the city, David felt responsible for whatever happened within its walls. This was an odd reaction, one David ruefully acknowledged. But he couldn't help believing that the dangers with Maon were somehow his fault. A Philistine spy was loose within the city, and David was determined to find him.

*But how?* If they were hiding in Gibeah, then they were well hidden. The only man he did find, and not by intention, was Doeg the Edomite. The red-bearded herdsman had returned to the city, and David had spotted him on a number of occasions, usually playing Dogs and Jackals on a clay gaming board with some of the off-duty garrison troops. Board games were a common part of society, but the way the Edomite played with a greedy tenacity set David's teeth on edge.

So it was with a measure of trepidation that David, while passing through the market, turned to acknowledge the raspy voice of the Edomite calling to him. He didn't like the man much, but maybe he had some information to be gleaned.

A far-off rumbling drew his attention to the sky. The afternoon sky boiled in the distance with dark clouds. A stiff, almost chill, wind had kicked up ahead of the storm, tugging at the goat-hair tents and their ropes. Some of the merchants were already pulling their wares under the safety of their tents.

The Edomite and his playing partners seemed unperturbed by the oncoming storm; their only concession to the approaching fury was to sit so as to better protect their playing board. Swallowing his discomfort, he turned and moved over to the shaded booth where the herdsman was playing Dogs and Jackals with a couple other men. One looked like a soldier, but the other two seemed to be herdsmen, probably underlings.

Doeg looked up as David stepped under the booth. "Well met, harper," he said, fingering a pair of dice carved from sheep knucklebone. "Care to join?"

David eyed the game board and pieces. He'd played enough at home to know the rudimentary tactics of the game, but he doubted he could compete with someone who undoubtedly spent as much time playing as the Edomite did. "Nay, I think not."

The herdsman's face tightened. "Perhaps we are too lowly for your taste now that you stand before our king." He shifted on the ground to face David more fully. "Being in the king's presence does not make one a king—or a prince—my young friend."

The words rang in David's ears, and his heart suddenly started thundering in his chest. The words struck a little too close to the truth for David's liking. "I'm just a harper," he protested quickly. "Or a shepherd if you like."

Doeg grinned. "Then sit with us."

David bit his lower lip and looked around. He'd come here trying to spy out Maon or his clean-shaven friend. Maybe Doeg knew of anyone hiding in the countryside. Resigned to talking to the man, he settled himself onto the hard earth.

"There's a good lad," Doeg acknowledged. He cast his dice onto the ground, read the numbers, and moved one of the pegs on the clay gameboard. His opponent grumbled something into his thick beard and picked up the dice for his turn.

"What news from the countryside?" David asked.

The Edomite gave him a short glance before looking back at his board game. "Summer is nearly upon us," he said, shrugging. He glanced at the sky. "Though it appears our unusual spring weather is not finished with us. Saul's herds grow, and even his stock of horses have foaled well this spring."

David was intrigued. Horses were rare in Israel. Most of them were owned by Saul, captured in battle or expensively traded for with other nations. Horses were used almost exclusively for chariots by most nations, though Saul had been training a tiny troop of horsemen for use in quick strikes and to break enemy lines. The common citizen, however, did not own a horse. A mule or ass was more likely to be found among the citizenry. "Do they truly run like the wind?" David asked.

"Aye," Doeg murmured, his eyes dreamy. "Nothing is faster or as spry. Mind you, I've only ever ridden one once, but the speed! You can feel the wind pushing against you, and the ground is a blur."

David felt jealous. He'd seen Saul's herds before as they moved by Bethlehem toward pasture land farther south, and he'd seen them run, frolicking and playing. He'd give anything to feel the wind on his face as the Edomite had described. But he needed to bring the conversation back to his purpose. "I'd love to ride one someday." He hesitated. "Have there been any reports of strangers about?" he asked.

"There are always strangers about, young one. Is there someone specific you had in mind?"

Curse the Edomite's tongue. Why'd he pick out David's intent so quickly? Well, nothing for it then. *I might as well just barrel on through.* "Aye, I've heard tell of a clean-shaven man who might be only part Hebrew."

"Heard tell?" Doeg asked, raising a bushy eyebrow. "I have heard no such tale nor seen such a man. What is this man to you?"

"I know not, herdsman. I saw him in the market some days ago. He struck me as out of place, odd. When have you heard of a Hebrew who shaved his beard? I wondered for what purpose he had come to Gibeah. I've searched for him within the city, but I've found him not."

Doeg nodded knowingly, ignoring a particularly violent gust of wind. "You think him a spy?"

*Curse the man!* David ground his teeth together. "Aye," he admitted reluctantly. "I know not his intent, but he didn't seem to be interested in the market so much as in the fortifications."

"Well then, he is surely a most incompetent spy."

David blinked. "Why?"

"A spy, you'd think, would seek not to be so obvious. Would not a spy grow a beard? Would not a spy look more Hebrew than a Hebrew? Would not a spy, perhaps, be seen as the blood and kin of a Hebrew?"

*Maon!* David instantly thought. The Edomite was right. The clean-shaven man was not the actual spy. Maon was the true spy. He squirmed, growing uncomfortable. He didn't like how quickly the Edomite had hit upon the truth. The man hardly seemed to be the sniveling cur David had seen groveling before King Saul. This man seemed confident…smug even. David didn't like it.

Doeg leaned closer. "It would not be strange for a spy to be within our very camp or that there would be among us one who would usurp the kingdom for his own. What think you on this?"

David kept his body perfectly still. He dared not give away or even hint that Samuel had indeed anointed another man to be king in Saul's place. "Such a man would deserve to die," David said firmly. "Lifting a hand against the LORD's anointed is the same as defying Jehovah Elohim. Such a thing ought not to be done."

"Well spoken," Doeg muttered, a smile playing across his lips. "Well spoken, indeed. But tell me, harper, you speak of Elohim. What of the other gods? You know me for an Edomite. My people worship many different gods. Do you think your Elohim can protect you against the gods of the Philistines or the gods of the Ammonites or Moabites?"

"Aye," David said firmly. "Elohim is the living God. These other gods you speak of are but things made of men's hands. They are dead."

"And what of the wizards and witches who deal with familiar spirits? Are they then powerless?" The Edomite's eyes bored into David's, and he began sweating.

"Nay, herdsman. There is power there, but it is as a valley brook compared to the sea. You know our history. You know how Elohim parted the sea, gave us this land, brought water from a rock. These things are testified of. Our people still remember, and the monuments still stand."

Doeg smirked and turned back to his game. "The Hebrew memory is short," he said. "Not that long ago your people worshiped Baal and even Ashtaroth. I've heard of high places yet in Israel where men and women still offer sacrifices to these gods. Tell me, shepherd, if your God is the one true God, why has your people so often turned from Him and sought out other gods? Is it because your God is cruel? I've heard tell of your law, of the way you are to live, of what you must do to turn aside Elohim's wrath. I wonder if so many of your people have abandoned Elohim because your God requires too much of you. Tell me, harper, how many of your own people has your God killed because they displeased Him?"

"Your tongue is vile," David snapped. "You are unworthy to speak His name. Do not do so again!" He glared at the herdsman who merely smiled slightly, unfazed.

The conversation had strange echoes of his and Maon's near the city wall a week ago. David wanted to give a more thorough answer, but he needed to think it through first. It was true that Elohim required more of His people than these so-called other gods did of theirs. What David knew of the law was what he'd learned from the priests and his parents. He'd never actually seen a copy of it as the few copies that did exist were carefully protected by the Levites. The priests read it once every seven years in its entirety to the people at the feast of tabernacles.[1] But he knew enough to acknowledge that other peoples and other gods did not live under the restrictions and commandments that Israel did.

Of course, some of these other gods required human sacrifice, which seemed to run counter to Doeg's and even Maon's argument. What kind of righteous god would demand human blood? But the Edomite's other point of how many Israelites had died because they had defied the living God was bothersome. One could argue that this was a type of human sacrifice.

"It is more than what you say, Edomite," David said softly. "We were chosen. Can you fathom what that means? Elohim sought out our forefathers to make us representative of His righteousness to all other nations.[2] These other gods you speak of? They are the creation of their own worshipers. Sacrificing to them is a means of power unto themselves. What power has Baal or Ashtaroth without the sacrifices of their worshipers? The Hebrews, however, sacrifice not to bring our God power but to stand in His wisdom and righteousness. These other gods? They are impotent without worshipers. Elohim is the living God. He needs not man to give Him power. He chose us to be His people because He loves us."[3] David looked up directly into the eyes of the herdsman. "Our greatest command, Edomite, is simple. We are to love Him too."[4]

Doeg opened his mouth to say something, but David cut him off, his face flushed with the heat of his passion, despite the chill of the approaching storm.

"Tell me, herdsman, what other god is so loved? What other god so loves his people among those false gods you speak of? That is the difference you seek. Should there not be a heavier burden for this privilege and honor? Should not His laws be righteous and holy, above the ken of man and other gods? Should not life and death be the cost of our vow to the true living God?[5] Those deaths of which

[1] Deuteronomy 31:9-13.

[2] Deuteronomy 4:6.

[3] Deuteronomy 4:37, 7:7-13, 23:5.

[4] Deuteronomy 6:5, 10:12, 11:1, 11:22, 19:9, 30:6, 30:16, 30:20.

[5] Deuteronomy 30:19.

you speak are of our own making. Our trespasses are our own. You are like a man looking in from outside. You can only see some of which I speak. I tell you that if you forsake these other heathen gods and turn with your whole heart to Jehovah Elohim, you will find the love and joy of which I speak."

The soldier that idled under the booth nodded. "Well spoken, lad! Well spoken!"

Doeg, however, had found his scowl. He wanted to say more, David could see, but the soldier stood up suddenly, hand on his belt knife. The Edomite swallowed what he wanted to say and forced an obviously fake smile upon his lips "Aye, it was well spoken," he rasped. "I ask only because it seems a peculiar relationship your God has between people, seer, and king. I confess, it is troubling in these dark days." He cast his die and moved his peg. His opponent looked troubled at the conversation, but he had chosen to say nothing.

"What more do you seek?" David asked.

"It seems many servants are breaking the bonds of their masters, seeking to replace them in these dark days. Your talk of spies has gotten me to think. Perhaps the king's life is in jeopardy even here amid his own people."

David frowned, trying to follow the twisting of the conversation. Something about it seemed off. The Edomite was not speaking words of his own. David had a strange feeling that the red-headed man was baiting him. *But for what purpose? What was the herdsman up to?*

Shouts from the gate caused them to look in that direction. David couldn't see, so he stood to his feet and stepped out from under the booth and into the force of the chill wind. Through the open gate, he saw Saul and Jonathan riding at the head of a column of soldiers. Both were hunched over as they rode into the wind, but David could see their bleak expressions.

Doeg stood up beside him. "The king has returned," he said unnecessarily. Something in the man's voice forced David to look at the herdsman. The man wasn't even looking at the king. He was eyeing David in a way that made him uncomfortable. "Perhaps the king would be well informed if we were to speak of these dark matters to him, harper."

David didn't understand. "We know not that spies are truly in the city, herdsman."

An evil grin sprouted on the Edomite's face. "Aye, that be true."

But David instinctively knew the man was lying. Suddenly nervous and with a sense of dread creeping up on him, David walked away to meet the king and his son. The herdsman had unnerved him, and he couldn't shake the feeling that he had missed something essential—something important in the conversation with the Edomite. *The man knows something. But what? What is he up to?*

Truly scared now, David hastened his steps as if to outpace the trouble trailing along after him. But before he could reach the king, David saw a clean-shaven man standing in the gloom of the wall near the gate. Two other men, both looking to be Hebrews, stood next to him, but all were watching the king with keen interest. Nothing at all was suspicious about that, perhaps, but then there had been a clean-shaven man who had met with Maon.

David hesitated long enough that King Saul and Jonathan rode past without seeing him, intent on returning home before the storm broke. Many of the soldiers following the king were wounded, some being carried on stretchers. The king had been in a fight, and his grim face didn't speak well of what had happened. *He's going to need me to play the harp.* Still, David lingered, watching the clean-shaven man watch the king.

It was more than possible that this was an entirely different man than the one David had seen in the dark shadows a week ago, but if not, if this was the same man, David felt it to be his duty to find out what the man was up to.

The king and his son disappeared up the hard dirt street, so David opted to try and see what he might learn. Despite the lack of a beard, Nasib, as David remembered the man's name—assuming it was the same man—looked entirely Hebrew. Only his accent had been foreign. He was shorter than his two companions, but his compact frame looked to be hardened by a life spent outdoors. David noted that he kept putting his left hand near his waist as if expecting to rest it upon something. A sword perhaps?

David moved off, trying to remain inconspicuous. Nasib turned to the other two men, gestured, and they walked out the gate, putting the wind at their backs. All three walked with the fluid grace of warriors. *Interesting.* David followed, keeping his distance.

Once out the gates, David moved swiftly to follow the men as they strode down the road to the base of the hill. They never looked back. By the time David reached the bottom, the first drops of rain began to splatter around him. David looked sourly at the sky and was rewarded with a drop that hit him square in his left eye. Shaking his head and wiping the water clear, he peered into the deepening gloom of the storm. He could see his quarry moving quickly ahead.

David considered turning back. The rain and wind would make for an uncomfortable trip, and besides, he wasn't prepared to be out in this weather anyway. But if he didn't go and something bad happened that he might have been able to prevent, then he would regret this day for the rest of his life. He briefly wondered if he should first seek help, but by the time he returned, he'd have lost the men in the rain. He had to act now.

Grumbling to himself, he pushed on, drawing his arms around his body. He wished he'd worn a tunic with sleeves. The spring rain harbored the last vestiges of winter in its watery fury, so it wasn't long before he was soaked and cold, but he pressed on anyway. Through the ever-harder rainfall, he kept an eye on the three men ahead of him. They, at least, had had the sense to wear cloaks. They had their hoods up protecting their heads, and the only positive thing for David was that they never looked back—probably because they didn't want to look into the blowing wind and rain. Well, praise Elohim for small things.

He trudged on, shivering and rubbing his arms in a vain effort to warm them. It wasn't really all that cold, but the biting wind somehow made it feel like the middle of winter. At least it wasn't snowing. He thought of the occasional times he'd actually seen snow. Usually, it lasted for a day and was gone the next. For the children, snow was an unusual treat. No, it wasn't snowing, but the rain didn't make walking much better. He was soaked through by this time, and the ground drank up the rain like a thirsty man emerging from a desert, turning the ground into mud which soon seeped up over his leather soles and made its way between his toes and producing a sucking sound with each step. He despised the mud, and—

He stopped, looking around. *Where did they go?* He couldn't see his quarry ahead. He turned around, trying to shield his eyes from the wind and rain, and peered back the way he'd come. He could no longer see the city in the rainy gloom. He saw no one on the road either. He examined the ground. If they had passed this way, there should be some sign of them in the mud, assuming the rain hadn't already wiped away any traces of it yet.

He glanced at his backtrail. He could see his own footsteps. He hadn't been that far behind the men, so he should still be able to see some trace of them. Worried, David ran a hand through his wet hair, brushing out some of the water. Deciding they must've turned off the road, he backtracked.

Now that he was facing the wind, his misery quadrupled. The wind bit at his face and eyes like tiny invisible whips. The rain followed the wind in great sheets, angled to hit him beneath his inadequate attempt to ward it off with his hands.

He was about to give it up when he saw the faint marks left by feet leaving the road and heading off to what might be an oak grove some distance off. David didn't even hesitate this time. If they weren't among the trees, at least he'd have some shelter to wait out the storm. These storms didn't usually last long, so he figured that climbing into the leeward side of an oak tree would be as secure as a house under these circumstances.

David quickly lost sight of any trace that someone had passed this way, but that hardly mattered. Anything that promised even some measure of protection from this awful wind and rain was worth it. He staggered around large rocks and low shrubs until he reached the first tree where he let out a sigh of relief as the wind and rain died down significantly. The oak limbs were low to the ground, but not so low that he had to duck under them. Warily, he moved farther in.

Large drops of water that had gathered in the boughs above splattered to the ground here and there, but otherwise, it was fairly dry. He crept along, looking carefully about, when he heard voices. Dropping to his belly, he waited and listened. The distant murmuring seemed to come from farther into the grove, so he wormed his way forward, his mud-slicked tunic sliding easily across the ground, grass, and dead leaves.

He took his time, not wanting to alert the men to his presence. He reached the trunk of one of the trees and guessed the men were just on the other side. Ever so slowly, he moved to one side and looked.

Three men huddled under a tent strung between the oak boughs. One of them looked to be trying to get a fire going by using a clay fireboard and a few sticks. David silently and sarcastically wished the fellow fortune in his efforts, finding pleasure in the man's futility. *Why should I be the only one to suffer?*

They weren't saying much other than to complain at one another about the fire-starter's lack of skill. Another had some cooking utensils ready as he waited impatiently. Nasib watched both men, his hands tucked away inside his cloak. The man seemed as disgruntled and irritable as David felt.

Suddenly, David felt this had all been a complete waste of time. These men were too cold and uncomfortable to do anything other than start a fire and cook some food. By the time they'd accomplished that, they'd probably be eyeing sleep. They weren't going to talk about their plans—assuming they were indeed the Philistine spies. The thought of Hebrews spying for the uncircumcised dogs made David's stomach churn. If he had any real proof, he'd do something about it himself. But as it stood, these were just three men camped out in an oak grove outside the city. Nothing was suspicious or unusual in that.

Sighing, David pulled his head back behind the tree and began edging back, until his feet hit something that hadn't been there before. Confused, he twisted around and saw two wide feet planted across his escape route. Before David could so much as shout in surprise, a fourth man jumped bodily on him, yelling, "Nasib! You was right! Someone did follow you!"

David grunted painfully as the large man landed on him. He tried to squirm out, and indeed his slick tunic almost allowed him to slip free, but the man cuffed him upside the head. David's ears started ringing, and his vision started to darken. The man must have iron fists!

Dazed, David felt his body being lifted off the ground. His vision swam, but he caught a vague impression of a huge, round face, bristling black beard, and small ferret-like eyes that eyed him with a mixture of menace and curiosity. "I founds a rat, Nasib. Come and see."

Only belatedly did David realize that the large lout had identified his quarry for him. The clean-shaven man he'd been trailing was indeed the man to whom his brother had been speaking. These were the Philistine spies.

He brought up his hand to try and push away his captor, but the huge man merely dropped David to his feet, where he wobbled unsteadily, still befuddled. The man measured him up and then punched David across the jaw with a tremendous swing of a meaty fist.

Mercifully, all his worries, caries, and fears exited his brain at the same time, and one of them thoughtfully extinguished the sun for David on its way out, and he knew nothing more.

# Chapter Eleven

Jonathan couldn't find David anywhere. He expected the youth to be in the king's house, but no one had seen him since late morning. No one seemed to know where he'd gone. He half feared that the lad had left and returned to his father's house, but David's cubicle was still furnished with his few meager possessions—including the harp.

Saul's mood had grown progressively worse on the trip home, and it became clear to Jonathan that the evil spirit was again upon his father. The combination of Jehovah's refusal to answer Saul's inquiries and the defeat at the hands of Goliath had invited the evil spirit to return once again. He needed David and his harp, but the lad had run off somewhere.

Jonathan ran a hand through his short beard, tugging at the end until he winced. The storm—one of those late spring rains that carried the last chill of a dying winter with it—continued to rage outside. Maybe David had gotten caught out in the storm and was waiting it out somewhere else. That made sense, but he needed the harper here, not out in the rain somewhere.

Michal, who seemed quite taken with the young harper, only knew that David had left late in the morning—something he'd been doing for the last week or so. Jonathan idly wondered why, but he shook his head as his first thought became a suspicion. Jonathan simply couldn't believe that David was up to something unseemly. The lad was very devoted to King Saul and the royal family. No, Jonathan was worried—for both his father and David.

There was no help for it. Jonathan would need to go out in the rain and look for the harper. He shed most of his armor. Walking would be difficult enough in the mud. *No sense in being weighed down.* He donned a clean tunic and heavy wool cloak to ward off the wind and rain. He strapped on his sword underneath the cloak and added a long dagger for good measure. These days, he didn't go anywhere unarmed. Dressed for the weather, he strode to the front door of the king's house.

There, he met the Edomite, Doeg, just entering the house. The herdsman looked like a rain-soaked dog. His beard was matted to his face, and his hair stuck out in unruly directions.

"My lord!" Doeg sniveled, bowing low before Jonathan. "I have news that I must impart to the king at once. Will he see me?"

"Doubtful, you're much too small."

The man blinked in confusion.

Jonathan sighed internally, irritation building. "Not now, herdsman," he growled, pushing past him. "Stay well away from my father. The black spirit is upon him. You have been warned."

The red-headed man licked his lips nervously. "But, my lord, the news is of great importance."

"I care not," Jonathan answered not looking back. "Unless you know where the young harper has gotten himself to, then keep that tongue of yours still."

"The one called David? Aye. I've seen him."

Jonathan froze, hand on the door. He turned about. "Where? Tell me."

The Edomite bowed low again. "I live but to serve, great one. It is of this man that I must speak—"

"Where?" Jonathan barked, hardly in the mood for the cur's groveling.

For just a moment, Jonathan thought he noticed a tightening of the lips and eyes on the other man's face. So, the man did have a measure of pride underneath all that sniveling.

Doeg bowed yet again. "I saw him in the market, my lord. We were both there when you and your father triumphantly returned from fighting the LORD's enemies."

Jonathan snorted. "Not so triumphant, Edomite. Where did he go then?"

"We watched as you rode by. David then left by the gate."

"Left the city?"

"Aye, my lord."

"In the rain?"

"Aye."

Jonathan gave the herdsman an incredulous look. "Was he prepared for the weather?"

The Edomite hesitated just enough to cause Jonathan's eyes to narrow. The man was up to something. "Nay," Doeg said at length. "He was not dressed for such traveling. It looked to me as if he were trying to meet up with friends who had already left the city."

Jonathan pursed his lips together. So David had followed someone from the city. But why? What was the young man up to?

"As I said, my lord, it is of the young harper that I must speak to your father."

"Nay," Jonathan snapped, "you will not approach my father while the black spirit is upon him." He looked the herdsman in the eye. "He may slay you. Leave well enough alone."

"I—"

Jonathan cut him off. "I have spoken, herdsman. Say no more. Await my return, and if your news remains important, I will hear it then and determine what my father should know." He wagged a finger in the herdsman's face. "Don't defy me, dog. You will regret it."

The red-headed Edomite nodded, clearly not very happy. Jonathan frankly didn't care. He needed to find David, and at least he had a place to get started. He left the herdsman in the hallway and walked out into the rain.

His cloak shed most of the water, but the driving wind carried the rain at odd angles, making it difficult to stay dry. Putting his back to the wind, he made his way to the market. Most of the merchants had already moved their wares under their tents, and only a few hearty shoppers were about. Ignoring these, Jonathan proceeded to the gate where several of his soldiers stood in miserable guard.

"What news?" he asked as he came up.

The guards stood in the lee of wall, trying to keep out of the rain as much as possible. They straightened as they took note of the king's son. One, a lean man matched with a thin beard, long face, and even longer jaw, bowed to Jonathan. "No news, my lord. All quiet."

"Has there been many who left the city this day?"

"Aye," he said. "The storm sent many scurrying to their homes."

"What of a young lad? He'd have left about the time my father and I returned this day."

The guard screwed up his face in thought, giving him a peculiar pinched look. He nudged his fellow guard. "Seen such a one?"

The other guard, perhaps a brother, since he too sported a long face, nodded slowly. "Aye. A lad left here right before the storm struck. He seemed ill prepared to venture into the storm, my lord. Should've known better I says to myself. But these lads nowadays think nothing will harm them."

Jonathan grinned at the young man, not much older than a lad himself. "I know what you mean." He turned to glance out the partially open gates. The road looked to be a muddy mess. Something told him that David wouldn't likely travel far. He was probably holed up somewhere nearby, trying to wait out the storm. *But what would possess him to venture forth into such a gale to begin with?* The herdsman had said something about other men.

Pulling at his damp beard, Jonathan decided to travel some distance on the road and see if anything presented itself. He didn't know why, but he felt anxious. The lad had more sense than to wander off in a storm like this.

"I'm going out there," he said to the guards. "Find two to replace you and come as my escort." He turned to look at the suddenly cheerless men. "Your reward will be a hot meal at my father's table."

"Well now," the first guard remarked laconically, his eyes lighting up. "We can't well refuse such a generous offer, my lord. We're your men."

"Hasten then."

They trotted off to rouse a couple of soldiers to take their place by the gate. Soon, the three of them were trudging down the muddy road, peering into the gloom. The initial fierceness of the storm had dissipated by this time, but the rain still fell steadily, and the wind had only died off from some of its earlier strength.

Jonathan really didn't know what he was looking for. Something simply compelled him to look for the missing shepherd. He trudged along the soggy road, his two companions walking behind him, saying nothing. No doubt they thought him crazy.

"Keep a close eye out," Jonathan said at one point simply to break the monotony.

"Aye, my lord," Long Jaw replied. The soldier hesitated and then asked, "If you don't mind me asking, my lord, but what is it that we're looking for?"

"The lad that left the city," Jonathan told them. "I have need of him."

"A thief, my lord? Truly, he was acting suspicious, like Dagon's own mistress, he was."

Jonathan started, barely stifling a laugh at the guard's profane words. Soldier humor. "Nay, the lad is no thief. He is needed at court. I would locate him if we can."

He didn't know whether the soldiers believed him, but they fell silent, swinging their heads from side to side to study the countryside through the gloom of the storm. Jonathan studied the road from time to time to see if he could spot the passing of anyone before him, but the rain had obliterated all traces that he could see.

He sighed. This might be a fool's errand. Only by the grace of Elohim would they be able to—

"My lord, look there!"

Jonathan followed the finger of one of the guards who stood looking at a copse of oak trees in the hazy distance. "What do you see, man?"

The guard squinted. "I thought I saw a flash of light. Mayhap a fire, my lord."

Jonathan stared at the trees for some time, searching their dark interior for any sign that someone might be camped within. He saw nothing. The guard, still squinting, backed up a step or two, still staring. Then he smiled. "Here, my lord. If you look from this spot, you might see the thinnest tongue of flame among the oaks."

Jonathan moved next to the guard, squinting. Sure enough, he spotted a sliver of light flickering in and out between two tree trunks. Move even a step either way, and the light was hidden from the road. "Jehovah has blessed our way," Jonathan whispered, grinning.

One of the guards frowned. "You think this lad has camped therein?"

"Only one way to find out." Jonathan stepped off the road and began a careful approach to the oaks. If David was within, he would find out soon enough. He still couldn't shake his anxiety and it put him on his guard.

Fortunately, the men with him had been trained to walk stealthily, not that Jonathan feared anyone would hear their approach. The rain and wind drowned out the slight noises they made in making their way across to the trees. What Jonathan worried about was sentries. If someone was watching the road, they would have easily noticed Jonathan and his men.

When they reached the trees, Jonathan drew his sword. His two soldiers took a single look at him and silently drew their own weapons. Jonathan indicated that they should spread out, and then they began creeping along toward the light of the small campfire.

Here under the trees, the rain and wind were muted enough so that Jonathan removed the hood of his cloak to give him a greater range of vision. He estimated that four hours yet remained until sunset, though he couldn't tell absolutely since the storm obscured the sun. Time enough to deal with this matter. When he was close enough, he saw four men huddled around a small fire. A tent had been strung between limbs, and a flap had been dropped to the windward side of the small clearing to protect their meager fire. The men seemed to be trying to cook something.

They looked like bandits to Jonathan, men who preyed on honest travelers. He didn't know why and he didn't have proof, but he knew these men were evil. Another figure lay right at the edge of the tent. The still form looked to be about the right size to be the missing shepherd, and instinctively, Jonathan knew he'd found David. In Jonathan's mind, David had stumbled upon some bandits and had paid for his curiosity.

He glanced to his left and right to see his two soldiers crouched behind oak trunks, swords carefully hidden to not reflect any of the firelight. They kept one eye on him, knowing that at his signal, they'd rush in. Shock and awe seemed to be the best tactic. Move in, cut down any resistance, and threaten mayhem if anyone else so much as twitched wrong. He lifted his hand and closed his fist, the signal.

All three burst from cover, and roaring like men possessed of devils, they charged the four bandits. Their surprise was complete. The four bandits looked up in stunned amazement, unable to react quickly to the sight of three sword-wielding soldiers bearing down on them. One did stand, a great oaf of a man with a round face. He started to say something, but Jonathan didn't give him a chance. He sensed they had hurt David. So he acted as his father had taught him, and he executed the king's justice.

Jonathan drove his sword nearly up to the hilt in the bandit's chest. The big oaf stared stupidly at Jonathan, his hands moving reflexively to grasp the blade protruding from his body. Blood bubbled up on his lips, and he opened his mouth as if to ask a question, but Jonathan jerked out his sword, being careful to sidestep the spray of blood, and kicked the man out of his way. The bandit fell limply to one side, gasping in feebleminded agony and died a moment later.

The other three bandits scattered like rabbits. In his panic, one of them tried to dart by the long-jawed soldier, who stabbed him in the side. The bandit screamed and fell to the earth, writhing in pain. The other two bandits managed to escape through the backside of the tent, running for their lives through the oak trees.

Almost did Jonathan pursue them. *Not yet.* He needed to see to David. He rushed over to the still form, worried that the bandits had already killed the lad but was relieved to see that the harper was breathing, even if shallowly. In the dim light, Jonathan could see the dark bruise on David's jaw. So, they'd simply knocked the young man unconscious.

"David?" Jonathan said, gently shaking the shepherd. "David, lad, awake."

David groaned weakly, stirring, but not waking.

The wounded bandit continued to scream and cry out for mercy. Irritated, Jonathan looked up at his two soldiers. "End it."

"Aye, my lord," replied one. He walked over and casually sliced the man's throat with a dagger. The dying bandit sputtered weakly, unable to force sound past his cut throat. He grasped desperately at his ruined throat until his struggles slowed and then ceased as he bled out.

"Thank you," Jonathan said to the man.

"My pleasure, my lord. I lost a cousin once to bandits such as these."

Jonathan nodded. Saul was doing his best to stamp out banditry, but many still skulked about the countryside. Destroying them along with witches and wizards[1] had been one of Saul's priorities after he'd taken the throne.

He nudged David again, and this time succeeded in getting the young man to open his eyes. David blinked unsteadily, and one hand went to his injured jaw. He groaned, trying to focus on the form bending over him. "Jonathan?" he asked weakly.

"Aye, lad, it is I."

"My lord, what happened?"

"It seems you fell in among thieves, harper."

David blinked, and his brow furrowed. Jonathan helped him to his feet, lending an arm to the unsteady shepherd. David glanced around the small clearing, noting the two dead bandits. He shook his head. "They weren't bandits, my lord. They were spies—Philistine spies."

Now it was Jonathan's turn to frown. "You are certain of this? These are not just common thieves and bandits?"

---

[1] 1 Samuel 28:9.

David stumbled over to the man whose throat had been cut. He studied the man's face. "Their master is not here," he told Jonathan.

Jonathan looked at the dead man. He looked Hebrew to his eyes. "Who was their master then?"

"The clean-shaven one. See you such a one?"

Jonathan considered. Yes, there had been a clean-shaven man among the bandits. He nodded. "He escaped with one other."

David rubbed at his jaw. His strength seemed to be returning. "I saw them watching you and your father when you returned from the battle. They seemed too keen upon you, my lord. I thought it best to follow. I—I overheard them talking. They are spies. Their master is one called Nasib."

*A Philistine name. Interesting.* Jonathan looked in chagrin at the dead spies. If he'd kept one of them alive, then they might have yet learned what they were doing so near King Saul's house. *That's what I get for being hasty.* He glanced at David. "How do you feel? Can you walk back to Gibeah?"

"Aye, my lord. I am strong enough."

"Good lad!" Jonathan nodded his approval. Something about David met with favor in Jonathan's heart. "My father has need of you. We must hasten...but first, let's spoil this tent and see what we may find."

They thoroughly searched the tent and the dead men's clothing but found nothing incriminating or interesting. Disgusted, Jonathan kicked dirt over the small fire, quenching it. "Come, let us return. My father needs us, and he may soon wonder where we are. Besides, my father must hear of these spies."

Jonathan noted that David looked strangely uncomfortable. Well, the lad had been most abused by those fellows. So his feelings weren't surprising. "Do not worry, harper," he told David, clapping him on the shoulder, "my father will root out their confederates, and once they have told us all they know, we'll put them to death either by the sword or by hanging. What say you?"

David's expression was unreadable, but he nodded. "Aye, my lord, a most deserving fate."

Jonathan grinned. "Well then, let us return and speak of these spies to my father. I love speaking of unimportant matters." His eyes twinkled with mirth as he beckoned them away from the camp. "Come. Besides, I promised these other two a cold meal at my father's table!"

The two soldiers' eyes lit up. "The promise was of a hot meal, my lord!" one protested mildly.

"Truly? How peculiar. Very well."

The soldiers returned Jonathan's grin. "It is well-promised and well-kept!" the other said.

As they walked away, Jonathan couldn't help but notice that David still wore a disturbed expression on his face. He wondered what had happened between him and these spies to so dampen his spirits. Elohim willing, David would still play the harp. Perhaps the music would bring cheer to more than just Saul.

# Chapter Twelve

Two more weeks passed after the incident in the oak grove. David, when he had time, still hunted for Maon and the elusive Nasib, but Jonathan's attack on their camp probably sent them scurrying from the country. In a very real way, David was relieved that Maon hadn't been at the camp. He didn't know how he would explain his brother's association with Philistine spies, and some part of him wanted to deal with Maon himself.

Most of his time was spent in Saul's court, playing the harp. The king's black moods were seemingly growing stronger ever since the battle near Aijalon where he'd barely escaped his encounter with Goliath. David had asked questions about the battle and about the giant, but those who had been there were strangely reticent. David saw fear in their eyes at the mere mention of the Philistine champion.

David didn't understand. True, he hadn't been there, but it shouldn't matter how big the giant was; he was still but a man. Elohim once delivered the entire race of giants into the hand of Joshua.[1] Why couldn't Elohim deliver one oversized and uncircumcised dog in the same way? He tried to bring it up to Jonathan once, but Jonathan simply shook his head and walked away. What sort of man was this Goliath that the worshipers of the living God would be so fearful?

It bothered David greatly, but with Saul's black moods and everyone else's refusal to talk about it, David was forced to let the matter go. Meanwhile, for the past two weeks, Saul had holed up in his house, refusing to hear any petitions or entertain any guests. Only his commanders talked and that consisted mostly of a military response to the inevitable invasion of the Philistine armies. David had been allowed into Saul's presence, but he never spoke to Saul; he only played the harp.

---

[1] Joshua 11:21-22.

This strange power David had to drive away the evil spirit that plagued Saul was something David really didn't understand. When he played, it was almost as if the Spirit of the LORD came upon him, and the evil spirit would flee in something akin to terror. They had even tried to bring in a few other instrumentalists to play for Saul, but only David's harp under his fingers could refresh the king.

As a result, Jonathan had yet to speak to his father of the spies they'd rooted out, probably unwilling to add to the king's burdens. Everyone walked lightly around the king, careful not to upset him or speak words that were offensive to his ears.

So it was surprising, but happily so, that on a day before the Sabbath, Saul held court for the first time since his return from Aijalon. David strummed the harp, playing softly in the background as petitioners approached the king to seek succor or justice. Saul's current mood was almost joyful, so David provided background music more than anything else. David watched carefully as King Saul gave his judgments on the petitions brought before him. He was impressed. Saul could often see right to the heart of a matter, and he rendered his judgment in the best interest of all.

A maid had been raped by a man from another city. Her father sought justice, knowing that finding her a husband after she had been defiled would be nearly impossible. The rapist denied the accusation, of course, but several witnesses testified against him. Saul commanded the man to take the maid as his wife, to care for her, and to give her father just restitution in cattle and sheep for his indiscretion. The man had to provide yearly evidence that he was abiding by the king's judgment or he'd be either hung or sold into slavery.

A pair of farmers brought a land dispute to the king, each claiming that a certain field belong to him and not the other as part of their inheritance. Apparently, the two farmers were distantly related, and both had claims on the field in question. Saul promptly took the field for the crown, leaving neither farmer with possession of it. Both farmers grew sullenly angry over this judgment, but when Saul then divided the field and gave half to each, they left feeling vaguely disgruntled at the king, but having forgotten their quarrel with each other.

David watched the proceedings in silent amazement. Being king wasn't merely about fighting battles or having your way. A king needed wisdom to guide the people. It was an important lesson for David—one he didn't intend to forget.

The next petitioner nearly caused David's fingers to stumble over the strings of his harp. Doeg, the Edomite, approached the king, bowing profusely. *Now what mischief is the mangy cur up to?* David silently wondered. The red-headed Edomite had all but avoided David over the past two weeks. But David had seen him often, loitering near the king's house and bothering Saul's servants for an audience with the king. Jonathan had grown so tired of the man's constant begging that he'd threatened to have the herdsman skinned alive if he didn't desist. Doeg had stopped asking at least, but here he was now, among the petitioners.

David felt uneasy anytime he saw the Edomite. A vague premonition of evil followed the man everywhere he went. David's own interactions with the herdsman had only reinforced that feeling. Honestly, he didn't know why Saul tolerated the man. Perhaps he was a superior herdsman, and his constant fawning around the king might have lulled the king into a false perception of the man. In David's eyes, the Edomite was cunning, shrewd, and entirely too dangerous.

"State your petition," Saul announced, waving his hand in a vague-like gesture of permission. The king was rubbing his forehead with his other hand, his eyes only partially open. He'd shown more interest in the previous petitions, but as soon as the Edomite had made himself known, Saul's attention started to wander. Perhaps the evil spirit was pressing upon him harder at the moment.

The Edomite bowed several more times before speaking, but when his mouth did open, his raspy voice grated on David's nerves. "My king! I bring news of a conspiracy. Spies lurk within your walls and even now seek to win your confidence, my lord, so that they may betray you."

Saul stopped rubbing his head and straightened up visibly in his chair, staring hard at the Edomite. "What is this? Have you learned something else of Samuel and his prophets then?"

The Edomite looked momentarily confused. Even David blinked at hearing this. Did Saul so fear Samuel?

But the herdsman was nodding his head vigorously. "Aye, my good king. This conspiracy does have some to do with the Great Seer."

Saul stood to his feet, his body quivering in rage. "Say on!"

The red-headed man flinched, his beard quivering under the impact of the king's command. "Three weeks past, my lord, I overheard spies within these walls. They spoke of Samuel and another—one anointed to be king over Israel. This man has of a surety leagued himself with the Philistines. They seek to usurp your crown and replace it with a man loyal to them, my lord. This I swear!"

David froze, his music dying into silence. Three weeks ago? That was when he'd confronted Maon! The other man, the one spying on them from the shadows…that had been Doeg? Everything became clear to David in an instant. The herdsman had overheard the conversation and had heard what Maon had guessed about Samuel's anointing of David. For a moment, David's heart threatened to climb up his throat and flee of its own accord. He fought it down, mastering his fear.

Deep down, he knew this day had to come. It would've been impossible to keep his anointing a secret, particularly if Elohim had ordained it. It was bound to come out, and Saul was bound to learn of it. David steeled his nerves, taking a deep breath. David would just have to rely upon his God to deliver him out of the hands of the king.

Jonathan, who stood off to the side, stepped up, his face flushed with anger. "You lying dog! You dare claim that Samuel has leagued himself with the enemies of God and of Israel?"

The Edomite cringed. "I make no such claim, my lord! I only speak what I have heard. I know not the Great Seer's involvement or intentions! I wish only for you to be the judge of what I've heard and what I know."

Jonathan nearly drew his sword right then, but a sharply raised hand by his father stopped him short. David sat behind the king, so he couldn't see Saul's face or the expression that he wore. But he could see the cunning light that came into Doeg's eyes as they glanced at David.

Saul took a step forward. "Nay, my son. Let the Edomite speak. I would hear and judge for myself the value of his words."

Jonathan stepped back, his eyes troubled.

Doeg bowed again. "Thank you, my lord. This is what I heard. Two men standing in shadows and speaking. One claimed to be a Hebrew, but a traitor. He had leagued himself with the Philistines and their gods. I tell you truly that I know not this man nor whence he went after I was forced to flee lest I be caught and foully murdered. It is of the second man that I have come to tell you, my lord. This man is close to you and claims to have been anointed by Samuel, the Great Seer, as the next king of Israel. I fear he means you ill, my king!"

David could see Saul trembling in rage. David sighed deeply, letting go of all his fear and anxiety. As had once happened before when he had fought the lion, a sense of necessity stole over David—a feeling that gave him sudden clarity of thought and insight. He knew instinctively that Doeg would name him as the traitor, and he knew that the moment to act was nearly upon him.

The king barked, "Name him!"

Doeg straightened, an evil smile curling over his twisted lips. "Your harper, my lord! The one called David!"

Saul fell back in his chair as if struck down by an unseen weapon. His body began to seize violently, and David heard a gurgle emanating from deep within the back of the king's throat. Everyone froze, uncertain. Jonathan's eyes went from his father to David, and David read the questions within. The servants backed away, some muttering superstitious chants to ward off evil. The petitioners fell back too, fear and uncertainty evident in their eyes—all except one.

The calmness that had stolen over David allowed him to see what everyone else had missed. One of the petitioners had edged forward, a hand hidden beneath his tunic. Now that David had spotted him, he recognized the man as one of the spies who had escaped from the oak grove two weeks past, and David knew without a doubt that this was the moment he was meant to act upon.

The petitioner jerked out a dagger and charged the incapacitated king, yelling some oath to Ashtaroth even as he brought up the dagger to plunge it into the breast of the helpless king. But David moved quicker. His body, seemingly controlled by something else, shot from his sitting position with such speed that the assassin never even saw David until the harper caught the knife-wielding wrist of the assassin even as it descended. The knife stopped mere fingerbreadths from Saul's unprotected body.

With strength David didn't know he possessed, he held the straining man's arm from moving even a fraction farther, and not a tremor of effort showed in his own muscles. The startled assassin glanced up in amazement at David. The young shepherd didn't give the assassin a chance to try something else. Still holding the assassin's wrist in a vicelike grip, he jerked the man's hand upward to slam into the assassin's own face. The hilt of the dagger struck the man in the eye with terrible force, sending him reeling backward with a piercing cry of pain, his eye bloody and his mind reeling from the shock.

David calmly stalked after the assassin, the need to protect the LORD's anointed overriding every other consideration. The assassin stumbled and fell to the floor but regained his feet and stared at the approaching harper with his one good eye. Amazement turned to implacable hatred. With a bellow of fanatical rage, he charged David, the dagger stabbing at David's face.

The assassin's motions seemed unnaturally slow to David. He easily sidestepped the clumsy attack and brought the heel of his palm sharply up under the man's chin as he stumbled past. A click, like a latch falling into place on a door, sounded clearly in the chamber. Then the assassin's one good eye rolled up in his head, and he crumpled to the floor groaning. Blood poured from the man's mouth, and David realized the assassin had bitten off part of his tongue. If someone didn't do something soon, the man would drown in his own blood.

Jonathan rushed over and jerked the failed assassin to his feet. "Guards!" he yelled, his eyes blazing in fury. David could tell he wanted to kill the man, but unlike the oak grove, Jonathan knew better than to kill the man without first getting some answers.

Two soldiers rushed up, their faces pale. They had almost failed in their duty, and they knew it. They grabbed the feebly struggling man roughly. The man spat out a bit of bloody flesh, but no one paid him much mind.

Jonathan placed a hand on David's shoulder. "You saved the king's life, David." Admiration shown in the man's eyes. "You saved my father's life. Thank you."

Everything returned to normal for David, and his body sagged a bit. His hands started to shake. "I—I couldn't allow him to hurt the king," he whispered. "He was one of those in the oak grove who escaped."

Jonathan glanced briefly at the assassin. "Is he their master?"

"No. Their master was clean shaven."

Saul jerked, still in the throes of his seizure. Jonathan moved halfway to his father and called over his shoulder, "David! Play and ease my father's suffering!"

David hesitated, wondering what his friend was going to do about the Edomite's declaration. Jonathan saw the look. "Is it true? Did Samuel anoint you?" he asked quietly for David's ears alone.

"Aye," David whispered.

The king's son nodded. "We will speak of it later then. For now, play."

David rushed back to his harp and began playing. He closed his eyes and shut out his fears of what might happen. He hadn't seen any condemnation in Jonathan's eyes, only understanding and gratefulness. That reaction gave him hope. The calming music filled the air, and slowly, Saul came back to himself.

This was the worst fit David had yet seen from the king. In most cases, the king would just fall into a foul, black mood, his temper dangerous and unpredictable. This time had been different. It was as if the king's rage had turned into something else, something so debilitating that even Saul's own mind had refused to acknowledge it and simply shut down. What that would mean for David once the king recovered was yet unknown. But David shuddered to think of what the king might do.

Long minutes passed as David played. Two guards held the groggy and dazed prisoner while the petitioners all huddled in a group near the back where other guards kept a wary eye on them lest another assassin be overlooked; the Edomite huddled among the petitioners. The servants hovered anxiously, unsure of what to do to aid their king. Jonathan knelt next to his father, holding his father's hand and speaking soothing words. At length, the king shuddered once and then calmed, his body relaxing.

He opened his eyes and looked about. At first, he didn't even seem to know where he was, but shortly he focused upon the bloody prisoner standing before him, held up by the two guards.

"What happened?" he asked Jonathan.

"An assassin, my lord. Hiding among the petitioners. Your servant, David, saved you, my king, and subdued the villain before he could do you harm."

Saul glanced over his shoulder at David, who bowed low over his harp while continuing to play. His heart began to pound again. *What will the king do?* Saul rose unsteadily to his feet and took David in with a long glance. "Rise, David. Stand before me."

David stopped his playing and rose slowly to his feet.

The king frowned. "You stopped the assassin?"

"Aye, my lord."

Saul turned to look again at the nearly unconscious assassin, and his fingers clenched as if seeking the hilt of a sword. "Jonathan, what advice have you? What should we do with him?"

"Have him questioned and then hanged before all the people. Let it be known what happens to anyone who would dare harm the king's person."

Saul nodded and rubbed his forehead briefly, wincing a bit in pain. "Sound advice." Then addressing the guards, he ordered, "Take him. Question him. I would know who his confederates are and if there is more to their ill intentions."

"Aye, my lord," one answered, saluting. He and his fellow dragged away the still bemused would-be assassin.

Saul then turned back to David. "It seems I owe you my life and my thanks, harper. Yet I confess to being somewhat troubled by the Edomite's words. He claims he saw you conspiring with spies in my own city. He claims Samuel has anointed you king. What say you to this?"

David swallowed. "The Edomite was mistaken in what he saw, my lord. That I encountered one of the spies is true, and it was this that he witnessed—but I did not conspire against you. Never that." David spoke those last words fiercely, his eyes gleaming with a holy light. "I saw the Edomite flee from the shadows though I knew not that it was him."

"And this spy? What happened to him?"

"He was known to me, my lord. A relative of mine. I sought to turn him from his path. I left him bloody and injured, but it was not in me to kill a blood relation."

Saul seemed to consider this explanation, glancing to the pool of blood and the tip of the man's tongue still staining the cobbled stones before his chair. Finally, he nodded. "That is well. But why did you hide it from me?"

Jonathan stepped up. "He told me, my king. I wished to tell you…but the evil spirit seemed to weigh heavy upon you, my lord. I decided not to burden you with it until we learned more. David and I destroyed a few of the spy's confederates some weeks ago shortly after our return to Gibeah from the battle."

David shot a grateful look at Jonathan. The lies were close enough to the truth that the king would learn of the Philistine conspiracy but be assured that neither he nor Samuel had anything to do with it.

Saul, however, regarded his son darkly. "It is not for you to decide what I should know, my son."

Jonathan looked properly chastised, and he bowed. "The fault is mine, my lord."

"And what of the claim of his anointing?"

Jonathan shrugged carelessly. "What of it? The Edomite's lies know no end, my lord. How can we know the full truth of the matter? But consider, Father, let us say it is true. Why would the Great Seer anoint a mere lad? What threat could he be to you or to us? If indeed he is anointed by Samuel, then the LORD has sent him to preserve the king's life. God is still with you, Father. What do you have to fear?"

The king seemed to consider this. He glanced once at the cringing Edomite, then he looked back at David. A brilliant and relieved smile blossomed on his lips. "Aye. What of it? You have preserved my life, David, and defeated the assassin. Tell me. How was it done?"

Jonathan briefly described David's actions, underplaying it greatly as was his nature, but Saul's eyes gleamed as he listened to the tale. When Jonathan finished, the king laughed. "You are indeed a mighty man of valor, David!" He stepped closer and kissed David on both cheeks. He then turned to face the court. "Know that I am pleased with my servant David. From henceforth, he shall be my armorbearer.[2] Let knowledge of his deeds be spoken to the ends of the earth. Let the people know. This I so decree!"

The guards in the room let loose with a cheer that David found quite satisfying, and he glowed with pleasure. Being the king's armorbearer was a great honor—one usually reserved for someone older. David wasn't old enough to go to war unless there was no other choice, being under twenty years of age.[3] But being the king's armorbearer may let him skirt that rule. And David felt a need to be

[2] 1 Samuel 16:21.

[3] Numbers 1:3, 26:2.

fighting the LORD's battles. Stopping the assassin had felt right. And this new position with the king was perfect to place David in the thick of the coming war.

The king gestured to Doeg. "Attend me, Edomite."

The man seemed to slink forward, his body trembling and his eyes darting furtively about as if seeking an escape.

When the man came to a halt and had flung himself on the floor, his forehead banging painfully on the cobblestones, Saul said, "You have been remis in your duties, Edomite. Are you not chief of my herdsmen?"

"Aye, my lord!"

"Then be about your duties, herdsman. See to my herds and come no more to my house unless it is of necessity." He paused then, his look spearing the herdsman whose grateful thanks died instantly on his lips. "Be warned, Edomite. The necessity must be great indeed for you to intrude upon my presence again. Do you understand?"

The man blubbered his understanding and when Saul waved a hand in dismissal, he slunk away in haste. David felt a relief in the tension the moment the spiteful fellow was gone. Saul stretched then, eyeing the remaining petitioners. "Return after the Sabbath with your petitions," he told them. "I am weary. Speak only of the assassin and my servant David's timely intervention. Speak of nothing else."

The petitioners as one nodded in agreement and shuffled out of the court, the guards prodding them along. Jonathan smiled then and looked at the blood on the floor. "I'll get someone to clean up the mess, Father. But shall we offer a peace offering to the LORD to thank Him for your safety?"

Saul's eyes lit up. "Aye, 'tis a good thought. Take the best of the Edomite's herd and call one of the priests. See that it is done."

Jonathan nodded.

Saul continued, "Tomorrow is the day of rest. We will speak of what transpired here no more until the Sabbath has passed."

With that, Saul dismissed the court and David too. As David left, he felt almost giddy. He was the king's armorbearer! Strangely, the first person he wanted to tell was Michal—or Merab. But Michal would likely be nearer, so giving in to the impulse, he set out to find her. They'd spent time together off and on, and David was beginning to feel a strong connection to her.

He'd like to bring it up with her father, but worried that the king would still look unfavorably upon such a union. He was the eighth son, meaning he would receive little inheritance and could ill afford to offer a proper dowry for the king's daughter. So why would the king want to have him as a son-in-law? Well, if nothing else, he could fantasize. He smiled and walked with a bit more spirit to his step.

# Chapter Thirteen

Three days later, a messenger sent by Abner relayed that the Philistine army was on the march. David, as the king's armorbearer, was permitted to attend the council of war that King Saul immediately convened. The messenger was told to stand ready to depart with a reply, and the lean fellow hovered near the door as if ready to bolt.

The king, Jonathan, and a room full of captains and scribes, the former of whom were among Saul's elite guard, had gathered in the court. A wooden table had been brought in and placed in the center of the room. Chalk was being used to draw a crude map across the top. David watched from his position off to the side, where he stood holding Saul's shield.

Jonathan stabbed his finger at a spot on the map. "Abner will intercept the Philistines somewhere along the Valley of Elah just east of Gath. If we don't stop them there, they'll be at Bethlehem's gates before we know it. What do you want us to do, Father?"

Saul rubbed tiredly at his temples. "We'll gather the outlying garrisons and meet Abner there. Doubtless, this is the Philistine's main push. Abner should have enough men to hold the Philistines in the valley for a time. They dare not allow our armies to get behind them or when they do lay siege to one of our cities, we'll grind them against the walls. No, they will go no farther. They'll be forced to stop and deal with us."

David felt a slight chill when he realized that the path of least resistance for the Philistine army would lead them right to Bethlehem. The Valley of Elah, wide near Gath, narrowed considerably as it ran nearly to Bethlehem, and a series of unbroken ridges provided an easy route straight to the city. If that route wasn't defended, Bethlehem would be endangered. The valley width allowed for a large army to march along it, but the valley was flanked by sharply rising hills to both the north and the south. Saul pointed to the northern hills. "Abner intends to meet the Philistines here.

The steeper slopes there should give us an ideal encampment from which to put the battle in array against these uncircumcised dogs."

He gestured to the messenger. "Find Abner and tell him that I will meet him on the north side of the valley. Tell him to hold until we arrive, and then we'll drive the Philistines back to Gath."

David wanted to cheer. *This is what being a king is all about—destroying the enemies of Elohim and of Israel!* Too long had the Hebrews languished under the heavy hand of the Philistines. It was time to send the heathen jackals back into the sea!

After the messenger left, Saul turned to his son. "Jonathan, lead the Gibeah garrison to the battle. Your brothers should already be there with Abner. I'll gather the garrisons at Ramah, Jerusalem, and Bethlehem. Send messengers to every city and call forth every man who can draw sword. We will need every man to repel the invaders."

Jonathan looked pointedly at his father. "Do you intend to seek Samuel's aid?"

Saul frowned, looking troubled. "I—I think not. Jehovah is with me, son. He protected me from the hand of the slayer. That is all I need know, and I no longer trust the seer. We'll send to the priests at Nob to offer sacrifices on our behalf and to call upon Elohim's favor."

Jonathan opened his mouth to protest, but a sharp glance from his father quelled whatever he had intended to say. David worried his lower lip. He didn't like this dissension between king and seer. In his eyes, the two were irrevocably tied together. Jonathan clearly disliked it as well and just as clearly wanted to say something about it. Instead, the prince asked, "What about the ark of the LORD, Father? Should we not take it?"

The other captains fell silent, waiting for a response. David held his breath. The ark of the LORD had been under the care of Abinadab of Kirjath-jeraim since the Philistines had returned it years ago.[1] But since then, Saul had not brought it forth. Rumors said that Ahimelech, the high priest, had once requested that the ark be

[1] 1 Samuel 7:2, 14:18.

brought back to the tabernacle, currently in Nob, but for some reason, Saul had refused. The ark remained in Abinadab's house in Kirjath-jearim,[2] one of the so called "hill cities" that pertained to the region of Gibeah.

Maybe Saul simply wanted the ark of the LORD close to him. Though truthfully, David couldn't understand the difference. Kirjath-jearim and Nob were both about the same distance from Saul's house. David had heard many rumors on why the ark had stayed in Kirjath-jearim, but nothing that he found acceptable. He'd never seen the ark of the LORD, and he felt a thrill at the possibility that the king would bring it forth once again.

"Nay," Saul whispered hoarsely. "The ark stays here to look over our people."

Bitter disappointment stabbed David. He'd so wanted to see the ark! The history! The tales of its power! Why wouldn't Saul take it? Of course, David knew his history. He knew that in the days of Eli the priest, the ark hadn't saved Israel out of the hands of the Philistines. Thirty thousand Hebrew men had died that day and the ark of the LORD captured.[3] True, the seven months that the Philistines had the ark in their possession had nearly destroyed them as a people.[4] *That* was the part of the story David liked.

The king had commanded, and even Jonathan dared not speak against it. The ark of the LORD would remain in Gibeah.

"We are adjourned," Saul declared. "Let us go each to his task. We will meet anon in the Valley of Elah and turn back this scourge that seeks to stain our lands with their unholy bodies. Make haste, my friends. The battle will soon be upon us, and each is needed. Now go."

The men scurried out, shouting orders to their seconds. Soon the large garrison of Gibeah would be on the march and messengers sent to the further reaches of the kingdom to call forth the Hebrew men to war. David found himself standing alone with the king. He

---

[2] 1 Samuel 7:1.
[3] 1 Samuel 4:10-11.
[4] 1 Samuel 5:1-12, 6:1.

swallowed his excitement, his eyes bright with fervor. "And I, my lord? What shall I do?"

Saul turned and looked upon him, and for a moment, David saw the love that Saul felt for him. Another thrill went up his spine. Saul dropped a strong arm atop David's shoulder. "You will return to your father's house until the matter is settled with the Philistines."

David's jaw dropped, and he stammered, "Bu—but, my lord! I am your armorbearer! I should be at your side in the battle!"

"You are valiant, my young servant, but I owe you a debt. I will not take you into battle and risk your life. Indeed, you are not yet of age to go into battle if I am not mistaken."

"I'm near enough, my lord," David protested. "Take me, I beg. I will not fail you."

"I fear not for your failure, David. I fear my own. I would not bring down your father's head with news of your death. Say no more. It is not in me to risk your life. You will accompany me to Bethlehem where you will abide. Tell…" he hesitated "…your father that you have served me well."

Saul had once again forgotten Jesse's name. Not that it mattered. David was much more concerned with the decision to leave him behind. *It's not fair!* He was the king's armorbearer, and he deserved to be on the frontlines protecting his king!

Saul noticed the disappointment and tried to give David a reassuring smile. "Go now. Prepare. We leave within the hour."

David bowed low, not trusting himself to speak. He left the court then, knowing that he had only a short time to prepare Saul's horse and equipment for the journey. He would need to gather his own things too. And say goodbye to Merab and Michal. There would be no telling how long the battle would last or when Saul would call for him, and his growing feelings for Saul's daughters would not let him leave without first saying goodbye.

And so nearly a day later, David and the entire Ramah garrison of troops walked behind the king's horse as he led them by the fortified city of Jerusalem. Few things in life had taken David's fancy as the fabled city of Jerusalem and its mighty fortress. Many of the

Jebusites still lived there, along with a portion of the tribe of Benjamin.[5] He didn't know why Saul hadn't made Jerusalem the capital of Israel instead of Gibeah. Jerusalem dominated the land around it, and its impregnable walls could withstand a besieging army for years if need be.

Having grown up so close to the fortress, David had spent many a day with the sheep and fantasizing about the fortress while looking upon its walls. David couldn't imagine a grander city in all the world.

Saul had sent messengers ahead of him to rouse both the garrisons at Jerusalem and Bethlehem and to prepare for his arrival, and so Saul didn't even need to stop at the fortified city—much to David's disappointment. The Jerusalem garrison had already mustered their troops, who were mainly Benjamite elite archers and slingers, and they were waiting for their king. They stood in companies as the king rode up. They cheered their king with a mighty roar of approval and support that inspired David.

The king gave them the same short speech he had given his captains and then led his growing army toward Bethlehem. Many of the men were eager, looking forward to finally closing with the Philistines and ending the threat they posed to family and friends. The more veteran soldiers kept a more realistic outlook, their demeaner more grim and determined than that of their younger companions. The only one truly unhappy and truly disappointed was David. The closer they got to Bethlehem, the sooner David would be left behind.

The evening wore on, and the sun began to set behind a thin line of clouds to the west. In the distance, the flickering lights of oil lamps marked the darkening city of Bethlehem as they descended from the higher elevation around Jerusalem.

Saul gave orders for his army to camp outside the city. He then smiled at David. "Your home, I believe," he said, gesturing toward

[5] Judges 1:21; 2 Samuel 5:6.

Bethlehem. "You have served me well, David. I thank you for my life. But as I have promised, you must remain here."

David knew better than to argue. He bowed to his king. "As you command, my lord."

Satisfied, Saul turned back to the city. A squad of soldiers from the Bethlehem garrison had been approaching since the army had come into view. When they drew close enough, David noted that their leader was none other than his brother, Abinadab, who commanded the local garrison.

"My lord king!" Abinadab greeted Saul, bowing low as he came to a stop before Saul's horse. "The garrison is mobilized and ready to march on the morrow as you have commanded. A house has been prepared for you. We will accompany you there, my lord."

"Very well," Saul acknowledged. "I hope you have talked to the elders of the city, captain. I rely upon them to ensure that we will be well supplied during this campaign. Other cities will contribute, but here is where the supply lines must hold fast." He hesitated, and Abinadab held his tongue probably realizing the king hadn't finished yet. "I fear a long campaign. I will rely upon Bethlehem for succor to keep us from hunger and thirst."

Abinadab nodded. "Your messengers were quite clear, my lord, and the elders have been apprised. They understand the need and have agreed to supply the army. They express only a fear that other cities will not deliver their goods in a timely manner."

Saul waved a hand. "I have taken care of that. Set up a depot to receive the supplies and put one of the elders, a man of wisdom and understanding, to see to the transportation and distribution."

David's brother saluted. "As you command, my lord."

"Very well. Let us proceed." He turned in his saddle to address another one of his men. "Camp here, captain. But off the road. We will be leaving at first light."

Abinadab dropped back to walk with David. He eyed the shield David carried. "The king's armorbearer?"

David puffed out his chest a bit. "Aye. I saved the king from assassination. He made me his armorbearer."

Abinadab grinned. "So we heard. It seems you've become something of a sensation since you've left us." His grin faded. "Are you then going to the battle?"

David's chest deflated. "Nay, the king would not risk me in battle. I am not yet twenty."

Abinadab took a deep breath. "That is well, brother. Father will need you home in the coming days."

"Why?"

"Eliab and Shammah will be going to the battle with me. Father will be in charge of the supply depot here, and our other brothers will be coordinating the supply runs from the other cities that the king has commanded to support the army. Maon is missing. We know not where he is. So you and our nephews are all that remain at home to help Father. Do you understand?"

David did. He didn't think it was fair, but he did understand. "I know my place, brother."

"It is well then."

Perhaps it was. Perhaps it was well. But down deep, David really didn't think so. Down deep he knew his place was by King Saul's side, fighting the enemies of the LORD. He hadn't mentioned what he knew regarding Maon, but he didn't intend to either. For whatever reason, David believed that Maon was his problem. The assassin David had stopped in Saul's court had not much to say before he was hung. He revealed only that Nasib was a Hebrew born among the Philistines. But as to either Nasib's or Maon's whereabouts, the assassin either did not know or refused to say.

David really didn't know what to do. For the moment, he would obey his father and wait. Perhaps opportunity would come.

The Valley of Elah
Where David Fights Goliath

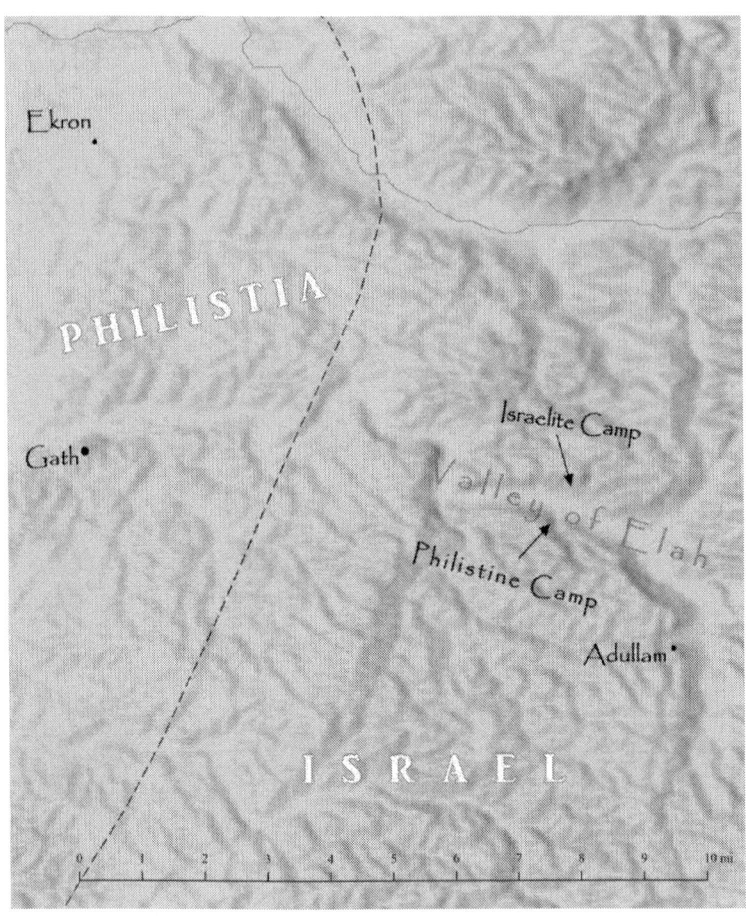

# Chapter Fourteen

Jonathan surveyed the valley, frowning at the smoke rising from seemingly thousands of campfires atop a hill across the valley to the south—too much smoke in his opinion. The Philistines had invaded in force, bringing more soldiers than the Hebrews had. From his position atop one of the higher hills on the north side of the valley, Jonathan had a good view of both the Hebrew fortifications right below him and the Philistines across the way.[1]

The Hebrew army, at Saul's command, were digging trenches. The hill they had chosen to entrench on had a steep slope that led down into the valley proper. The slope and trenches would prevent the Philistines from executing a frontal attack, unless they wanted to be cut to ribbons by Saul's well-placed archers.

The wadi Elah, a small brook that only ran with water during the springtime or after heavy rains in the hill country, wound its way through the valley in lazy curves, but straightened out directly below and hugged the hill below the Hebrew fortifications. The brook wasn't much of a barrier, but it was a source of water if the Hebrews needed it.

Abner stepped up beside him. The older man looked tired. It had been his responsibility to intercept the Philistines and stop their advance into Israel. He'd succeeded, but there had been casualties. He didn't look like he'd gotten much sleep recently.

Jonathan spoke, "You're certain the Philistines won't continue their march up the valley? I don't see how we could hope to stop them if they wanted to."

Abner shook his head. "Recall your lessons, my lord. If they do such a foolish thing, we would be able to disrupt their supply lines and chew away at their flanks. By the time they got near Bethlehem, they'd be hungry and bloodied to the point where we could easily

[1] 1 Samuel 17:1-2.

finish them off. Nay, the Philistines know better than to allow us such an opportunity. This was their plan all along."

Jonathan did indeed remember his lessons. He just wanted to distract his father's cousin from the burdens and trials they faced. However, this last statement caught Jonathan by surprise. "What do you mean this is what they had planned?"

"The Philistines knew we were waiting for them to invade. They weren't going to take us by surprise, and they knew it. They wanted to draw out our army and engage us. Defeat the army of Israel and the entire country will be open to them. This…this battlefield is exactly what they wanted."

"They outnumber us," Jonathan muttered, understanding. "They plan on destroying us here."

"To a man." Abner nodded.

"That's why you're digging in. You're trying to avoid a pitched battle that commits all our reserves."

"Aye. We'll still fight in the valley when it is tactically sound to do so, but we dare not bring our full force or linger long in an engagement. If we're caught out there and destroyed, nothing will prevent the dogs from marching to the gates of Bethlehem. This is now a battle of attrition. We're going to weary them and bloody them when we may. Perhaps in time, they'll think more of their homes than of us."

Jonathan worried at his lower lip, pulling lightly on his short beard. He suddenly felt old. He remembered a time when the numbers wouldn't have bothered him at all. The LORD, he knew, could save by few or many.[2] He'd even put that to the test and had won a great victory nearly singlehandedly against an entire Philistine garrison.[3] But things were different now. Back then, Saul had the Spirit of the LORD upon him, and both the ark of the LORD and the Samuel, the seer, had been with the people. Now, however, the ark had remained behind, and Samuel refused to even speak to the king.

---

[2] 1 Samuel 14:6.

[3] 1 Samuel 14:13-14.

Where were the blessings of Elohim now? Dare the Hebrews risk themselves if the LORD was not with them?

Saul's deliverance from the hand of the assassin had convinced his father that the LORD God was still with him, but Jonathan wasn't so sure. Perhaps the LORD had been with David rather than Saul. Jonathan missed David. He wished the young lad was with them. Had has father made a mistake in leaving the harper behind? Jonathan wasn't sure, and it worried him.

Jonathan surveyed the valley again. The valley made a sharp turn around the base of the Hebrew's hill, allowing Saul's forces to dominate a wide swath of the valley and maintain easy control of the ridge that led to Bethlehem. Even if the Philistines tried to march farther up the valley, they would immediately be outflanked. It was an ideal location to wait out a siege. Jonathan shuddered. He hated sieges. Give him a good fight any day, but this cat-and-mouse game just irritated him.

Abner laid a hand on Jonathan's armored shoulder. "Come, my lord. Let us go to your father. The Philistines will probe our defenses, looking for weaknesses." He hesitated. "And then there is their champion."

Jonathan went cold. "The one called Goliath?"

"Aye. My scouts have spotted him within the Philistine camp. The Philistines revere him like a god. In fact, they believe he is a god incarnate, invincible. They will rely upon him to break our lines. Fortunately, we control the heights here, and I think he fears our archers. But out there in the valley, he is a danger for which we must be watchful when we put the battle in array against the uncircumcised dogs."

Jonathan nodded, and together they left the hilltop and made their way down to the Hebrew fortifications. A pair of watchmen remained on the taller hill with horns to signal and warn of any movement among the Philistines.

They found King Saul overseeing the trench building. The hillside was sparsely covered with large terebinth trees,[4] and old Elah nuts crunched beneath their leather sandals as the pair came up to Saul. Both Abner and Jonathan bowed.

"Is everything satisfactory, my lord?" Abner asked.

"You have done well, cousin," Saul said, looking around with satisfaction. "The Philistine dogs cannot get past us without being destroyed." He stared for a moment at the cloudless sky. "Pray that the weather holds. Our supply line is longer than theirs."

"The route is well defended, Father," Jonathan pointed out. "The elders of Bethlehem have already begun sending supplies. I don't think the weather will stop them."

Saul frowned. "Aye, they dare not fail me."

Jonathan started. Why such a harsh thought? Was the evil spirit coming upon the king yet again? Jonathan fervently wished his father hadn't left David behind in Bethlehem.

Saul seemed to lose interest in the topic of conversation. He moved out in front of one of the trenches, staring across the valley and lapsing into silence. He stood beneath an old terebinth tree, one hand resting on the gray, haggard-looking trunk.

For a moment, Jonathan thought the old tree and the old king shared much in common. The trunk had deep fissures running up its length, making the tree look haggard and worn. The king's face was deeply lined with worry, giving him a similar appearance. Both stood silent watch over the valley like statuesque sentinels weathered by time and hardship. It was an illuminating moment for Jonathan. Deep in his heart, he knew his father's time was coming to an end. Saul wasn't the same man he once was. There was a brittleness to him now that, like the battered old tree, threatened to consume him.

A horn sounded from the hill behind, shattering Jonathan's musings. He leaped across the trench and stood at the edge of the steep hill, looking across the valley. The Philistines were stirring, flowing out of their encampment; thousands of them gathered at the

[4] *Elah* is the Hebrew word for the "terebinth tree" and is what the valley is named for. It bears a pistachio nut.

base of the valley. Their colorful, tall headdresses gave the impression that the hill beyond was covered in flowers. Chariots, archers, spearmen, and swordsmen all prepared for a push against Saul's defenses. Looking at the huge army, Jonathan wondered how the Hebrews could possibly stop or even stem such a vast tide of humanity.

Saul shook himself and moved away from the tree, barking orders, and Jonathan ran to his command. He already knew what to do. His armorbearer caught up to him there and helped strap on his round shield. Jonathan moved to the forefront of the line of foot soldiers who were to hold the western side of the slope. Here the Philistines would focus their attack. If they could break the Hebrews, then they could crush the army and open the way to Bethlehem. The chariots and horses of the enemy would be useless against the steep slope, so it made sense that the Philistines would try to lure the Hebrews out of their positions and into open battle on the valley floor. This had to be avoided at all costs.

The pounding of drums, a deep sound that penetrated flesh and spirit, echoed through the valley, prophesying of death and blood. The Philistines marched out to the middle of the valley, gathering like a swelling raincloud, and then with a roar, they burst forth, charging in one great mass.

"Steady!" Jonathan yelled, holding up his fist. The charge was bait. Battle lust could overwhelm soldiers in conditions such as this, causing them to behave unwisely. Many an army had allowed it to overwhelm their good sense. "Steady!"

The enemy soldiers howled as they bore down on the Hebrew position. When they nearly reached the base of the Hebrew slopes, Abner cut loose with a withering shower of arrows. Scores of enemy soldiers cried out in pain and fell out of rank only to be trampled by those coming behind. Another flight of arrows cut into the mass, stalling the charge and creating confusion when the Philistines came up against the steep slope and found no easy way up to the deadly archers.

"Attack!" Jonathan roared, leaping off the edge and sliding down the slope into the mass of soldiers milling about in confusion. His attack came so unexpectedly that Jonathan had time to set his feet and sweep about him in great arcs, knocking men aside like clay bowls stacked too high on a shelf. His men, shouting in glee, followed him, and hundreds of Hebrews smashed into the disorganized ranks of Philistines at the base of the slope.

Seeing their enemy within reach, the Philistines rushed to converge on Jonathan and his men, howling and shrieking their hatred. The confusion blocked the enemy chariots from engaging or Jonathan would've likely been trampled under. Once the enemy had committed, Jonathan and his men, following his father's battle plan, began to work their way to their left, pulling the angry enemy soldiers after them like flotsam in a ship's wake. At that point, Saul's company smashed into the Philistine rear, taking the enemy completely by surprise. Jonathan saw its effect more than witnessed the actual charge.

Cries for help began to rise from the far flank of the enemy army, generating even more confusion as soldiers became indecisive as to which way to turn and meet the greater threat. In the meantime, more arrows descended upon the hapless Philistines. A hearty few tried to return fire, but Abner quickly isolated them and cut them down from his superior position up high.

That's when, with another great shout, a third company of Hebrew infantry, led by Jonathan's brother, Ishui,[5] descended off the slope to hit the Philistine forces between Jonathan and Saul's company. Soldiers died by the score on both sides. Men screamed in pain and agony; blood stained the ground and the stones of the brook.

Jonathan reached Ishui's side. "Fight well, brother," he roared, blocking a Philistine thrust and countering by driving the point of his sword under the fellow's chainmail. The man's face blanched,

[5] 1 Samuel 14:49.

and he staggered back. Jonathan let him go since more of the enemy immediately filled the gap.

Ishui favored a heavy spear which he wielded in short, dangerous thrusts. He drove back a pair of Philistines and then retorted, "I always fight well, brother. By my spear, I vow to have the greater tally of slain heathen this day!"

Jonathan laughed at his impetuous brother, and together they pressed forward into the enemy. Soon both were blood-splattered and had left a trail of bodies as they continued moving their men to the east. For thirty more minutes they fought thus, Saul's hit-and-run tactics played havoc on the Philistine command who could not react quickly enough to entrap the Hebrews, for wherever they turned, a stinging flight of arrows broke up formations and sent Philistine warriors scurrying to get away.

Then Goliath entered the fray. Jonathan saw him coming. The man couldn't be missed. He was like a leviathan of old. The gigantic man, his tattooed head swinging ponderously back and forth, thundered forward, his spear sweeping aside any who got in his way. Jonathan's heart nearly turned to iron in his chest. He vividly remembered what Goliath could do. His men knew too. They began crying out in fear,[6] and the Hebrew lines wavered. But Saul was prepared for this. A horn sounded, and Jonathan barked a command to his men.

Immediately, they pulled back and rushed away, seeking the hidden paths back up the slope to reach the trenches and the protection of the Hebrew archers. They left a fuming giant stomping around the battlefield with no one to fight. A few of the injured Hebrew soldiers who were not quick enough, were crushed under Goliath's rage, their broken bodies falling among the other dead and dying, but for the most part, Goliath's wrath had nothing to focus upon.

Jonathan signaled to his armorbearer who had remained atop the hill for exactly this moment. Another company of Hebrew

[6] 1 Samuel 17:24.

infantry, hidden among the trenches, launched themselves forward and struck the other Philistine flank—well away from Goliath. When the giant stormed in that direction, the Hebrews melted back up the slope only to appear in another sector.

No one would win a fight like this. The Hebrews were like menacing wasps buzzing about the head of an infuriated bull. They could sting, confuse, and torment the bull, but they couldn't destroy him. The Philistines, for their part, swatted ineffectively at the Hebrews who struck first in one place and then in another, running back to their fortifications the moment either Goliath or the Philistine chariots appeared on the field of battle.

Finally, the Philistines had had enough.

They withdrew to the center of the valley, leaving behind hundreds of men dead and dying. Scores of Hebrews also lay among them. Goliath then turned and faced the Hebrew fortifications. Jonathan walked to the edge of the slope, breathing heavily from exertion. He stared at Goliath, but even looking at the man from a distance sent small stabs of fear up his spine. His father and Abner joined him there, and it took much of Jonathan's strength to keep his eyes steady on the giant, trying not to allow his fear to show. But he could see the hatred reflected in the eyes of Goliath. Here was a man whose sole desire was to kill every Hebrew he could get his hands upon.

The huge man stepped forth from his men, his size dwarfing the Philistines who watched him as one would a god. Jonathan noted for the first time that the giant's armor was unlike the rest of the Philistines. He wore a chain shirt where the standard Philistine warrior sported the ribbed leather straps, studded with iron to protect their torso. The giant wore a beaten breastplate above the shirt and instead of the typical colored headdress, he wore a helmet that left the tattoos on his face and forehead visible.

The Philistine warriors began banging on drums and shields as their champion stood forth, and in a booming voice, bellowed, "Why do you not fight me? Am not I a Philistine and you servants of Saul? Come now! Choose a man from among you and let him come down to me! Let us fight here before our armies—we two champions of our people! If he is able to slay me, then we will be your servants!" He spat on the ground when he said it, clearly indicating what he thought of that possibility. "But if I prevail against him and slay him, then you will be our servants. Why should any more die this day? Is not one life sufficient?"[7] He spat on the ground again. "I defy the armies of Israel! Where is your God this day?" He banged on his chest, the bronze armor vibrating under the powerful blow. "Come, give me a man that we may fight together!"[8]

Jonathan wanted to take up that challenge. He wanted to face the giant, but a fear he could not describe froze his limbs. It was as if a great weight had been enfolded him unlike anything he'd ever experienced before. How could one man have so much power over him? Out of the corner of his eye, he saw his father drawing in great ragged breaths, his nostrils flaring in anger, but he too stood rooted to the ground unable to move.

Facing the giant was their duty. As the king and firstborn son of the king, it was their duty to face the giant. But neither could. Both knew that the giant would cut them down like so much kindling. The man was very nearly a god. Maybe...maybe if the Great Seer had stood with his father. Maybe...maybe if the ark of the LORD had been brought into the camp...maybe then he could've. But not now.

So father and son, Israel's two champions, stood there and said nothing as the giant cursed them, their people, and their God. Eventually, the giant tired of yelling his challenge and led the Philistines back toward their encampment.

Thus began a daily ritual. Each morning and each evening,[9] Goliath marched alone, except for a single man to bear his shield, to the center of the valley and cried forth his challenge, demanding a man be sent to him to fight, the victor becoming master over the other nation. His challenge was most effective, eating away at the

---

[7] 1 Samuel 17:8-9.

[8] 1 Samuel 17:10.

[9] 1 Samuel 17:16.

confidence of the Hebrew warriors, instilling fear and worry in their ranks, and imprisoning them in their trenches.

And each day, Jonathan and Saul stood atop their fortified hill and listened, stony-faced and impotent—neither able to answer the Philistine champion.

## Chapter Fifteen

David was bored. After being around King Saul's court, tracking down spies, defeating assassins, and being the king's personal armorbearer, David found little excitement in watching his father's sheep.[1] The last ten days had been lonely and dull. Jesse had been consumed with the other elders in sending a constant stream of supplies to the embattled Hebrew soldiers in the Valley of Elah. David's older three brothers were with Saul, fighting the LORD's battles. His other brothers, except for Maon, were organizing supplies from other surrounding hill cities, and all of David's nephews were, like David, watching other flocks of sheep or tending to the fields. David had barely seen anyone in his family over the last ten days, and he'd heard little of the battle and of King Saul.

The only positive that David could draw from his situation was that he had plenty of time to commune with the LORD God of his fathers. He spent hours in prayer, praying for his family, for King Saul, for Jonathan, and for Israel. He composed songs and sang to the disinterested ears of the sheep, but it was at such times that he felt closest to the LORD.

But then there were the times between, where the monotony and frustration of not being allowed to fight the LORD's battles gnawed on him like a dog worrying a bone. He grunted in frustration and threw a rock far down the hill where the sheep grazed. A few of the sheep looked up, startled, and gazed at him reproachfully, but generally, the creatures had little room for more than a single thought at a time, so most simply kept grazing.

With nothing better to do, David considered the sheep and their need for a shepherd. Without a shepherd, the sheep would stray and most likely die. He'd seen sheep wander lost and thirsty just over the hill from water but lacking the instincts to find it for themselves.

[1] 1 Samuel 17:15.

He wondered if that was how Jehovah Elohim saw people…as wandering sheep. As much as David desired to honor the LORD God, he knew how often he failed. But if there was one thing he'd learned, staying under the protection of Jehovah was the safest place to be.

He thought then of Maon. He hadn't seen his brother since the confrontation near the wall of Gibeah. No one in the family had seen him either, but that wasn't surprising. Maon had abandoned the LORD God and had turned to the false gods of the Philistines. His brother's actions saddened David and angered him at the same time. He was saddened for Maon and angered at the insult to Jehovah Elohim. Frankly, David couldn't understand it. *Why would anyone abandon the truth? Why would anyone willingly walk away from the one true God?*

In one of the few chances he'd had to talk to his father, David had told Jesse of his confrontation with Maon. He wished now he hadn't. The pain in his father's eyes had surprised David, and it had taken him a moment to realize what the revelation about Maon likely meant for his father. Maon would be stricken from the genealogies, his name blotted out as if he'd never been…never been part of the people of God.[2] History would record only seven sons of Jesse instead of eight.[3] It would be an unending grief of the heart and mind for David's parents.

No, David didn't understand Maon at all. Having personally experienced God's favor and attention, Maon's actions and thinking were as foreign to David as some of the peacock feathers he once saw imported from somewhere far to the east. He just couldn't fathom it. He did wish that his brother would return. If nothing else, David could use a good argument to relieve the never-ceasing boredom. And maybe, he could turn Maon from his ways and restore him.

*Yeah, right.*

---

[2] Exodus 31:14; Leviticus 7:20, 18:29.

[3] 1 Chronicles 2:13-15.

He chucked another rock, startling a young lamb that instantly began bawling for its mother.

Maon was lost as long as he thought he'd gone too far to ever come back. David didn't believe anyone could go so far that they couldn't come back, but if Maon did…if he believed that, then the odds of him returning to a true worship of Jehovah was nonexistent. He just wouldn't do it.

That worried David.

He picked up another rock and froze. Something large and draped in the shadows of a tree crouched at the base of the hill. The oblivious sheep continued grazing, but David's heart began to pound as adrenalin surged through his body. He carefully shifted to bring his sling to hand. Dropping the rough rock he'd picked up, he opened his pouch and pulled out a smooth stone, one much more aerodynamic, and dropped it into the sling.

The creature at the base of the hill shifted, coming partly into the sunlight. A bear! The animal looked huge to David, dwarfing the nearby sheep who still hadn't spotted the predator. It's light-brown fur almost looked grayish in the sunlight, helping the animal to blend in well with the dirt and other terrain features. Its snout lifted, sniffing, and its small, greedy eyes and small rounded ears shifted as it considered the grazing sheep.

The beast looked hungry.

David mentally measured the distance. The sling had a range that exceeded the bow and arrow, though its stopping power at such a long distance relied more upon gravity as compared to an arrow's ability to pierce flesh. Still, the bear was in range, and David had made similar shots in practice many times. Hopefully, he could sting the bear enough to drive it away.

Hopping to his feet, he set the sling in motion, gauged the necessary trajectory, and let fly. The missile flew true, arching high into the air and then falling to strike the bear along the flank.

The bear roared more in anger than in pain. The sheep took one startled look at the enraged bear and panicked. They scattered, one even stupidly attempting to run right by the bear. This was just too enticing to the large predator, and despite its pain, it swatted at the passing sheep sending it tumbling head over heels.

*By the blood of Abraham, Isaac, and Jacob!* He slipped his hand into his pouch and brought out another stone, this one a bit heavier and larger than the first. He charged down the hill toward the bear, sling already spinning. There were too many cursed bushes and boulders in the way! He dodged and weaved but couldn't get a good angle on the bear who had turned and was swatting at the injured sheep.

Muttering under his breath, David leaped to the top of a boulder that fell away sharply on the other side, and without even pausing, launched himself into the air. The bear had heard him coming and turned its head to see what manner of mad creature would be charging a full-grown adult bear—and inadvertently presented David with a perfect target. David let fly with the stone.

The smooth rock smacked into the bear's jaw with crushing force, sending a spray of blood into the air as its head snapped back under the impact. Injured and pained, the bear was not yet finished—only enraged.

David landed from his leap on the sloped hill and tumbled the last few cubits to the base. He rose to his feet just as the bear turned and reared up on its hind legs, growling and snapping with its bloody and ruined jaw. The bear didn't stand much taller than David this way, but its bulk clearly out-massed him by a significant amount. One swipe of those deadly white claws could decapitate David.

They stood about fifteen cubits apart. David reached for another stone and loaded his sling, sending it spinning into a blur of motion. Fortunately, because the bear had risen to its hind legs, the animal couldn't charge him easily, and the stance made for a much larger target.

The stone caught the bear a glancing blow to the side of the head, right under the eye, but its thick fur and fat prevented the stone from doing much more than bruising the already angry animal. The bear dropped down on all fours and charged.

David yelped and scrambled away, dodging around boulders and frustrating the bear's efforts to catch the fleet young man.

Arming the sling again, David, jumped atop a white boulder and slung another missile at the charging bear. This time, he hit the bear squarely in the back hip with bone-cracking force. The bear snarled in pain and tumbled over sideways. When it came back to its feet, the bear moved with a noticeable limp.

*Good.* Grimly, David began the process of battering the bear to death. It was much like a stoning, except the rocks struck with a force beyond what a human could muster alone. The sling could be a terrible weapon in the hands of someone as skilled as David. Four more well-placed stones put the bear out of its misery. When the bear finally stopped struggling, David walked over and, for good measure, slit the beast's throat with a knife that had been a gift from Jonathan.

He stood over the kill, his body still flushed with energy and power. He'd killed a bear![4] He thought back to the lion he'd killed all those weeks ago. Now he had killed both a lion and a bear! The bear had been less challenging since all he had to do was run around and sling stones at a distance, but he doubted many people could claim they'd killed both!

He had heard of other lion and bear attacks, but twice now, Jehovah Elohim had protected him and delivered him. He uttered a word of thanks and vowed to offer a sacrifice of thanksgiving to the LORD for His goodness.

So caught up was he in the euphoria of his victory, he never heard the footfalls of the two men who walked up behind him until it was too late. Some sixth sense or premonition from the LORD warned him, however, and he turned in time catch a heavy fist right in his jaw.

Pain flashed through David's head, and he cried out as he tumbled backward. He hit the ground and lay stunned, so he didn't move when the man who had hit him marched up and casually kicked him in the ribs. David grunted, feeling a rib crack. A shadow

[4] 1 Samuel 17:34-36.

fell over David, and he blinked up at his assailant, trying to understand what was happening.

"Look upon me, boy," the man standing over him hissed. "Know me."

David squinted, trying to see through the tears of pain that had gathered in his eyes. Blood dribbled out the side of his mouth and ran down his cheek. The man above him had a stubbled chin—the result of several days growth of whiskers, and his accent…David recognized it from somewhere.

The man squatted down beside David and placed a dagger at David's throat. "I had the chance to slay you once," the man said, "and how I wish now that I had. You stopped my man from slaying the king. You ruined everything."

David knew him now. Memories came flooding back. "Nasib," he spat out.

"So you know my name," Nasib said, frowning and scratching irritably at his whiskers. The man hadn't shaved in days. "I despaired of having my revenge upon you. Dagon be praised, I met someone who knew your whereabouts."

David looked past Nasib to the second man. "Maon," he whispered, feeling dread clench at his stomach for the first time. He didn't fear Nasib, but his brother's presence spoke volumes of his brother's heart condition. Maon hadn't simply betrayed Jehovah Elohim; Maon had now betrayed David too.

Nasib looked back at Maon, his face troubled. "He knows your name as well. Why is this?"

Maon shrugged. "I told you once that he was my brother. Did I not tell you where he would resort to? How do you think I knew? He is here as promised."

Nasib grunted and turned back to David, glancing curiously at the dead bear. "You slew a mighty beast, boy. This is a feat spoken around campfires, but you're not going to get the chance. I'm going to slay you, meddler and your brother is going to watch as the life leaves your body. You would've been wise to remain far from our business. The man Saul hung was a friend, and we'd long planned that assassination. Your meddling ruined many months of planning and preparations." He paused to slap David sharply across the face with his free hand. David's head rang from the blow. He tried to shake his head, but Nasib grabbed his jaw and held his face firm, the dagger still poised at David's throat. "My masters will not be pleased with me, and I don't intend to face them without a gift. Your head will have to do, meddler."

Nasib raised his dagger to strike and end David's life. David tensed, trying to prepare his body to act, to call upon the strength and power that he had at various times been granted by the LORD God, but he never had the chance.

The spy suddenly stiffened, his arm still raised for the killing blow. His mouth worked wordlessly, and a dribble of blood appeared at his lips. The dagger suddenly fell from listless fingers and dropped harmlessly to the ground beside David.

David rolled over and came painfully to his knees, facing the wild-eyed assassin. *What is going on?* Maon stood behind Nasib, his face a study of implacable and emotionless lines and angles. David's brother stepped back then, pulling out a long knife he'd stuck into Nasib's back. Nasib shuddered once and fell over onto his face where the light faded from his eyes forever.

David stared at his brother in amazement. "Why?" he finally asked, the movement of his jaw bringing a stab of pain.

"I like you not, brother, and I agree with you less on many things, but it is not in me to allow this one to slay a brother of mine." Maon's face, still damaged from David's fight with him those weeks ago, looked bleak and determined—and perhaps a bit sad.

David sat back on his heels, trying to shake the cobwebs of the attack out his mind. "You once said that such bonds had been broken."

Maon shrugged. "I lied."

Grunting, David wiped some of the blood from his mouth. "Then if you were of a mind to slay him, why wait until after he'd beat on my face?"

Maon smiled sardonically. "A bit of revenge for the beating you gave my own face, brother. I owed you that. You could've slain me then, but you didn't."

"I seriously thought about it," David admitted, watching as Maon moved over to Nasib's body and began searching him.

Maon nodded, pocketing a few silver shekels he'd discovered. "And I seriously considered letting Nasib slit your throat. I guess neither of us could do what we should. I have a feeling that letting you live will be a most serious mistake, brother. I know about Samuel's anointing. If you become king one day—how that could be is still beyond me…" his voice trailed off as he looked at the dead bear and then at Nasib. "Well, perhaps it is not so impossible after all. Yet, your love for your Elohim will not endear you to the Philistines. I think I could save them much grief—me, too—if I'd let you die."

An awkward silence descended between the two. David didn't know if he should thank his brother or curse him. Instead, he asked, "Where will you go?"

Maon stood up. David also climbed warily to his feet, watching his brother closely.

"I will go to the Philistines. The border is mostly clear now that Saul had to pull the army to Elah to confront the Philistines. I should have no problems slipping over."

"You would ally with our enemies, brother?"

Maon smiled coldly. "Have not I been for some time, brother?" He shrugged. "It is the only path for me now. Too many people here know of my involvement with the assassination attempt on King Saul. I must flee."

David swallowed a lump in his throat. "I told Father, Maon. He knows."

Maon sighed deeply, looking truly troubled for the first time. "I wish you had not. It would be better if Mother and Father had never known."

"You know what this means, do you not? You'll be cut off. Outcast. You'll be as if you'd never been born, your name blotted out."

The brothers looked solemnly at each other for a long moment, dark thoughts clouding each other's minds. Finally, Maon nodded. "So be it. Farewell, brother. I pray we never meet again." He turned, slung a pack over his shoulder and began walking away. He never once looked back.

David watched him go until he was little more than a speck in the distance. Finally, he sighed, knowing he had to gather the scattered flock and look after the injured lamb—not to mention his own injuries. "Farewell, brother," he whispered. "May you find your way back to your true God."

# Chapter Sixteen

A month after the incident with Maon, Jesse stopped David early one morning[1] as he was preparing to drive one of the flocks of sheep back up into the hills around Bethlehem. "Leave the sheep to Joab, my son," Jesse said, taking David by the arm and pulling him out into the covered courtyard of their ancestral house where a cart hitched to a short-tempered ass, stood ready to depart.

"What is this, Father?" David asked, surprised.

"I want you to find your brothers who followed King Saul and take their pledge. I would know how they fare." He went over to the cart and pulled back a woolen blanket. "There's an ephah of corn and ten loaves of bread that you are to give them. Find out how they fare and if they need anything else."

David's eyes narrowed. This behavior was unlike his father. Nearly forty days had passed since the siege in the Valley of Elah had begun. *Why now? Why is he worried now?* Not that David was complaining. His jaw and ribs had mostly healed from the beating he'd taken from the Philistine spy—the incident had been covered up easily enough and blamed on the bear—so David was itching to do something other than watch those stupid sheep!

Word had been slow in coming out of the war camp, and what they did get was often garbled and sheathed in rumor. Armed clashes happened frequently, and Saul's forces were more than holding their own, but rumors of a Philistine champion who was challenging the armies of Israel abounded. David wondered if this was the same champion who had almost trapped King Saul some months ago.

David's brothers had sent word back with the caravanners when they could, and a messenger had arrived from Eliab just four days ago, so something must have happened for Jesse to send David to check on them.

[1] 1 Samuel 17:20.

"Father, what's wrong?" David asked.

Jesse combed his fingers through his long, white beard. "I'm uneasy, my son. I would check on them myself, but I fear my days of roaming over ridges and hills are long past.[2] I…I want to know how they truly fare. I didn't like the tenor of your brother's last message. I would send one of your other older brothers, but I cannot spare them. You must go."

"Yes, Father," David said quickly. He didn't want his father to change his mind.

"There are also ten cheeses. Deliver those to your brother's captain with my compliments.[3] That should get you through to see your brothers and take their pledge of how they fare." He gave his son a shrewd look. "I know you're anxious to see the battle, but promise me you'll return quickly with word of your brothers."

"I swear it, Father." Anything to get going.

"Then hasten, my son. More supplies are going out this morning, so you can travel safely with the caravan. Do you know the way?"

"Aye, Father." The route followed a ridge until it reached the valley. About a day's walk, but he fully intended to do it quicker than that.

"God speed then, my son. Oh…I packed several meals for you on the ass. Your mother would not see you hungry when you return."

"Thank you." David picked up the ass's reins and began tugging the beast toward the courtyard gate. The cursed beast had his own idea of how fast he wanted to travel, but David was not about to be undone by a silly animal, and before long, they were moving quickly through the town.

Once beyond the city walls, he went quickly to the depot where a supply caravan was preparing to pull out. A troop of Saul's soldiers had arrived to escort the caravan, but they seemed to be taking forever to get organized. David waited a few minutes, and then

---

[2] 1 Samuel 17:12.

[3] 1 Samuel 17:18.

impatient, started off on his own. He knew the way. He'd traveled the ridgeline several times and had looked out over the Valley of Elah once or twice, so he didn't figure there was much sense to waiting around.

The path atop the ridge had been worn down by centuries of feet, hooves, and cart wheels. The broad wound its way along the ridge top straight from Bethlehem and eventually merged with the Valley of Elah to the west. It was this route Saul guarded. If the Philistines gained control of this passage, they would have easy access to Bethlehem and many of the other cities of Israel.

Much to the ass's chagrin, David set a punishing pace. He frequently had to threaten or bribe the stubborn ass, but regardless, he made good time and along toward late afternoon, he came out atop the ridge to see a valley stretched out before him. His breath caught. From across the valley, the Philistine army was gathering. The grass along with the yellow and blue flowers that populated the valley floor at this time of year had been repeatedly trampled between the two armies, so it was obvious where each army had chosen to camp. David could see chariots, horsemen, and foot soldiers mustering in rank upon rank on the Philistine side of the valley. The sight was breathtaking. He'd never seen so many men at one time before.

The Hebrews had not yet advanced to meet them.

His heart pounding with excitement, David practically pulled the ass along the trail. Not so much farther on, he found the quartermaster depot. The quartermaster himself, a burly man with muscles that seemed to sprout out all over him, directed him to an unloading platform. David left the cart there, and forgetting about the corn and bread for his brothers, he darted off toward the trenches. He could see the various tribal standards now and moved quickly to the Judean standard where his brothers would likely be.

He got there just in time to see the Hebrew forces launch a counterattack against marching Philistines. David watched in awe as the two forces clashed in brutal mayhem. The soldiers of Judah were not in this fray, for Saul had decided to hold them in reserve, so it didn't take long to find his three brothers.

Abinadab stood atop the trench directing men into position in case they were called upon to help with the battle below. Eliab and Shammah waited in the trench, fingering short, wicked-looking spears as they watched the battle below. Only Abinadab had a sword, but it was belted to his waist. For the moment, he used a spear to direct his men.

Eliab spotted David first. "David! What do you here?"

David didn't answer. He didn't even hear. He stared in fascinated horror at the battle unfolding before him. Men screamed, cursed, and died. Flights of arrows flew out from the Hebrew fortifications to rain down upon the Philistines. Answering flights of arrows struck back at the Hebrews, one arrow smacking into the ground not so far away from David. He didn't even notice.

But even with the apparent chaos, David detected a peculiar status quo that had been established between the two armies. The two forces almost seemed as if they were poking at each other rather than trying to destroy each other. The Philistines had grown wary of the Hebrew fortifications, and the Hebrews were reluctant to venture too far away from the same fortifications. This resulted in a bizarre and deadly game of touch-me-if-you-can. Men still died and men still fell away wounded, but it didn't appear as if either army wanted to fully commit themselves.

And that's when the giant appeared on the battlefield.

David blinked, trying to reconcile the man's size with that of the other soldiers. If the giant was normal, then the men around him were mere children. The Hebrew soldiers took one look at the giant, turned, and fled, swarming up the steep slope to their fortifications, scrambling and tearing at the earth to help climb. Fear fell over the camp. David glanced at his brothers and saw it in their faces too.

The Philistine army fell back, leaving the man named Goliath and his shield bearer as the sole owners of the battlefield. The sun reflected dully off the man's bronze helmet, mail shirt, and breastplate. A huge sword hung from the giant's waist, the length of which looked to be twice that of a normal sword. Bronze greaves protected Goliath's legs, and the spear he held casually in one hand looked more like one of those communal weaver's beams where many women could work on at once. His wide head swung to take in the whole of the Hebrew defenses, his tattoos visible even from where David stood.

David was impressed. Never had her seen such a large man decked out in that much bronze armor. No wonder the Philistines revered him as a god. But David knew better. Even as impressed as he was, he knew the giant was nothing more than a man—a man who could bleed as freely as any other man. Why else the armor—if not to protect sensitive flesh?

The giant lifted his spear to the sky and bellowed, "I defy the armies of Israel. Send me a man that we may fight! Where is your God? Why has He not fought for you? Come, send me a man! Let us fight, and let our gods determine the outcome! How long will you cower in your trenches, Hebrew pigs!"

David bristled, and his eyes fastened on the giant with an intensity and anger that David had rarely felt before. He then glanced at the men around him, saw their fear, and heard their muttering. Shock momentarily replaced anger. He tried to find one man who looked as angry as David felt, but all he saw was fear. David didn't understand. "Why hasn't someone killed that uncircumcised Philistine?" he demanded, forgetting his place.

One of the soldiers, without taking his eyes off the giant below, said, "Look upon him! No man can stand before him. Surely, he is come to defy Israel."[4]

David stared flabbergasted at the man. "No one has yet answered the giant's challenge?"

The soldier finally turned to look at David, noted his youth, and sneered dismissively. "Feel free to do so, lad. The king has promised great riches and his daughter to any man who can slay the giant. All debts will be forgiven, and his father's house will be made

[4] 1 Samuel 17:25-26.

free in Israel. So has the king promised the man who will slay that Philistine."[5]

"Then let me go," David snarled, glaring at the giant. "I will slay him!"

Eliab, David's oldest brother, leaped out of the trench and shoved David backward. David grunted in surprise and swung around to face his brother, but Eliab never even gave David a chance to say anything. He grabbed David by the front of his tunic and pulled him to within a fingerbreadth of his own face. "Enough of this foolish talk, David! Why have you really come here? With whom have you left the few sheep in the wilderness? The herd was your responsibility, David. Father needed you there! Why have you come here?" David struggled to say something, but Eliab shook him. "I'll tell you. I know the naughtiness of your heart. You've come to see the battle."[6]

David knocked his brother's hands away and stepped back. "What have I done, brother? Is there not a cause?"[7] He glared at Eliab. "Someone should've already gone down there and removed the dog's head from his body."

"He's a giant, David!" Eliab shouted. "He's slain all who have gotten near him."

"He is but a man!" David shouted back. "A man only! We are the armies of the living God. Elohim will protect us."

Eliab swore and pointed to the battlefield of dead and dying. "That means not that you won't die, David. Look at bloodied field below. Look at what the Philistine have done to the armies of Israel. Would you be among them?"

David clenched his teeth and backed away from his brother. They'd gathered an audience now. Most of the soldiers in this sector of the trenches were staring at the two brothers wonderingly, not saying anything, simply watching. Everything that had happened to David over the last few months gathered in his heart and narrowed

[5] 1 Samuel 17:25.

[6] 1 Samuel 17:28.

[7] 1 Samuel 17:29.

down to one overriding truth: the LORD was with him. He knew this irrevocably.

Maon' arguments had forced David to see things in a new light. He was no slave to Jehovah. A slave was one who had no choice but to serve his master. David was no slave to Elohim. He was a *servant.* He wanted this life. He wanted to serve his God. More than that, Jehovah had chosen him and had anointed him for this task. He knew beyond any measure of doubt that this battle was his to fight. This was what God had been preparing him for. This was what God had raised him up to do.

David spread his arms wide. "I will go. I will slay the giant and remove the reproach from Israel. Is there any other here who would deny me this?" The men began muttering among themselves. David nearly lost his temper altogether and shouted at the men, "The king seeks a man to fight the Philistine, is this not so? Has he not promised rewards?"[8]

The men nodded, and a few ayes were shouted back to him.

"Then I am that man. I will fight him!"

The commotion atop the Hebrew fortifications must have gained Goliath's attention. He stood his ground, looking curiously at the Hebrew army. "Is this then the day you send me a man at last?" he roared to the Hebrews. "Send him then! I shall wait!"

David very nearly started down that instant, but his brothers intervened, standing between him and the giant. "David," Abinadab said softly, "don't do this. You are ill-prepared for this battle."

David looked sadly at his brother. "You are wrong, brother. I have been prepared. This fight won't be mine, brother. It will be Jehovah's. You should know this." He took all three of his brothers in with a glance. "I am able to defeat the giant."

His brothers stared back wordlessly. David could see their doubt, their confusion. He looked at the rest of the soldiers who still watched him. They too looked doubtful, but David also saw shame

[8] 1 Samuel 17:30

in their eyes and rightfully so. David was willing to do what they were too frightened to do.

A squad of soldiers bearing the standard of Benjamin thrust their way through the soldiers of Judah. Their leader was a man David recognized. Abner looked David up and down, his craggy face showing his surprise and uncertainty to discover the cause of the commotion was a lad. "Come," he said to David at length, "the king wishes to speak to you."[9]

David turned without a word and hurried after Abner. He could feel his brothers' eyes on him until he was lost from sight. Abner led David to a large tent that had been pitched behind the fortifications. Inside, David stood before King Saul and Jonathan.

"David?" Saul said almost in disbelief. "You are the one who wishes to fight the Philistine champion?"

David nodded. "Let no man's heart fail because of the giant, my lord. Your servant will go and fight with this Philistine."[10] David wasn't completely sure where such boldness had arisen from, but it felt right. He did not fear the Philistine. Truly, he'd been well-prepared for this battle. Both the lion and the bear had been mightier than David, yet the LORD God of Israel had delivered David out of their paws. The giant would be no different. Besides, the giant looked slow—and the inkling of a plan began to form in David's mind.

The king was shaking his head. "You can't fight the giant. You are just a youth, and Goliath has been a man of war from his youth. What chance do you have?"[11]

David bowed. "Then let the king know. Your servant kept his father's sheep. There came a lion and a bear and took a lamb out of the flock. And I went out after each, and smote them, my lord, and delivered the flock from their mouths. And when the lion arose against me, I caught the lion by his beard, and smote him, and slew him. I also slew the bear, my lord. This uncircumcised Philistine will

---

[9] 1 Samuel 17:31.

[10] 1 Samuel 17:32.

[11] 1 Samuel 17:33.

be as one of them, seeing he has defied the armies of the living God. The LORD God that delivered me out of the paw of the lion and out of the paw of the bear, He will deliver me out of the hand of this Philistine."[12]

Saul stared at David, his expression one of amazement. "This is true what you say about the lion and bear?"

"Aye, my lord," David said. "Doeg the Edomite was witness to the lion. I but slew the bear not a month ago."

Jonathan stepped forward and placed a hand on David's shoulder. "Father, I think this can be done."

For some reason, Jonathan's endorsement meant much to David. He smiled gratefully at his friend. He had grown close to Jonathan since they'd met in Saul's court, and if David needed any additional support, then Jonathan's was all he truly needed.

The king looked from his son and then back to David. He nodded then, a slow nod filled with all sorts of emotions that David could only guess at. "Go," he whispered, not even really looking at David, "and Jehovah be with you."[13] Saul glanced at his armor sitting in the corner of the tent. "But I would not that my servant go so unarmed. Come here."

David followed the king curiously. "You want me to wear your armor, my lord?"

"You've seen the giant, David. You know what you face. I would not have you go unprotected."

David eyed the armor uncertainly. He'd never worn anything like it before, but the king did have a point. So with Jonathan's aid, he began putting the armor on. Many of the leather straps needed to be tightened since David was shorter and smaller than the king. Finally, the bronze helmet was put on David's head and Saul's sword strapped to his waist.[14] David squirmed, trying to settle the added weight about his body. The helmet nearly spun an entire circle

[12] 1 Samuel 17:34-37.
[13] 1 Samuel 17:37.
[14] 1 Samuel 17:38.

around his head, and the armor was heavier than he would have expected.

He took a few steps and then stopped and looked directly at Saul. "I cannot go with these, for I have not proved them."[15]

"Would you go unprotected then?" Saul asked, his face disapproving.

David began to remove the armor. "It's not that, my lord. When I fought the lion and the bear, I succeeded because I could move quickly. I have no experience with these, my lord, and I have little experience with the sword. I fear, I must rely upon other weapons."

"Such as?"

David retrieved his staff and sling.[16] "Just these, my lord."

Jonathan and Saul exchanged a long look. "This does not bode well, David," Saul reproved him. "How can you defeat the giant with so little?"

David grinned again, thinking of his plan. "Watch and see, my lord. I do not think you shall be disappointed. Besides, I go with God. The giant is the one who faces me with little."

The king's eyes closed. "I hear your words. I see your heart, but I still fear to send you, my son. I fear what the giant will do to you. You have yet to witness his great strength." He hesitated. "But I do believe the LORD is with you. I pray that He is. Our honor, our nation, our lives rest upon you, my servant. Go, and Jehovah be with you."

David left the tent, but only Jonathan followed him. "Do you have a plan, David?" the eldest son of Saul asked.

"Aye, my lord. The giant is large. He walks the ground like an ox. I will be like the deer—or the wolf."

"I'm not sure I understand, but I give you warning. Even an ox, when angered, can be exceedingly dangerous. Stay well, my friend, and bring us the giant's tattooed head."

---

15 1 Samuel 17:39.

16 1 Samuel 17:40.

Both men grinned at each other. Jonathan walked over to a pole that bore a flag of challenge. It had lain unused on the ground for these past forty days, but now Jonathan hoisted it high and slammed the butt hard into the earth to steady it. The red flag waved defiantly in the small breeze of the late afternoon.

A roar of approval rose from the ranks of Hebrew soldiers, and from the valley below, Goliath beheld the challenge flag and beat upon his breastplate in pleased battle lust. He shouted, "Come then! Send me a man that we may fight!"

David took a deep breath, eyeing the monstrous giant. Then he bounded down the slope to meet his fate and fulfill the duty of his anointing.

# Chapter Seventeen

Jonathan watched David bound recklessly down the slope. The lad's enthusiasm was either born of innocence or arrogance—to face the giant with naught but a sling was the height of foolishness! Still, Jonathan recalled a time when he had possessed the same enthusiasm. Filled with zeal and the Spirit of the LORD, he'd ventured off with no one but his armorbearer to challenge an entire garrison of enemy soldiers in a similar reckless endeavor. Together, they had slain twenty of the enemy warriors and put the fear of Elohim in the hearts of the enemy.[1] What had happened to that younger, more energetic man?

Watching David go, Jonathan felt a stab of guilt. *I should be the one facing the giant—not that ruddy-faced youth who doesn't know how to handle a sword or wear armor properly. What is my father thinking, letting David fight the giant?* If David lost, then where would they be? Would Saul truly surrender to the Philistines as Goliath had demanded?

David reached the bottom of the slope and temporarily disappeared into the trees near the brook. Out in the valley, Goliath waited impatiently, occasionally bellowing more curses and demands. He'd wanted this fight for the last forty days.[2] He'd finally get it. Jonathan could only hope the giant would be disappointed.

Saul and Abner stepped up beside Jonathan. Both looked solemn as they beheld the waiting giant. His father had not yet donned his armor. *Strange.* He wore his kingly robes instead.

Suddenly, he leaned toward his craggy-faced commander and asked, "Abner, whose son is this youth?"[3] He hesitated. "I know it was told me before, but I cannot recall."

Much had been clouded for Saul over the past months. The man who had delivered Israel from the crushing grip of the

[1] 1 Samuel 14:14.
[2] 1 Samuel 17:16.
[3] 1 Samuel 17:55.

Philistines had been consumed by this angry, distant, and bitter man. Abner looked troubled. He had not been in court over the last few months to know this. "As thy soul lives, O king, I cannot tell. I never learned of his father."[4]

"Inquire whose son he is for me,"[5] Saul stated, still not looking directly at his commander. "I would know in case…" He trailed off.

Jonathan understood. If David were to fall, Saul wanted to honor the lad's family. If by some miracle David won, then the king would still want to know. While David had only been a harper in the king's court, his family name hadn't mattered all that much. But David represented all Israel now. The lad was their champion. For good or ill, all eyes were on him. Live or die, he would be remembered.

David stopped when he reached the brook that formed a shallow moat of sorts at the base of the hill. The brook only had a small amount of water flowing through it, and under normal circumstances, the brook would have tinkled merrily along, but now the ravages of war had marred its picturesque tranquility. Blood-spattered rocks littered the brook on all sides. Rotting bodies, left by the Philistines, lay bloated and black among the rocks and trees, and swarms of flies and flocks of greedy carrion-eating birds filled the air or covered the bodies.

The smell nearly made David retch, but he fought down the impulse. He had a mission to complete. He emptied his pouch of the stones he normally carried, knowing for this task they were probably too small. He needed something bigger that would do damage to a larger foe, and the brook provided a source of limitless ammunition for his needs.

---

[4] 1 Samuel 17:55.

[5] 1 Samuel 17:56.

He quickly selected a smooth rock that fit easily in his fist. It would fit in his sling snugly, and David knew the round shape and smoothness would allow it to fly easily through the air. He hunted around until he found four others and slipped them into his pouch—all the pouch could conveniently carry. Only one of the stones was relatively small. He would use that one first, sting the giant and knock him off balance. Then the others would do the real damage. He was ready.

His plan was simple. The giant was so big and so weighed down with armor that Goliath would never be able to catch David. All David needed to do was run around beyond the giant's reach and sling stones at him until he was brought down. It would be just like the bear, except Goliath looked slower than the bear had been. And if David needed more than five stones,[6] well, there was an entire brook full of ammunition. He could pelt the giant all day if needed and never come within range of that huge spear or heavy sword.

The shield-bearer didn't look to be much of a threat, David decided. The man had all he could do to carry that huge shield around. David should have little problem dodging around the burdened shield-bearer to take potshots at Goliath. With Jehovah Elohim guiding his arm, the giant wouldn't stand a chance.

His confidence burgeoning, he skipped out of the brook and emerged from the trees to face the giant. Goliath took one look at David and began to laugh. It was a deep, raw guffaw, like one hears from someone too long at the wine—a mocking laugh that immediately set David's teeth on edge and his blood to boiling.

The giant took a dozen steps forward, facing not David, but Saul and his army atop the hill. His face was dark and flushed with fury beneath his bronze helm. "Am I a dog?" he roared at King Saul. "Is this the man you send me to fight? A boy? I will see your head on my spear for this insult!" He spat on the ground and then snarled at David, "Why has your master sent you to die at my hand? Am I a dog that you come to me with staves?"[7] He barked another mocking

[6] 1 Samuel 17:40.
[7] 1 Samuel 17:43.

laugh and cursed David by his gods. "Come then! Come to me, and by Dagon, I will give your flesh to the fowls of the air and to the beasts of the field![8] If your master wishes you to die, then so be it! Come!"

David marched closer so that everyone in both armies could see him and hopefully hear what he had to say. Goliath's defiance had struck a chord deep in David's soul. Like with the lion, the bear, and the assassin, a sense of necessity descended over David, and the Spirit of the LORD infused him once again. This giant had defied the armies of the living God and had mocked Jehovah long enough.

"You come to me with a sword, a spear, and a shield," David announced, his voice somehow carrying easily to both armies. It was as if nature itself had stilled to lend an ear to David's voice. "But I come to you in the name of the LORD of hosts, the God of the armies of Israel, whom you have defied. This day will the LORD deliver you into my hand, and I will smite you, and take your head from you, and I will give the carcasses of the host of the Philistines this day unto the fowls of the air and to the wild beasts of the earth that all the earth may know that there is a God in Israel." David flung his arms out wide, staff in one hand, the other empty to encompass both armies in his proclamation. "And all this assembly will know that the LORD saves not with sword and spear—for the battle is the LORD's—and He will give you into our hands."[9]

Goliath laughed again, but this time, the laugh was mixed with anger. David's words had struck home. "Enough talk, child! Come and let my spear feast on your blood!"

David started running straight for the giant.[10]

As he ran, he discarded the staff. He wouldn't need it for what was coming, and it had already served its purpose. Goliath had focused on the staff, thinking it to be David's primary weapon. He couldn't have been more wrong. Still running at full speed, seemingly straight to his impending death, David took out his sling, dipped his

---

[8] 1 Samuel 17:44.
[9] 1 Samuel 17:45-47.
[10] 1 Samuel 17:48.

hand into his pouch, and slipped the smallest of his missiles into his real weapon.

The giant lumbered into a run, more of a trot really, but one full of immense power. Goliath's grin widened as he approached, and a roar of victory began to sound on his lips. The hapless shield-bearer ran before the giant, shielding most of the giant's body from the sling, but Goliath had not reckoned on the might of the LORD's favor upon David.

Several score of paces away, David leaped into the air to gain a bit of height and launched his missile with terrifying speed and accuracy. The zipping sound carried clearly to every ear in the valley as the smooth stone cleared the shield-bearer and rose to slam into Goliath's forehead, one of the few unprotected spots on the giant's armored body. A crack of bone breaking was immediately followed by the sickening sucking sound of the rock burrowing into the giant's brain.[11]

David already had a second, larger stone in his sling and had it spinning for another shot as he scooted sideways to get a different angle around the shield-bearer, but it wasn't needed. Blood poured from the wound in the giant's head as the giant staggered unsteadily to a stop. Goliath blinked stupidly at David, his tattooed face filled with confusion and pain. Then his eyes rolled up in his head, and he fell flat on his face, unmoving.

David let his sling stop spinning. *That was it?* He could hardly believe it! He knew he would defeat the huge lout…but…but on the first throw?

Jehovah Elohim.

That was the only explanation. God had directed the rock as surely as anything David knew to be true.

Every man, both Hebrew and Philistine, in the valley stood in frozen shock. The human god had fallen, slain by the hand of a youth with a sling and a single stone. Impossible. David surveyed the two

[11] 1 Samuel 17:49.

armies and knew he had one more thing he needed to do—one more thing to irreversibly destroy the Philistine's faith in their human god.

He strode past the stupefied shield-bearer who flinched violently away, but David gave him no heed. He came upon the body of Goliath and slowly drew the huge sword from the sheath. Up close, the giant seemed even more imposing in size, but lying face first in the churned-up ground of the battlefield had crushed all fear of the man out of the hearts of the Hebrew armies.

Standing above the fallen giant, David deliberately began the gory task of chopping off Goliath's head with the man's own sword.[12] David needed more than a few swings of the heavy sword to sever the huge head from the gigantic body. But at last the head fell free. Dropping the sword, David yanked off Goliath's helmet and lifted the severed head up with both hands by the hair. He then climbed atop the corpse and raised his gory trophy to the sky.

An earthshaking cry of victory rolled over the valley as the entire Hebrew army broke ranks and charged down the hillside. The Philistines' spirit, shattered by their Champion's ignoble fall, saw death approaching. They had revered Goliath as a god in human form—an emblem of their superiority and deity. It was too much for their superstitious minds. As one man, they turned and fled westward, abandoning their tents, chariots, horses, and much else.[13]

The armies of Israel and Judah flowed around David like a river parting around a boulder and charged on with fanatical ferocity. After forty days of endless stalemate, David had shattered their fear with one sling of a rock. They gave the Philistines no quarter. The slaughter continued all the way to the gates of Ekron.[14]

David kept his pose on his fleshly dais—a beacon standing above the flow of men, an inspiration for the weary armies of Israel. When the last soldier passed in his pursuit of the enemy, David turned and began trudging up the slope to where a few men had remained behind. He toted the gaping, staring, tattooed head of the

---

[12] 1 Samuel 17:50-51.

[13] 1 Samuel 17:51-52.

[14] 1 Samuel 17:52.

Philistine champion with him. They watched him coming with something akin to wonder and awe. Never had they seen the like.

Abner reached David first and took the grisly trophy from him. He looked deep into David's eyes, his own blue ones reflecting wonder—and relief. "Well done, young one. You have upheld the honor of Israel this day." A tear of gratitude escaped his eye, a true concession to the normally emotionless man. "Come, let us speak to the king."

The cagey commander led David to where Saul awaited him. Jonathan stood nearby, his eyes locked onto David in a way David had never seen before. The harper approached the king and fell on his knees. "Your servant has returned, my lord. The LORD God of our fathers has delivered the Philistine champion into our hands."

Saul placed his powerful hands on David's bowed head. When he spoke, his voice was thick with emotion. "Whose son are you, young man?"[15]

David already knew that Saul had forgotten who his father was, so he didn't even hesitate to say, "I am the son of your servant Jesse the Bethlehemite."[16]

"Then, son of Jesse, you have done your king and your people a great service this day. You have slain the giant and delivered us out of the hands of the Philistines."

"The hand of Jehovah, my lord, delivered us. I was but His vessel in this matter."

King Saul nodded. "As you will, son of Jesse. We will honor our God with this victory. This I swear."

"Then all is well?" David asked, his tone betraying a bit of anxiety. He had no idea what should happen next. Goliath was the first man he'd ever killed and standing there on the giant's body with the bloody head raised to the sky had been more emotionally draining than David had imagined. He realized, perhaps a bit belatedly, that he had been somewhat presumptuous in his challenge of the giant. Perhaps he should've waited for Saul or Jonathan to

15 1 Samuel 17:58.

16 1 Samuel 17:58.

answer the challenge. Perhaps he had somehow insulted the king by taking up the giant's challenge without realizing it.

But Jonathan interrupted before the king could say anything. "Is it well?" he practically gushed, "it is more than well! A great victory has been wrought here!" Jonathan reached down and pulled David to his feet. He spun David about so that they faced each other squarely. "Do you bear witness, Father?"

King Saul looked startled and fell back a pace. He studied his son for a moment, obviously trying to understand his intent. Then he nodded. "I bear witness."

David and Jonathan looked into each other's eyes, and something profound passed between them. A bond formed between the two in that instant that David would never be able to explain. Jonathan began to unbuckle his armor, and as he placed it upon David,[17] he said, "This day do I swear to be a brother-in-arms with David, the son of Jesse. We will be as one, he and I, all the days of our lives. From this day forth, let no man sully his name or disparage his person. Any who do so does so to me, and I will be avenged upon such a man. My blood is his blood."

David straightened, feeling the binding power of that oath[18] as the words were being spoken. He gripped Jonathan's arm tightly as his friend finished buckling his sword around David's waist. "My blood is your blood," he repeated to Jonathan. "I too will be avenged upon the body of any man who disparages your person."

The king's son glanced at Saul, waiting. The king's face was unreadable to David. He couldn't tell whether or not the king was happy with the oath. But at length, Saul said, "I am witness."

Jonathan and David then embraced, and if the loss of Maon as a brother had been painful, the gaining of Jonathan as a brother was doubly joyful in contrast. A love had been born between the two men that would become legendary.[19]

---

[17] 1 Samuel 18:4.

[18] 1 Samuel 18:3.

[19] 1 Samuel 18:1.

For the first time since Samuel had anointed David, he felt his way ahead was clear and free. Jehovah Elohim was indeed with him. What exactly that meant for the future, David could not say, but for this moment, all was as it should be.

# Epilogue

Saul's jubilant mood began to sour as the armies passed Bethlehem and entered the hill country and cities that made up the core of the nation of Israel. Yes, they'd won a great victory against the Philistines and smashed their ability to wage war for years to come. Yes, they'd pillaged the enemy tents[1] and were bringing back much spoil that would go a long way in alleviating the economic hardship brought on by any war. Indeed, the Hebrew armies were generally intact. They had suffered losses and men had died, but the laughter outweighed the sorrow; the victory outweighed the loss. And the Philistine champion was dead. No more would the giant plague Saul's dreams. No more would he need tremble at the sight of him.

But something, like the intangible beginnings of an illness, had begun to bother Saul. He struggled to put his finger on it and to understand why he couldn't rejoice with his people in the great victory that had been wrought over Israel's enemies. To be sure, he was pleased with the overall outcome, but he kept coming back to a single mental picture that stung like an infernal mosquito addicted to his flesh.

He kept seeing David standing on the body of the giant, holding high Goliath's head like a standard. Saul's soldiers had rallied to that standard and had crushed the Philistines. *Why should that bother me so much? I sent David to fight the giant.* The boy had only done what his king had commanded. The victory was as much Saul's as it was David's. *Did not David serve me? Did not the harper bow to me? Am I not the king?*

He also kept seeing his beloved son, Jonathan, making a covenant with the son of Jesse. Saul had never seen his son so passionate before—so caught up by anyone's deeds. *Was not Jonathan a hero in his own might? Why would my son bind himself to the son of Jesse?*

[1] 1 Samuel 17:53.

These questions gnawed at Saul like a pack of wolves chasing an aged and terrified deer.

Word of their victory had run before them like animals before a wild fire. Rumors of people gathering along the road to Gibeah to welcome home the victors had already trickled back to Saul. He looked forward to it. The people knew who kept them safe. They knew who fought for them. In the back of Saul's mind, this would be his vindication. David may have killed the giant, but Saul had been fighting the enemies of the LORD and of Israel for years. He was due his proper recognition.

David rode just behind the king, next to Jonathan. He rode poorly, Saul noted with some satisfaction. The son of Jesse had obviously never before ridden a horse. He looked awkward and uncomfortable whereas Saul looked confident and in charge. Yes, the differences between them was fitting roles for the returning heroes. It should provide the right impression and put David in his proper place. It would do good for the son of Jesse to be reminded of such.

Then the road that led up to Jerusalem began to fill with people, laughter, music, and singing. Saul soaked it in. It was good for his people to rejoice. He glanced at the tall pike where Goliath's tattooed head had been stuck, lifted high for the people to see. The giant's armor had been granted to David as spoils of war,[2] but that mattered little. Who could possibly wear such large armor anyway? Goliath's head, stuck on a pike, preceded them all—a testament to Saul's leadership and kingship. And clearly the people knew it. Though he didn't know why, Saul determined to have the head displayed above the gates of Jerusalem.[3] He didn't feel comfortable with the head being displayed at Gibeah. Jerusalem would be just fine.

Saul finally let himself relax and smile. David would know his place. In fact, Saul intended to keep the shepherd close from now on. No more would he be allowed to return to his father's house.[4]

[2] 1 Samuel 17:54.

[3] 1 Samuel 17:54.

[4] 1 Samuel 18:2.

David was now Saul's servant, and everyone would know it. He lifted his hand in greeting as the marching armies came up to the crowd of people.

They shouted when he did so, cheering their king—and rightfully so. *Yes, this is a good day!*

Then a large group of women flanked the road. Half stood on one side and half the other. The army would pass between them. Saul's chest swelled. His saw his wife and concubine, Rizpah,[5] among them, but it was his daughter, Michal, who stood foremost among the women. This pleased Saul. A daughter should honor her father. They were dancing and singing as they played upon tambourines and other instruments.[6] Saul laughed along with them. It did his heart good to see them honoring their king!

Then women on one side shouted in a singsong voice as they played and danced, "Saul has slain his thousands!"

The king's chest swelled at hearing such words. But then the other side instantly responded in kind, "And David has slain his tens of thousands!"

Saul's face froze even as all the air left his lungs as if he'd just been kicked by a mule. His smile remained—a mere caricature of a real one. Unbridled anger surged through him like a flashflood down a narrow stream. Surely, he had heard those words wrong! Surely this could not be the song the women sang!

But then, laughing, the woman, led by his own daughter, Michal, shouted to each other again, "Saul has slain his thousands!" and the answer roared back, "and David his tens of thousands!"[7]

Saul's mind worked furiously. *They have ascribed to David tens of thousands, and to me they have ascribed but thousands!* Saul's teeth clenched until they hurt. *And what can he have more but the kingdom?*[8] The king then remembered Doeg the Edomite's revelation that Samuel had indeed anointed David to be the next king of Israel.

[5] 2 Samuel 3:7.
[6] 1 Samuel 18:6.
[7] 1 Samuel 18:7.
[8] 1 Samuel 18:8.

It was all true then. Every bit of it. Samuel meant for David to be king in Saul's place. Samuel's betrayal was now complete. If the Great Seer had his way, what then would become of Saul's family? Of his sons? Saul trembled in barely contained rage. This son of Jesse would not take the kingdom! No, if necessary, he would die first!

And so Saul eyed David from that day forward.[9]

# The End

Thus ends book one of the Davidic Chronicles. In book two, *Valiant,* David struggles to survive the deadly intricacies of King Saul's court while facing a vengeful Philistine nation bent on slaying him.

---

[9] 1 Samuel 18:9.

# Additional Biblical and Historical Explanations

## Facts Versus Interpretation to Discover Truth

Stating a fact and interpreting that fact are not the same thing. By themselves, facts do not represent truth; they are merely facts. Truth is a fact that has purpose and meaning—often what is called a philosophy—that gives the fact a means to interact with your life and become relevant and meaningful to you. This then becomes a truth for you.

For example, take a fact: dinosaur bones. This fact coupled with either the philosophy of evolution or creationism will present two entirely different and opposing truths. Each side considers theirs to be true and their opposite to be false. But the core "fact" is still a bone. The interpretation of that fact leads to our perspective, views, understanding, and ultimately the truth to which we cling.

Jesus said that He is truth, which means that when we see life through His eyes, we find purpose and meaning that cannot be found unless we can view that perspective. Jesus is indeed truth—my truth, and I trust your truth as well. But even among Christian circles, that perspective varies enough that our "truths" are often not quite aligned with someone else's. Welcome to individual soul liberty.

I say this to explain that though I try to incorporate *all* the facts that the Bible speaks of in this series of novels, I am still going to interpret what those facts mean for the characters and events described. Not everyone will agree with my conclusions. For example, a fact: David took five smooth stones with him to fight Goliath. Why five? This is where we begin to interpret the fact. Was it because Goliath had four brothers, and he possibly would need one stone for each? Or did David merely want more ammunition, thinking it would take more than one shot to bring down Goliath?

When you interpret the fact, your "truth" of the event shifts. Your understanding of it changes, and how you relate to the fact and how it becomes meaningful to your life also changes. This becomes your truth of the story mentioned in the Bible. Preachers do this all the time.

These novels represent my interpretation of those facts into a cohesive and, hopefully, noncontradictory story that will entertain but also spark your fascination for the Bible, the characters, God's interaction with men, and ultimately your own relationship with Him.

I do not expect everyone to agree. But I do hope these novels will inspire you to delve into God's Word in a much more personal way and to see that the characters in the Bible had real lives and that it is those lives to whom God wanted to introduce you.

**Scripture and the Law**

The Hebrews of David's day had only the first five books of our Bible to guide them—and possibly whatever Samuel wrote, though it is doubtful that Samuel's writings would've been considered scriptural canon in his day. Right and wrong, therefore, were based on their understanding of the Law—the Torah.

Only the priesthood and the king had an actual written copy of the Law. Most families taught their children by oral tradition or by what the priests would have taught. Religious understanding would have been firmly wrapped in ceremony as a means of passing down truth from one generation to another. What David knew would have been delivered from his father and from the local priests living in Bethlehem. Occasionally, pilgrimages to the tabernacle would have been made, but this would likely happen no more than twice a year for a religious holiday such as the Passover and the Feast of Tabernacles.

Physical copies of the Law were rare and expensive to produce. In fact, not so long after Solomon's death, all copies of the Law disappeared and weren't discovered again until Hilkiah the high priest found one in the temple (2 Kings 22:8).

Monuments, markers, ceremony, and oral tradition would have been the primary educational methods employed to inform the next generation about God and the Law.

## Fictional Characters, Characteristics, and Events

I try to use characters that the Bible already speaks of. The story is already in place, and I believe the main characters should remain the main characters of the story. Where possible, I use characters the Bible already mentions.

But I still introduced several fictional characters into this story. Maon, David's brother, is fictional. There was an eighth son of Jesse, but the Bible does not mention his name. The Chronicles mentions only seven sons of Jesse, but the Samuels mention eight. Maon is the fictional name of a real son of Jesse who was never named. His role in the story is purely fictional.

The Philistine spies and David's interaction with them are also fictional. I imagine there were spies as the two nations were in a state of war, and it seems that an attempt on Saul's life would make sense, but those events are purely fictional and are designed to help explain how some of the facts in the Bible may have been connected.

The battle where Saul is nearly trapped by Goliath is fictional. The purpose of that scene was to help explain why the Hebrews, particularly King Saul and his son Jonathan, were so terrified of Goliath. No doubt Goliath's reputation had reached Saul, and it seems likely that Saul would've witnessed Goliath's prowess at some point before the events in Elah. So the fictional scene is my guess as to how that might have happened.

The priest in Bethlehem is fictional. No doubt a priest lived within the city, but his role, influence, name, and family are unknown to us. His role in the story was to show how people often inquired of the LORD.

Doeg the Edomite is a real person who really was the chief of Saul's herdsmen. The Bible does not actually mention him until later in David's life, but he was a villain of sorts. So I used him to help explain how King Saul would have been introduced to David and his skill with the harp. That David would have met Doeg before the Bible introduces him is very possible.

Some of the roles that characters play, such as David's brother, Abinadab, being captain of the Bethlehem garrison, are fictional. It could have happened, and it could be true, but we don't know for certain. Jesse's role of organizing the supply depot at Bethlehem is also possible, but fictional. There are other instances like this throughout the novel meant, again, to bridge and connect facts in a logical way to bring a possible, fuller story to light.

The Bible facts are footnoted and referenced. The fictional elements are not footnoted and are designed to connect the facts in a logical cohesive story that entertains and hopefully inspires you to see the Bible in whole new lights.

**Timelines and Timeframes**

The biblical account is often vague on the actual timeline of events presented in this novel. Perhaps if there is any area that I take more liberties, it would be with the timeline. For example, when David is anointed by Samuel, we get the sense that only a short time elapses between that moment and when David kills Goliath. Indeed, that is how I presented it in this novel, but that doesn't mean it was so. There could have been several years between the point where David is anointed and when Saul sends for David to play the harp for him. Also, we really don't know how long David stayed in Saul's court before war with the Philistines broke out.

I had to make a choice, and for the sake of the story, I chose to tell this story so that it all takes place within a couple of months. I freely admit that arguments could be made for a different timeframe to wrap the story in. Unfortunately, the Bible doesn't make it clear.

In fact, there are only two timeframes given in the entire story leading up to Saul's death on Mount Gilboa. The first is found in 1 Samuel 27:7 and says that David hid among the Philistines for a year and four months. That hardly helps. The other is found in the New Testament. Acts 13:21 is part of Paul's sermon to the Jews at

Antioch. He claims that King Saul reigned for forty years. It is possible, of course, that Paul was under the inspiration of the Holy Spirit when he said those words and so the forty years of Saul's reign is a fact, but it could also be just as true that Paul repeated what he'd heard from his training. It may be that Jewish tradition held that Saul reigned for forty years, but it may have been considerably less.

Since we don't know how old any of the primary characters were when this story takes place, it is difficult to reconcile exact timelines and timeframes. Saul calls David a youth, so we can be fairly certain David was not yet twenty when he killed Goliath. But other ages are not so easily determined. I believe, for example, that Jonathan was at a minimum ten years older than David since he was a man of war long before we even hear of David.

I leave it to the reader to decide what is right, and pray you have mercy on my decisions.

**Brass, Bronze, and Iron**

My only biblical source for this story is the King James Bible. There are many reasons for this, but an important one is based on the flow and cadence of the language in sounding more "godly" than any of the modern versions being published. I structured much of the dialogue of this story in a similar pattern and cadence. It provides a particular rhythm that is almost captivating in its flow.

That being stated, when the King James Bible was translated, the word *bronze* had yet to enter the English vocabulary. The KJV translators rendered the Hebrew word *nechôsheth* as "brass," but modern-day brass did not exist in David's day. The alloy used was copper and tin which, today, is commonly known as *bronze*. As stated already, the term *bronze* had not yet been introduced into the English language at the time of the KJV translation, so "brass" was used to describe any type of copper alloy. This means Goliath's armor was bronze, not brass, in today's usage of the words.

I settled on using the word *bronze* so as not to confuse the reader who would automatically think of brass differently than the actual metal of Goliath's armor. The confusion exists only because the KJV translators did not have access to the word *bronze* at the time.

Saul's reign marked the beginning of the Iron Age for that region. The Philistines had either killed all the smiths or crushed the trade so thoroughly that the Hebrews, even to get their farm instruments sharpened, had to go to the Philistines for all smith-related needs (1 Samuel 13:19-22). Only Saul and his son had swords at first. Goliath's spear was made of iron (1 Samuel 17:7), but his armor was made of bronze. This was very common for the armor to be made of bronze and the weapons to be of iron.

Iron wasn't necessarily a superior metal over bronze. In fact, most rulers and kings preferred bronze over iron. Bronze could be cold-molded, beaten into shape without having to heat it up and without affecting its strength or durability. Iron was more unwieldy as a metal to shape and heavier. Good for weapons, but often too heavy for armor. The reason iron eventually supplanted bronze is because bronze requires two metals to produce: copper and tin. Stop the import or mining of either of the metals and you could prevent your enemies from having bronze. Iron was more prevalent and thus easier to attain, requiring only the one metal, which is why the Iron Age supplanted the Bronze Age.

Common soldiers eventually had iron for weapons and parts of their armor. The rich and the powerful still retained bronze armor when they could—even after the Iron Age was in full effect. The story in this book takes place at the beginning of the Iron Age, so there is quite a bit of crossover. Both iron and bonze were rare in Israel, and both were expensive. Much of the plunder of Saul's victories no doubt included the Philistine's bronze and iron armaments.

It would've taken time for smiths to be reinstated in Israel, but this no doubt began to happen under King Saul's rule.

## Locations and Maps

I attempted to be as accurate as possible with the distances and locations mentioned in this story. I also attempted to be as accurate with the description of said places and locations, being careful to consider all facets of the terrain and locales to explain possible military tactics, travel conditions and times, economic impact, and the ease or challenges of communication.

For example, five east-west valleys provide natural corridors of travel between the land of the Philistines and Israel. The Valley of Elah was one and the one most accessible to the city of Gath from which the invasion in this story was launched. The valley gave access to an unbroken ridgeline that ran right to Bethlehem. This would explain why Saul stopped the Philistines where he did and why the battle was so important.

I did not include any fictional cities in this story. I used only known cities and places of the time to tell this story. Their locations and geographical descriptions are as accurate as I could make them.

**Wine and Strong Drink**

The men and women of this period had only the Law to guide them regarding the consumption of wine and strong drink. Vineyards were very prevalent, and the production of wine was one of the largest commodities of that time. Wine and strong drink was only ever forbidden to two groups according to the Law: the priesthood when they were in service to the tabernacle (Leviticus 10:9-11) and a Nazarite who was still under the conditions of his or her vow (Numbers 6:1-20)—though the Law expressly gives the Nazarite permission to drink wine *after* his vow was finished (Numbers 6:20).

Unless you were one of those two groups of people, the men and women of this period had no inhibitions to drinking wine or strong drink. In fact, wine was used extensively to help purify water since water was often undrinkable in that time. They would cut their water with a small portion of wine to make the water potable. Wine was used in many of the Hebrew religious ceremonies, particularly the drink offerings (Exodus 29:40; Leviticus 23:13; Numbers 15:5-10). And at least one permissible part of the Law allowed Hebrews to take their tithe and purchase wine or strong drink, whatever they desired, and to drink it while sharing with the stranger and the Levite (Deuteronomy 14:22-29).

The pasteurization process that we hold dear today to keep grape juice from fermenting wasn't invented until A.D. 1869 by Thomas B. Welsh, a Methodist. Therefore, the Hebrews of David's day had no ability by which to keep grape juice from fermenting. The fermentation process would begin within a few hours of the pressing. Honey and other substances were added to the juice to produce certain types of wines and flavors.

It is likely that nearly every single person of that period would have drunk wine or strong drink, including children. The only exception would be one who maintained a lifelong Nazarite vow, such as Samuel. I expect he was the rare exception—not the rule of this period.

Drunkenness would have been a common occurrence, as it is today, so the Hebrews would have fully understood the dangers of drunkenness, and indeed, Solomon wrote about it later in the book of Proverbs. But the use of wine and strong drink was very common and something that nearly every Hebrew participated in and few would have thought to be wrong, even among the most devote and religious.

### Violence and Warfare

Life was cheap in David's day and violence a part of everyday life. The early kings of Israel did not maintain prisons as we understand them today. In many cases, an infraction resulted in a physical punishment—an eye for an eye, a tooth for a tooth principle. More serious infractions or violations often resulted in death. Saul, and then David, often executed people for even minor violations of disloyalty.

King Saul, for example, killed all the priests of Nob for the simple fact that they had helped David. Saul felt that such a drastic action was well within his rights as king, and no one chastised him for it either. David killed an Amalekite man who had admitted that he'd helped King Saul commit suicide. The man was lying, but David didn't take the time to find out the truth of the matter. He let the man's mouth be his judge and ordered him killed. On another occasion, David set out to kill every person associated with Nabal because he felt slighted and insulted by the man. Only Nabal's wife, Abigail, succeeded in turning away David's wrath just in the nick of time. When Nabal died a little later, David felt no remorse and saw it as vindication of God's favor.

These examples were not exceptions. They were the norm for that period. Violence and death were common bedfellows, and a simple way to eradicate malcontent was to kill the malcontented. I tried to keep this aspect of common society in the story. David was a bloody man according to God, and death and violence followed him.

Warfare was also part of everyday life which I tried to portray in the story. I studied the arms and armaments of the period along with common tactics and strategies. I did my best to keep them as accurate as possible in the story.

Overall, I hope to have portrayed an accurate way of life that reflected the character and life views of the period.

# Sources and References

Much research goes into a novel like this. I wanted to stay true to the biblical account but also to stay true to the era and times. This meant I had to learn how they built their houses, what their clothes were made of, and many other customs and facts. The sources below represent the majority of the information about customs, manners, and geography that I incorporated into this novel. Those not mentioned only corroborated what I found in the following sources.

*Disclaimer:* Undoubtedly, I have missed or didn't learn many facts about ancient life, and so the astute reader may discover historical and geographical errors. Feel free to write me about them, as long as you corroborate them with sources, and I will attempt to incorporate them into future editions of the novel.

**Sources**

- The King James Bible
- www.biblicalarchaeology.org
- www.ancient-hebrew.org
- www.gci.org/bible/hist/weapons
- en.wikipedia.org/wiki/Sling_(weapon)
- www.gotquestions.org/Jehovah.html
- www.theoldtestamenttimeline.com
- www.israelbiblicalstudies.com & blog.israelbiblicalstudies.com
- www.jewfaq.org
- www.bible-history.com
- www.biblewalks.com/info/trees.html
- www.netours.com/content/view/241/26/
- www.bearsoftheworld.net/syrian_brown_bear.asp
- en.wikipedia.org/wiki/Asiatic_lion

- www.bibleatlas.org
- Jan H. Negenman, *New Atlas of the Bible* (New York: Doubleday & Company Inc., 1969).
- Rand-McNally Bible Atlas - Published in 1910.
- Smith Bible Atlas - Designed and edited by George Adam Smith, 1915.
- Jan H. Negenman, *New Atlas of the Bible* (New York: Doubleday & Company Inc., 1969).
- Fred H. Wight, *Manners and Customs of Bible Lands* (Moody Bible Institute of Chicago, 1953).
- Boyd Seevers, *Warfare in the Old Testament* (Grand Rapids, MI: Kregel Publications, 2013).
- Chaim Herzog and Mordechai Gichon, *Battles of the Bible – A Military History of Ancient Israel* (Barnes and Noble Publishing, 2006).
- A. Van Deursen, *Illustrated Dictionary of Bible Manners and Customs* (Grand Rapids, MI: Zondervan, 1958).


**Commentaries and Dictionaries**


- James Orr, M.A., D.D., General Editor, International Standard Bible Encyclopedia.
- John McClintock and James Strong, Cyclopedia of Biblical, Theological and Ecclesiastical Literature (1895).
- Canne, Browne, Blayney, Scott, and others, with introduction by R. A. Torrey, Treasury of Scriptural Knowledge (1834; public domain).
- John Gill's Exposition of the Bible (1746-1766, 1816; public domain).
- Jamieson, Fausset and Brown Commentary - A Commentary, Critical and Explanatory, on the Old and New Testaments (1871; public domain).
- Adam Clarke's Commentary on the Bible (1810-1826; public domain).

- Joseph Benson's Commentary on the Old and New Testaments (1857; public domain).
- Albert Barnes' Notes on the Bible (1847-85; public domain).
- Matthew Henry's Commentary on the Whole Bible (1708-1714; public domain).
- W. Robertson Nicoll, Sermon Bible Commentary (1888-1893; public domain).
- John Wesley's Notes on the Bible (1755-1766; public domain).
- F. B. Meyer, Through the Bible Day by Day – A Devotional Commentary (1914; public domain).
- W. Robertson Nicoll (Editor), *Expositor's Bible Commentary* (1887-1896; public domain).

# About the Author

Greg S. Baker has been writing novels for over twenty years. His books are widely read and enjoyed. His primary focus lately has been on his stellar Biblical Fiction novels and his engaging young adult adventure novels. He has written a number of other helpful books for the Christian life. He has a passion for expanding the Kingdom of God within the kingdom of men.

He lives in the southwest with his wife, Liberty, and their four boys. Much of his writing has been for them, desiring to provide entertaining stories that teach and inspire.

He attended Bible college in the late 1990s, pastored a Baptist church in Colorado for thirteen years, and now works as a writer, a freelance Christian editor, and a programmer from his house. He remains active in his church, serving God in a variety of capacities, but focusing mainly on teenagers and young single adults.

He loves chess, playing sports, and rearing his teen boys.

You can connect with Greg through his website www.thedivineingredient.com. He loves hearing from people and engaging them as an active part of the writing process for his future books. If you love reading, then stop on by.

www.TheDivineIngredient.com